'An [illegible]
ingredi[illegible]s.

The Bookseller

'McCaughrean has the gift of making remote times and places unfold as if before the reader's very eyes . . . what a novelist!'

Independent

'McCaughrean tends to be an armchair traveller while researching her books, but her Madagascar springs off the page, equatorial, relaxed, full of exotic flowers, animals and superstitions. Ruthless and blood-thirsty pirates are no match for three young teenagers and their paradise found.'

Daily Telegraph

'a truly exotic adventure of pirates and deception. The characterisation is full of subtleties along with the growth of the three main characters . . . Swashbuckling galore, and the final chase, well . . . '

Books for Keeps

'This must be the finest adventure story for years . . . A brilliant read.'

Guardian

'its two opening chapters, in which Nathan and Maud discover that they have been orphaned and decide to run away with the son of a pirate, are electrifying.'

The Scotsman

'This swashbuckling adventure is not to be missed!'

Daily Telegraph

'This story has a very different theme from most fiction now on offer and I enjoyed it very much.'

School Librarian

'told with swashbuckling bravado that leaves you laughing and breathless'

Times Educational Supplement

'beautifully written . . . an absolute joy to read for the language alone'

In Brief

'There [illegible] a plenty to hold [illegible] readers . . . One feels that the research has been thorough and the richly descriptive writing gives a convincing ring to the authentic picture of another place and another time.'

Junior Bookshelf

'the literary equivalent of the best all-action, technicolour movie . . . A wonderful read.'

Shelf Life

'an action-packed novel full of piratical swagger'

Lancashire Evening Post

'a rip-roaring historical adventure . . . The colours and scents of the island are ever present in this richly atmospheric story for older juniors while the deeply satisfying ending brings the story full circle'

Junior Education

'My overall opinion of this book is that it is quite simply brilliant . . . this book succeeds in every way, the descriptive quality is exceptional and I would suggest that it allows this story to be enjoyed by a wide range of readers. I am sure this book will be both interesting, entertaining and a big hit! It is without doubt the best book I have ever read.'

Bookstop! (Blackwells) Review ed. by pupil of Cokethorpe School

Plundering Paradise

Other books by Geraldine McCaughrean

One Thousand and One Arabian Nights
Saint George and the Dragon
The Canterbury Tales
El Cid
The Odyssey
Moby Dick
A Little Lower than the Angels
A Pack of Lies
Gold Dust
Forever X
The Stones are Hatching
The Kite Rider
Stop the Train
Smile!
Not the End of the World
The White Darkness
Peter Pan in Scarlet

GERALDINE McCAUGHREAN

Plundering Paradise

OXFORD
UNIVERSITY PRESS

OXFORD
UNIVERSITY PRESS

Great Clarendon Street, Oxford OX2 6DP

Oxford University Press is a department of the University of Oxford.
It furthers the University's objective of excellence in research, scholarship,
and education by publishing worldwide in

Oxford New York

Auckland Cape Town Dar es Salaam Hong Kong Karachi
Kuala Lumpur Madrid Melbourne Mexico City Nairobi
New Delhi Shanghai Taipei Toronto

With offices in

Argentina Austria Brazil Chile Czech Republic France Greece
Guatemala Hungary Italy Japan Poland Portugal Singapore
South Korea Switzerland Thailand Turkey Ukraine Vietnam

Oxford is a registered trade mark of Oxford University Press
in the UK and in certain other countries

First published 1996
First published in this edition 2007

British Library Cataloguing in Publication Data available

ISBN: 978-0-19-271994-2

1 3 5 7 9 10 8 6 4 2

Printed in Great Britain by Cox & Wyman Ltd, Reading, Berkshire

Paper used in the production of this book is a natural, recyclable product made
from wood grown in sustainable forests. The manufacturing process conforms
to the environmental regulations of the country of origin.

For Ron and Dorothy

At his return to Madagascar, White . . . nam'd three
Men of different Nations, Guardians
to a son he had by a Woman of the Country,
requiring he might be sent to England . . . by
the first English ship, to be brought up in the
Christian Religion, in hopes he might live a
better Man than his Father . . .

Captain Charles Johnson's *A General History of the . . . most notorious Pyrates . . .* (1724)

1

Graylake School 1717

Cold gnawed on him like a rat. Around him, the dun and grey blankets of the other beds rose and fell like the swell of a bleak, dirty sea. Nathan had no idea what had woken him—he was still exhausted—and yet some upheaval had washed him up above the waterline of sleep. He was afraid, without knowing why.

A master's black gown hung from a peg on the wall. It had hung there, unclaimed, for as long as Nathan could remember, threadbare, almost transparent with age, like the ghost of a hanging man, swaying in the draughts. As many nightmares as moths had fluttered towards Nathan out of that black gown swinging, swinging from its hook.

He thought about his sister. This was the only time of day when it was acceptable to think about a sister. Once the day had got under way, there would be no excuse to mention her. For Nathan to mention Maud to one of the other boys would be like referring to his nursery hobbyhorse or teething ring. Secretly, Nathan thought it rather a betrayal of sisters, to pretend they did not exist. So he made a point of thinking about Maud, in the privacy of first light: mousy little Maud, keeping house, cooking and supervising meals, polishing spoons, and reading to her father.

With their mother dead, all such housewifely duties had settled on Maud like an inch of dust, obscuring the pictures Nathan carried in his mind.

When he tried to remember how she looked, he had difficulties distinguishing her dress from the drab parlour curtains, her face from the white plates on the dresser. Mousy Maud. She never played with him now, in the vacations: her duties left her no time. She did not smile much, either.

A bird came and sat on the window of the dormitory, half in and half out. Birds never flew in, despite the lack of glass. They seemed to sense the difference between inside and out. And they had the choice, of course. The bird's shadow fell on Nathan's chest, and when it fluttered away, the shadow fluttered, too, like a soul leaving a dead man's breast . . .

It was the clanging of the morning bell which had disturbed the bird. The other boys began groaning and wriggling under their brown blankets, like moles who burrow away from noise. The beadle, who came to ensure that everyone obeyed the bell, was in fact startled to see Nathan already on his feet and dressing. Boys are not commonly so easy to wake.

The boys' boots were all out in the courtyard, lining the cloisters, as if they had set out early for breakfast without waiting for their owners. Bare feet paddled across the cobbles and squeezed into them; the leather was rigid with frost. Gibbering boys pulled their jackets over their convict-shaven heads, so that they looked as if they had no heads at all, clumping along to the refectory with boot-laces lashing loose, unwilling to spend time in the cold, tying them. Besides, their fingers were numb. Some wore woollen gloves, which was permitted. Only the head and feet had to be kept cold, in the interests of education. Headmaster Thrussell abided by the precepts of John Locke.

Thus, Nathaniel Gull, aged fourteen, sat in a

draught, while the eminent masters of Graylake School, speaking Latin, erected over him towering pinnacles of knowledge: history, the classics, mathematics and divinity, rhetoric and philosophy. He felt the moisture in his eyes congeal, the facts lodge in his brain like rats in the neck of a python, indigestible.

So inside his head, he was fighting pirates.

Further back, in a desk in the fourth row, a real pirate sat—the son of a pirate, at least. To Nathaniel Gull, son of a country parson, Tamo White seemed as exotic and strange as a basilisk or giant orc. To be the son of a pirate! Not that Nathan had ever spoken to him, not above a few words. He was real, after all, and the whole point of pirates (as far as a boy in a Greek lesson is concerned) is their far remove from reality, their Romance!

Pirates were meat and drink to Nathan, their treasure caves somewhere he daily chose to spend time, rather than listen to his lessons. He knew the names of more buccaneers than saints. He knew their ships, their ports-of-call, their homes and histories. He knew which had fallen into piracy by bad luck, and which had been driven to it by the sheer wickedness in their souls. He knew what pirates ate and wore, and the oaths they spat from between gold teeth. He knew how they died, craven or penniless, begging forgiveness for their crimes. He had read it all in Exquemelin's *Bucaniers of America* and Dampier's *Discourse of Wind.* And during Greek lessons he imagined himself a sea lord, with letters from the king urging him to purge the oceans of pirates. While Mr Pleasance, the Greek master, chanted lists of irregular verbs, Nathaniel Gull fought pirates, blade-to-blade across the wooden desk-tops of a forty-gun carrack. *'Surrender, foul wretch, scourge of the main! Throw down your flintlock and tell your men to pray for your scurvy soul! It's Gallows Hill for you, you rascally cut-throat!'*

'Gull? Gull!' the master had to say his name several times, and even then Nathan thought it must have to do with irregular verbs. But a junior boy had brought a note from the headmaster, a summons. 'Gull, you are to attend on the headmaster at once.'

His stomach ached with sudden foreboding. He searched his conscience for anything he might have done wrong. But he could find nothing. He did nothing wrong. He never, never did anything wrong. He was a parson's son, for God's sake! He was Nathaniel Gull, for Heaven's sake. What had he ever done wrong but be born puny and vile: an insignificant full-stop in a black night sky.

'Salve, magister,' said Nathaniel. He found he had pulled his hands up inside his sleeves, and could not latch the door behind him. There was no answering, *'Salve.'* The headmaster was on his feet, resting his knuckles on the desk, glaring. In front of him, Locke's *Some Thoughts Concerning Education* lay on top of the Bible. Locke on the Bible. Nathan fixed his eyes on the book, abject.

Before speaking, Thrussell walked twice round Nathaniel, flicking his fingers against the baggy blue jacket, the blue, veiny skull. 'I see no patches, I see no rags,' he mouthed, as if he were declaiming in the Roman Senate. 'Lift your boots, boy! I see no holes in these soles! No threadbare coat-tails!'

'Thank you, sir,' said Nathan. He knew it was not the right answer. The hand holding his ankle, like a farrier shoeing a horse, gripped so hard that the ankle-bones clicked.

'Gull. Son of Gull. Should I not have hesitated as I entered that name in the rolls of this academy? Should I not have said to myself: Hold, Dr Thrussell, will not this Gull, son of a Gull, not gull us in time? Will he not prove us gullible in our hospitality? May he not snatch, like a herring gull, the perfect eggs of knowledge, uncouth and gluttonous and cruel? Well, sir, you have gulled us indeed, sir! Indeed, you have gulled us, Mister Gull!' The pun seemed to give Thrussell too much pleasure for him to leave it behind and move on. Nathan sensed he was not intended to smile at the doctor's wit. 'Gulled us, I say! Tricked and deceived us! We who believed—too gullibly, I see!—that a man of the church might be relied upon for honesty and plain dealing!'

'Father?' said Nathan. 'What's the matter with father?'

'Oh, nothing! Nothing! *He* has simply quit the field! He has escaped the consequences of his actions! He has left others, such as me, to suffer the difficulties wrought by his perfidiousness!'

'Where has he gone?' asked Nathan, trying to guess. It was like trying to grab the spoke of a turning wheel.

'Heaven, we must assume,' said Thrussell, adenoidal with sarcasm, 'since the mercy of the Lord is infinite. And there, I dare say, he continues *passing himself off* as a godly man, a man of religion!'

The room took a sudden swing to the left. The floor heaved. The windows bulged like eyes. A horse in the stables beyond shrieked with shock.

' . . . though he will find few friends, I venture to suggest, when it is discovered what manner of man he truly is!'

'My father's dead, sir?' said Nathan.

'Dead, sir. And destitute. Penniless. In debt. A pauper, sir. But then, you would know as much . . . '

'Papa's dead, sir?'

' . . . overspending, living beyond his means . . . sponging upon those fooled by his masquerade of affluence.'

'I know we were never rich . . . ' Nathan did not mean to argue, but he had to find something to say, something to stop the torrent drowning him. 'Did he tell you he was rich?'

'Did Satan warn Eve of his wickedness? Does the criminal speak aloud of his plans to thieve?'

'I'm sure he didn't mean . . . Can I see him? Can I go and see him?' If he was quick, he felt, if he ran all the way and did not waste time on breathing or crying, he might be in time to see his father's face smiling at him, to throw his arms around him.

'Go where you please, sir, so it lays no more expense on this school! This school, which has nurtured you like a viper in its bosom, boy! This school, which your father died owing *two terms' fees*! Go, boy! Before my Christian patience fails me and my righteous wrath smites you where you stand!'

Nathaniel backed towards the door. He felt sick and leaden. His boot-laces flickered round his ankles, like vipers, stinging his calves. With his hands still inside his sleeves, he fumbled with the latch, and banged his head on the opening door. As he stumbled down the corridor, Thrussell's voice bellowed after him: 'And you can leave that jacket when you go! We are not here to clothe the indigent poor in best worsted!'

He went back to the classroom. Because he had nowhere else to go. When he failed to sit down again at his desk, the boys looked at him with pity, thinking he must have been flogged. Little Goody Gull flogged? Unheard of! Extraordinary! He took off his jacket and bundled it under the lid of his desk. His shirt sleeves dropped even further past his fingertips. Only as he tried to shut the lid did he catch sight of *Bucaniers of America* among the primers and copy books.

The Greek master looked at him, eyebrows raised, derisively asking permission to proceed with his interrupted lesson.

'It's my father. He's de—' said Nathan, dazed.

The master stepped forward at once and laid a hand on his shoulder. 'I'm sorry, boy. My sincere sympathies. That's a terrible loss for any son to bear.'

Nathan waited a few seconds to wake up from the bad dream he was in. But it did not end. 'I have to leave.' The class stirred, ready to be indignant on his behalf. 'There's no money. My fees weren't . . . ' There was no alteration in the face of the Greek master, but the class of boys stirred with a different murmur now, a single shocked intake of breath. Gull was not worth two halfpennies. Gull was a pauper.

'Sit down,' said the master, pressing a little harder on Nathan's shoulder.

'I have to go. I'm not allowed . . . ' But his mind was on seventy other things more real—vacations, coach rides, birthdays, conversations, all fallen irrevocably into the past. He must put right the mistake—rush home and prove to himself that his father was, in truth, perfectly well, really grafting apple trees in the orchard, or writing a sermon in the study.

The Greek master took the pirate book from under Nathan's arm and, opening it at random, placed it on the desk, bending the boy's head over it, giving him time to take in the dreadful news while the lesson flowed on round him, ignoring him, sparing him. When all the other boys were dismissed, and clattered out of the room, Nathan was still sitting with his book, eyes fixed on the same page, seeing nothing.

'Where will you go, child?' asked the master. He was powerless to offer more than sympathy. He knew how much Thrussell hated poverty—hated and feared it, as though it might rub off if it came too close, as though it could infect the very schoolhouse like an epidemic of smallpox. The parents who sent their sons to Graylake did not intend them to jostle with the poor, share a dormitory with unfortunates such as Gull. That is one of the privileges money expects to buy. 'I'm deeply sorry for you, boy. Have you no relations who might . . . take over your father's responsibilities?'

No, Nathan had no one, no one in the world except Mousy Maud and his father, in Heaven. *Our Father, which art in Heaven: the Reverend Gull, deceased debtor of this parish . . .*

They were waiting for him outside. Though the teacher had meant to help by making Nathan stay, he had simply given the older boys time to brood and conspire. A beggar in their midst? Gull must be taught a lesson for polluting their wealthy sanctum. They were waiting for him in the dormitory—Betterton, Wase, and Fitzgerald senior, Beaulieu and Southern and Hawkwood. Their blue jackets dangled from their fingers, their eyes were full of malice.

They waited, without speaking, for Nathan to drag his travelling box out from under his bed, before they slowly closed in on him. He tried to ignore them.

Even when the jackets started to pound on him, with their metal buttons and thick cuffs, he tried to go on dragging the box towards the door. He dropped *Bucaniers of America* from under his arm, and though it was his dearest possession, he hoped, as they grabbed it and broke its spine and kicked it from one to another across the dormitory floor, that it would at least give him time to escape.

But as the book disintegrated the boys turned back towards Nathan, twirling their jackets again, baring their teeth. They broke open the flimsy box containing all his worldly goods, and began flinging them about. Beaulieu pocketed the half-sovereign, Betterton the bag of pennies. They threw his commonplace book through the window, his good quill into the grate. They snatched the black gown off its peg on the wall and wrapped it round Nathan's head as they bundled him into the box and slammed the lid on his back. Down the stone staircase they bumped him—'Let's sail him down the river!' 'Let's set him alight!'—until the joints split and the wooden sides bowed and the lock dangled by a single nail. And all the while, the boy inside said not a word, uttered not a sound but for the grunts forced out of him each time his lungs were knocked empty. Who was there to call on for help? No one. He had no one in the world. He could not breathe. *'Our Father, who art in Heaven . . . '*

'Stop!'

It was not a master speaking.

'Stop, or I'll split you!'

It was a boy's voice.

The chest had rolled on to its lid, and Nathan had to squirm his way out of it, like a tortoise from under its shell, sliding blindly down the remaining stairs before he could untangle his head from the black gown and see who had saved him from suffocation.

Tamo White, the pirate's son, stood on the bottom stair, a silver sabre in his hand. The light from the stained-glass window in the main hall threw down swathes of transparent red, purple, and green across his foreigner's face and long black hair. He was wearing a fur waistcoat under his baggy school jacket. Nathan noticed that, particularly.

'His old man's died a pauper! He's not worth anything but a pack of debts!' protested Southern.

'Didn't even pay his fees!' said Betterton, as if it were ample reason to kill a man.

'While the rest of us would pay good money not to be here,' said White softly. 'Come with me, Gull. Let's go and dine.'

' . . . masquerading as a gentleman!' whined Wase as the boys turned to go.

'Yah! Trust a mongrel to be looked after by his own kind!' jeered Hawkwood.

White turned and made a single lunge. The blade stopped a half-inch short of Hawkwood's ashen face, and he took off up the stairs, best speed, barking his shins on the broken box, skidding on the torn black gown. The rest followed, either howling or whining, promising vengeance on White, calling him 'a half-breed and a cannibal'.

They are only children, after all—only little boys, thought Nathan, now that he saw them on the run.

White turned the broken box over with his foot. 'Did they take anything of yours?' he asked.

'No. No,' said Nathan. 'No. Leave it.'

Then the pirate's son (to whom Nathan had barely spoken, in all his time at Graylake) put an arm round his shoulder, and together they walked down the school drive.

Tamo White lived outside school bounds, in a rented apartment in the town. Such things were permitted to older boys with large personal allowances or money of their own. White had a bank account with eight hundred pounds in it, and some guardian with even bigger sums in trust.

'My father wanted me to live a blameless life,' said White. 'But he also wanted me to have the proceeds. The proceeds from his . . . working life. Never saw any paradox in that, the old man.'

In place of the sabre, he held now a red-hot poker newly pulled from the grate. He plunged it into an earthenware jug of red wine. Nathaniel's eye never left the poker, reflecting the steam, the bubbles that spilled over, the shine of the silver tankard.

As Nathan studied the art of mulling, Tamo studied the boy he had rescued. Sleeves dangling, his shoulders slumped forwards; whenever he turned to look at something he did not swivel his head, but turned the whole set of his body, with a cautious, anxious stiffness. The blue veins made his shaven head look like a Stilton cheese, and his nose was red and sore at the tip.

'I wasn't there, either, when mine died,' said White. 'I don't know if they did things right. I've never even seen his grave.'

'Oh! A grave. I never thought,' said Gull. 'There has to be a funeral, I suppose.' He lifted the tankard to his lips and scalded himself on the hot wine.

'My father took it into his head, when he got sick, to send me back to England for a good education and a respectable life. He put me in the charge of three guardians, and shipped me out before the sickness finally took him. I fooled myself for a year or more that he got better after I left—made an unexpected recovery, and that he'd send for me, to have me back. But he was dead, all right. Must've been dead before I was three days out of Tamatave.'

The pale boy swivelled his body towards Tamo White, but all he said was, 'Why have you still got your hair?'

Tamo poured himself more wine, tucking the hair in question absently behind his ears. It had a wiry quality, crinkled, voluminous, like the mane of an Abyssinian lion.

'Oh, Thrussell and Locke. Locke and Thrussell. Hang Locke for a barbarian. Who was ever better off for wet feet and a cold head? The way I argue it, nothing ever hatched out of an egg without it was kept warm!' And he laughed—a bright, dazzling laugh that freed the hair from behind his ears again. 'Thrussell's a barbarous pig. Slander a man who's just died? And to his own son? What kind of a pig does that?'

'I suppose he feels cheated out of his money,' said Gull feebly, and Tamo snorted with disgust, prepared to write off the spineless little creature slumped in front of his fire.

'Is that what you really think?'

Gull frowned. 'No,' he said, thoughtfully. 'No.' And then, 'I think I think,' he ventured slowly, 'that he ought to be tarred and hung up by his tongue in the Great Hall; and his body wrapped in chains and his school burned down round him, and Locke used for kindling. And all his aunts and uncles stuffed with paper and put out in fields for scarecrows. And Betterton and Wase to be waiting in Hell for him, with their blue jackets. And his ashes to be mixed with molasses and used to caulk rum barrels. For saying those things about Papa. Even if they were true. Which they weren't.'

Tamo swallowed. 'My word!' he said, and took the earliest opportunity to remove the jug of wine into the bedroom. Locke, in *Some Thoughts Concerning Education,* forbade wine or strong drink, and with a needy vicar for a father, it was probably the first time Goody Gull had tasted alcohol. Another tankard and the lad would either pass out, or go looking for Thrussell to punch him in the mouth.

As Tamo came out of the bedroom, carrying a jacket of his own for Nathan to wear, he was asking what Nathan meant to do next, whether he had anywhere to go, someone who would take him in. But there was no answer.

Gull had slithered out of the chair on to the hearth mat. He was asleep, in a drunken stupor, only his head on the chair-seat, his wet boots hissing among the embers.

2

The Pirate's Son

When Nathan woke, he could not judge where he was, and knew nothing except that his neck was stiff. He seemed to be inside a larva of some kind, waiting to hatch. Then it occurred to him that the cloth round his head was canvas and must be a shroud, and him stitched into it. He shouted and writhed and struggled, turned over . . . and crashed from a great height on to a bedroom floor. The hammock which had spilled him out swung gently to and fro above him.

'I've got a suggestion,' said Tamo White from over by the window. 'Why don't you come with me?'

'Why? Where are you going?'

'Home. I've had enough. I hate England.'

'Hate England?' It was too much to grasp, with a head full of searing headache.

'The cold. The rules. The little tyrants. I miss home. Why don't you come? There's nothing to keep you here.'

'Where's home?'

'Madagascar, of course. My father was Thomas White. I thought you knew. Soft-hearted Thomas White of the Indian Ocean.' His voice was full of self-mockery, and Nathan presumed that the whole idea of leaving was a schoolboyish flight of fancy, not to be taken seriously. 'Two of my guardians are dead—the ones who promised my father to keep me in good order. The third one, he thinks I should have done with schools by my age. He already thinks I'm more educated than the King. If I tell him I want to pay a visit home before I go into business, he'll take me back on his ship. Once I'm there, nobody's going to prise me loose.'

'Would you really go and live among pirates?' Nathan whispered, in awe. He recalled the woodcuts in his mangled book, the gurning faces, the cutlasses, the peculiar tortures, the dens of wickedness.

'No!' snorted Tamo, dragging his own travelling box into the middle of the room. It was a real sea-chest, with iron bindings and a curved lid. Inside it were men's clothes, not boys' but men's clothes. 'Madagascar's a big place—vast. I could go back to my clan village—a crocodile village. No need to go among the crew.'

'Live with the savages, you mean?'

Tamo regarded him coldly over the rim of the trunk, waiting for him to apologize. But Nathan had no idea he might have given offence. 'I am a savage. My mother was a savage. It's only my name that's White, you know.'

'Oh, but your father . . . '

'My father didn't want me to be like him. That's why I'm here. He didn't want me to be Thomas White the Second.'

'No, he wanted you to be a gentleman!' Gull did not mean to be quarrelsome, but he was very sensitive, just then, to the subject of fathers. He longed to have a father he could ask: 'What shall I do? Where must I go?'

Tamo kicked the trunk. 'Well, that's one thing his gold can't buy him, isn't it!'

Nathan shrank inwardly. Such a heat of hatred! He felt lost—cast adrift. The whole world had lost its temper with him—he who had only ever striven to please, to avoid unpleasantness! He fell silent and watched the pirate's son pack.

Of course, it was preposterous of White to talk of Gull going with him. People would have plans for him. People would, at any moment, tell him where to go, what to do, how to live, what life held in store in the new scheme of things. God had plans for Nathan; his father had always told him so. At any minute, those plans would become plain. In his newly humbled state (and he had never been much other than humble), he was perfectly willing to accept God's instructions.

But as he sat there, watching the pirate's son wrap a pair of flintlocks in chamois leather and stow them between clean, lace-collared shirts, he shivered in the cold draught of panic. It blew in under the door. It rattled at the window. *Hooo. Hoo?* Who in the world was left to tell him God's will? Not his father. Not his school. Not friends or relations. Not even the slow, steady pressure of Time pushing between his shoulder blades, moving him on from one day to the next. Suddenly, he had to decide—he, Nathan Gull—had to decide where to go and what to do, in order to put food in his belly and a roof over his head.

'Come with me,' said White, seeing the younger boy's mouth crumple. 'What's to keep you here?'

Nathan opened his mouth to say no, but the word would not come out. He opened his mouth to say yes, but did not dare, for fearful faces popped up at the window sneering and jeering at his contemptible day-dreaming. Go among pirates? Nathan Gull?

He stood up abruptly, bumping into the door frame as he left the room. He could not understand why Tamo White followed him, not realizing he had himself said, 'Come with me!'

Nathan ran back towards the school. On the way, he passed three churches, for none of them would serve his purpose. After attending Graylake school chapel for so many years, he could not help but think of God as a public school God. He ran up the drive again, keeping to the wrong side of the great beech trees, so as not to be seen. And he tumbled breathless into the monumental chapel building, the one endowed by the King himself.

'What are we doing here? What are you doing?' panted Tamo White.

'I'm asking!' said Nathan, still out of breath. 'Father told me.' He had clambered on to the base of the lectern, and was struggling to open the great leather cover of the Bible. It was chained shut. A lock on the Bible. But he could still just get the pages apart a little way. 'Ask the Lord, in thy perplexity!'

His father had said it once. Nathan could picture him now, eyes shut, pointing finger poised over the open Bible and the other hand clutched to his breast, the teacup on the table rattling with zeal: 'Ask the Good Book, Nathaniel! Seek out the Lord's will, in thy perplexity!'

The cold run to the chapel, the trespass on to the lectern, had used up Nathan's burst of daring. He knew what he would really do. He knew he would borrow a few coppers from White, so as to get home for the funeral. And if anyone was at the funeral—the family solicitor or grocer or some busybody neighbour—he would let them tell him what to do with his life. He was only a schoolboy, after all, and schoolboys are not supposed to decide for themselves. Even so, his icy hands scrumpled the thin paper of the part-open book, his cuff scuffed the edges. He poked his sore, wet nose close to the opening and peered inside.

'What are you *doing*?' asked Tamo White.

'My father . . . '

'What, did he write the book?'

'Don't be ridiculous.' (He had forgotten Tamo was part-savage.) His hand lay spread on a page. He read between his fingers. ' . . . *Of the children of Asher after their families: of Jimna, the family of the Himnites: of Jesui, the family of the Jesuites: of Beriah, the family of the Berites . . .* '

Nathan tried again—somewhere in the New Testament, the Gospels. The words within the crevice crawled about like ants disturbed by the lifting of a rock. But at last he pinned a single verse into place with his fingertips, and his eyes focused:

'Leave the dead to bury the dead.'

The words struck him such a jolt that he fell off the lectern and up against Tamo, who caught him and stopped him crashing to the floor.

'I'll come. I will come. I will come with you to Madagascar!' he said, and his voice boomed within the hollow nave, off the carved mahogany and the startled faces of plaster angels.

'What are you boys doing in here?'

They did not stay to see who had spotted them, but ran out through the vestry, letting the door bang behind them. That bang set the royal chapel reverberating like a drum. Nathan did not hear it, though, for the throb of blood in his ears. He was going to live among the pirates! He was going to live out his day-dreams, on a far-away island, living among savages!

Back down the drive they ran, through a fine, sleeting rain, weaving in and out of the noble beech trees, grazing their hands on the bark. He was going to drink rum and eat coconuts and build a hut from palm leaves! God had given his approval!

Then, just at the very moment when Nathan felt the weight of terror and misery fall from his heart, he caught sight of her.

Her little spoon-shaped face was the colour of corroded tin, her lank hair plastered to her skull by the rain, her nose red from crying and cold. His sister Maud stood with her hands grasping the school gates, her forehead resting against the bars as she hoped, without expectation, for a sight of her brother: the only person she had left in the world.

Just for a moment, Nathan hated her. She had only come to scupper his hopes, to sink his glorious daydream.

He had forgotten her—as everybody did with Maud—had overlooked her. A half-hour before he had been craving one soul on Earth who belonged to him, was family to him. But why had Maud had to come now and remind him that he did have family, after all? He skidded to a halt, just as she caught sight of him.

'I can't go.'

Tamo White gave a howl of exasperation. '*Now* what?' he said.

They were so close to Maud that she could hear what they were saying, and yet she did not venture in through the gates; that would have been presumptuous and unseemly. Her face crumpled into renewed tears. Her thin-wristed little hands reached through the gate, imploring her brother for comfort. Nathan walked slowly down the drive, with Tamo snapping at his heels—'Now what? *Now* what's wrong?'—and opened the heavy gate. Maud pitched herself against his chest, sobbing dementedly. The rain was turning to hail.

'I can't go. I have a sister,' Nathan explained to the pirate's son.

'Well, bring her with you!'

They stood there, being pelted by the hail. The granules of ice rested momentarily on Maud's head then melted into her wispy hair. The fur of Tamo's waistcoat glistened with diamonds of sleet.

Nathan shook his head dismally. Take his sister to live among savages a thousand miles from home?

'Bring me where?' snuffled Maud, shuddering with cold.

Tamo White bowed to her with an elegant flourish. 'To Madagascar, madam. I am returning home, and invited your brother to accompany me.'

Nathan sniggered despite himself—a rictus of misery. Take Mousy Maud to Madagascar? A million miles from Christian decency? Among cannibals and lonely sailors and diseases and wild beasts? 'Take no notice,' he advised his sister. 'It was just a fancy. Just me being fanciful. You know me.' Nathan comforted himself that he would shortly die of an ague caught standing about in the rain; then all his troubles would be at an end.

'I fear we could not afford to pay for our passage, sir,' Maud was saying to the pirate's son.

'There is no requirement, ma'am. My guardian owns a ship. I was thinking to sail with him.'

Nathan took his borrowed jacket off and put it round his sister, although it was so wet that this was hardly an act of chivalry—more like hanging a blanket round a bird cage to stop the bird squawking.

'Very well, sir,' said Maud. 'We are greatly obliged to you for your kind invitation,' said Maud. 'When do we sail?'

Doctor Thrussell, returning from evening chapel, his thumbs in his armholes and the blackbirds singing all around, contemplated the arrival of a new student the following day. The child of very eminent parents. The honour and the revenue to come solaced him somewhat for the criminal behaviour of that villain Gull. Dead, indeed, and destitute! What was the Church of England coming to? At least God had done His best to recompense the school for the fraud perpetrated upon it.

His foot struck a half-empty canister, and some of the contents splashed his ankles. Thrussell sniffed; a foul, butcher's-yard smell. He bent to inspect the contents of the can. Pigs' blood, he concluded. Soon after, he found the stick Tamo had used to spread the blood—and, straightening up, saw the words daubed along the wall of the royal chapel.

'Gull!' The name burst from his mouth like a cough.

Even the fact that the Latin was correct gave the headmaster no relief from the rage which crammed his body and set his feet dancing on the spot. A new and prized pupil arriving next day, and all along the chapel wall were daubed the words, in pigs' blood, *DE MORTUIS NIL NISI BONUM.*

Never speak ill of the dead.

3

Madagascar

Warmth sat on his chest like a cat. Around him an azure and green sea breathed with soft undulations on its muscular back, and now and then flying fish leapt through the glassy surface before falling back against their own reflections. Nathan did not see them, for he had his eyes shut, but he could hear Maud cry out each time, her wonder as great as at the first. Porpoises were leaping in convoy beneath the dipping prow, escorting the ship towards Madagascar. From time to time, fear dropped out of the shrouds and pierced Nathan like a marlin spike: Madagascar. But for the most part he was too comfortable, too relaxed, to think ahead. The present was sufficient.

Tamo White, on the other hand, had barely stopped being seasick for one hour since leaving England. He was less inclined to live in the present.

'When will we get there?' he kept asking the captain. 'How much longer?'

To distract him, Captain Sheller, his guardian, was trying to teach him seamanship, navigation and so forth. But the fact that he smoked a clay pipe, and blew his smoke generously into Tamo's face as he spoke, meant that the lessons rarely lasted long.

Of Tamo's three guardians, the Frenchman had died of typhus in Marseilles; the Dutch-American, a shipbuilder, had gone down in one of his own vessels on the Bermuda reefs. That only left Captain Sheller, a jolly, florid man inclined to such vagueness that it was not plain where or on what business he plied his three-master the *Tenderness*.

'What were you doing on the island when father asked you to be my guardian?' Tamo had asked him.

'God's work. God's own work, son,' Sheller said, which made Tamo think of him as a missionary.

Sheller wore a tartan waistcoat under a red jacket, and a tricorn hat, a flat side rising from his forehead and the corners jutting out over both ears and the back of his neck. It made his head look gigantic, his capacity for thought far greater than other men. And yet he gave the impression of a rather vague and absent-minded man, muddling along through life's complications, rarely reaching the end of a sentence without forgetting where it had been heading. In fact he could not even seem to recollect where his ship was ultimately bound when he agreed to take Tamo and his two friends back to Madagascar. Nathan had half expected the guardians Thomas White chose for his son to be pirates, with black moustachios and a shortage of eyes and teeth. Captain Sheller was clearly no pirate. He scarcely touched strong drink, and kept a Bible in a cork box wedged between the spokes of the ship's wheel. His cheek was invariably smooth, and he smiled at the children with a doting fondness every time one of them looked his way.

'Uncle Jacques—before he died—he said there are pirates all the way from Tamatave up to the Bay of Antongil these days,' said Tamo, 'and at Masselage and St Augustine and Matitanana, too.'

'Then I'd best set you down somewheres else, my dearheart, hadn't I?' the captain had said with a breezy chortle, and chucked his ward under the chin. 'Trust your Uncle Noah to look after you.' And he had locked Tamo's sea-chest in his own cabin—'You can never be too careful these days, my dearheart . . . such rogues in the world.'

'I'd forgotten,' said Tamo to Nathan. 'I'd forgotten about the seasickness. Going to England I didn't mind it so much. It stopped me thinking. You can't cry when you're being sick.'

Nathan pulled his knees primly to his chest. He was rather appalled by talk about such things. Things like crying. Graylake boys did not cry. 'Didn't you want to go to England, then?'

'And leave everyone I knew? Never see them again? My mother, for instance. Did you know your mother?'

Nathan swallowed. Did he have to talk about such things? He was not a great one for sharing confidences.

His father had always told him: 'Nobody wants to know your troubles, lad. People have troubles of their own.'

He swallowed again and said, 'She died when Maud was born. Sometimes I think I do, but it's only what I've been told. Probably only what I'd been told. There was a blue dress . . . Anyway, I wasn't two when she died.'

'I remember mine,' said Tamo categorically. 'I remember her pushing a canoe down the beach, pushing it out through the surf. It was too heavy for her. I was afraid. She came paddling out to the ship. She was wearing her red cloth—red and green. She called up to me. The canoe kept bumping against the ship: I was frightened for her. I said, "Go away,

Mama." She had a necklace of crocodile teeth she wanted to give me—for good luck—but the ship was so tall and she was so low down . . . A sailor was washing the decks. I asked him to let his bucket down, so she could get the charm to me. But he didn't understand. I took the bucket from him, but I was so little: I was too clumsy. When I let it down, the bucket banged against her head. And when I tried to pull it up the necklace fell out and I lost it. Mama was holding her head, and I thought she'd be angry with me—for hurting her and for losing the amulet. So I ran away—to the other side of the ship. And when I looked again, she was rowing back to the beach. And I was afraid for her. The sharks, and so on.'

'Sharks?' Up until then, Nathan had imagined Madagascar in a hundred different ways. Now he could picture only sharks. Sharks and crocodiles. He wanted to ask, 'What else? What else haven't you told me about? Am I going to have to spend day and night hiding up a tree from wild beasts?'

But Tamo was thinking about his mother, and it would have sounded selfish, not to mention cowardly. So instead Nathan said, 'Does your mother know you're coming home?'

Tamo snarled at him oddly, the tears flowing easily and openly down his cheeks. 'How could she? You think I could send a letter? You think my mother went to Graylake? You think she can read the King's English? Or maybe you think she's waited on the beach five years? She'll be gone away! She wouldn't stay. After the old man died, she wouldn't stay with those scum. She'll have gone back to her own kind. How do you propose I find her, Mister Gull, sir? Stand on a hill and whistle?'

Maud looked away from the flying fish when she heard Tamo's voice raised in anger. She scurried over from the rail, and placed herself between the two boys, her hands demurely clasped in front of her waist. She was accustomed to reacting in this way to raised voices. In the last months at home, when money had been short, she had often had to defend her father from the anger of tradesmen who wanted paying. 'We will help you look for her, Mister White,' she said, smiling sweetly at the pirate's son.

Tamo was exasperated, but he was too unused to girls to argue with one. 'You people. You don't understand. It's big. Madagascar's big. It's big like England. Much bigger than England. It's big like France! Or Italy! Or Russia!'

Maud put her hands on her hips and looked down at him, sceptically. She was clearly not convinced of the bigness of Madagascar.

Inside Tamo's head, the vastness (which he had proved to himself with globes and charts and atlases) vied with his memories. The Madagascar inside his head was a row of huts, a noise of chickens, a dish of rice, a melon patch, and a smell of cordite as his father sat shooting button-quail from a chair in a doorway. He longed to get home to familiar surroundings—but would he know anything at all when he got to some strange new stretch of shoreline, somewhere other than Tamatave? He might know nothing, nothing more than these two English. To put an end to the discussion, he said, 'I won't see my mother again. Not a chance. Now leave it.' Then the ship altered course slightly, and took a rolling turn in the trough of a big wave. Tamo White bolted for the ship's rail.

* * *

Nathan, too, felt his ignorance like a pain. He wished he could have had time to read books about Madagascar, to know what he would eat, to know what would eat him, to know *anything* at all! He wanted to join in Tamo's lessons in navigation, but did not like to impose on the captain's kindness or time. 'People will like you best, Nathaniel, for saying least,' his father had always told him.

So he struck up a friendship with one of the two ship's navigators, Charles Hardcastle. If he knew nothing at all about Madagascar, he might at least learn a thing or two about the sea which surrounded it. Charles Hardcastle, a Tilbury man, was more than glad of the company. For he had learned, just before signing aboard, that his wife was expecting her first child. It had given him a whole new perspective on children, and he looked upon Nathaniel as a wonderful chance to find out more about them.

'I hope my boy has your brains,' he would say to Nathan. 'I hope my boy can make shift as well as you, if he's left all alone in the world.' Being almost a father himself, he found it ineffably sad to think of Nathan losing his, and let Nathan babble on about the Reverend Gull for hours, while he leaned over his charts and made busy calculations of tide and wind.

'You see, father guaranteed a loan for one of his parishioners—that means he promised to pay the money back if the borrower couldn't—and when this man lost all his money, father had to pay—even though *he* hadn't borrowed the money in the first place. Well, Maud says he tried to pay the interest with the money from his living. But it wasn't enough, and he had to borrow more from his own bank, and he couldn't afford the repayments. He never had any savings, and the parsonage wasn't ours to sell, and there wasn't anything left for us to live on, and no one knew except Maud, because Papa didn't want me told, because it might upset my studies, and of course he thought something would come right: God would make things right. Maud says he prayed a lot for God to put things right.'

'I hope my boy remembers me as fondly, after I'm gone,' said Charles Hardcastle.

It was odd that there were two ship's navigators. Even Hardcastle did not understand it, for he was being paid well above the standard rate himself. 'It was the only thing that persuaded me to leave Heskia alone at a time like this. I asked Captain Sheller—why two of us?—but he didn't quite seem to know, himself.'

'Yes, woolly-headed, isn't he?' said Nathan, grinning.

'I doubt that,' said Charles Hardcastle, and coughed politely into his hand.

'Where exactly are you bound, uncle?' said Tamo. (He had always called his guardians 'uncle'.)

'Oh, here and there. Here and there, son,' said Captain Sheller.

'You're so very kind,' said Maud, for the hundredth time. 'To go out of your way, for us, captain. I do hope it won't be dangerous for you.'

'For a pretty lady like yourself, dearheart,' said the captain, looking at Maud with such tenderness that his head listed to one side, 'I'd sail to China and pluck the emperor's beard.'

She smiled and coloured, and clasped her hands in front of her stomach. In secret she was knitting the captain a pair of woollen hose, she liked him so much. But Nathan could see that she hated to attract attention, and diverted the conversation away from her. Besides, he really wanted to know.

'Hey, Tamo. Those crocodile teeth—are there really crocodiles? I mean, do you . . . meet them very often? I mean, how do you kill a crocodile?'

'Kill them? You don't!' exclaimed Tamo White, stunned with disgust. 'They're *fado*! Some people's ancestors are crocodiles! Would you kill another man's ancestor?'

Brother and sister looked at one another, and when they turned back to look at Tamo, both their mouths were open to speak.

But Tamo had smelt the captain's clay pipe, and was making for the rail again.

'Where did you say the ship was heading, Captain Sheller?' said Nathan.

'Oh, here and there, lad. Here and there.'

Madagascar appeared like a gigantic crocodile asleep along the horizon. It was as green as privet and might have been as big as France or the size of a garden. But three hours of sailing scarcely brought it nearer. It remained a green mirage, lacking all detail. Nathan began to think it must be moving away from them, borne on the tides, or swimming like whale: they would never set foot there. He was barely sorry.

'Let me see, uncle,' said Tamo, as the captain scanned the coastline with a telescope.

'Nothing to see, boy. Nothing but trees.'

Nathan wandered away, to find his friend the navigator. Hardcastle was easing a chart out of a leather tube, and clearing a space for it on his table by piling things into his hammock—rulers, ink bottles, pens, cups, a plate, a telescope. 'Do you know these parts very well?' said Nathan, getting in the way.

'Pretty well. I was an East-India man before this. I've steered past it many a time . . . Not as well as Sheller, mind. He's plied these waters all his life, so I hear.'

'Going where? Where does he go, exactly?' There was a rising hope in Nathan's breast that he might be able to stay on board and reach some more civilized, far-off spot on the globe. Even if it meant parting from his new friend, he owed it to Maud to ask, at least. There was the matter of the sharks and the crocodiles to be considered.

'Go? Well, to Madagascar, naturally.'

'No, no. I don't mean this time. He's just putting Tamo White ashore there. Where will he go on to, after?'

'On? Why nowhere, boy. It's back home from Madagascar. Can't be soon enough for me. Oh! Any day now, Nat! Imagine being eight thousand miles from dear Mrs Hardcastle at a time like this.' And with that he pushed a parallel ruler across the map, plotting their present course and projecting it directly into the heart of the word *Tamatave*.

'You mean that's his destination?'

Charles Hardcastle wagged his eyebrows and blew through his lips like a horse. 'When a man can earn what Captain Sheller earns from one trip here, why should he dent his keel anywhere else? Beautiful place. Beautiful, by all accounts. I'll think very well of it, I dare say, when I'm home snug in Tilbury.'

Nathan pointed at the map. 'But not there. He's not going there. That's where the pirates live. He's going to drop us along the way from there,' said Nathan. 'Somewhere there are no pirates.'

Hardcastle seemed surprised by that. 'Said nothing

to me about it.' Turning to examine the chart, he ran his finger over its topcoat of varnish crazed and brown, tracing the coastline. He was interrupted by a knock at the door.

'Captain Sheller wishes a word, Mister Hardcastle,' said the deck-boy.

'That's what he wants to tell you,' said Nathan, confidently.

After Hardcastle had gone, Nathan stood about in his cabin, waiting. He sat on the stool beside the desk and studied the chart entitled *'Madagasikara'* with its reefs and islands, and fringe of place-names. It was as if the interior were utterly uninhabited, for not one word appeared on the uplands, away from the coast. But then seamen need to know nothing about a place beyond its safe harbours, shoals, coastal landmarks.

The names were preposterous, half a mile long and shaped like words a magician might use: *Ambodifototra, Farafangana, Helodranon i Mahajamha*. 'Abracadabra,' muttered Nathan, and turned to look out of the porthole, which lit the map table with a round beam of sunlight.

He squinted against the sun-jagged water. Then he recalled that one of the things Hardcastle had tossed into his hammock was a telescope, and fetched it. He poked it out through the porthole. The ferrules were sweetly oiled. The lenses were strong. As Nathan searched about for the horizon, a circular image crisped suddenly out of a blue blur. A ship.

A ship was bearing down on the port bow—a ramshackle hull of pitch-black timber wearing every stitch of sail on the mainmast, nothing at all on the fore mast, which wagged at a drunken angle to the deck. From the after mast hung a black flag made from something unsuitably heavy which did not catch the wind.

Nathan's stomach turned over within him. He fumbled his grip on the telescope and it slipped out through the porthole, plummeting into the water without the vestige of a splash. Nathan peered out with his own unaided sight, and the ship was still there. It seemed so far off now that he could not so much as see the flag at the masthead . . . He must warn Captain Sheller. He must warn Tamo and Maud.

Pirates!

4

Tamatave

'Pirates! Pirates!' he yelled, as he thudded along the wooden decking. *'Pirates! Pirates!'*

He should have known from his reading what to expect. Sheller had sailed too close to a pirate lair, and they had caught scent of him: easy prey. 'Pirates! Pirates!'

Maud gave a little squeal and covered her face. Tamo, unable to see anything, began to climb the side-rigging. Captain Sheller did not stir. 'Where's that then, lad?' He polished the eye-piece of his telescope with meticulous care, using a corner of his plaid waistcoat, then laid it unhurriedly to his eye. He scanned the horizon, beginning on the starboard side, though Nathan kept pointing the other way. At last the telescope settled on the distant ship.

'There! Yes! You see? You see! Pirates!'

Captain Sheller folded his telescope away and slid it into a long pocket behind his coat-tails. 'Just an island trader,' he said. Maud still had her eyes shut in terror. Tamo White dropped back down on to the deck and scowled at his schoolfriend. Nathan looked around for Hardcastle, but he was nowhere on deck. He clambered up on to a capstan and tried to make out the ship against the black-dazzle of the glittering sea. He could just see it, making away from them now, heading back towards the land. He sank down, astride the capstan, and sat there until Tamo came by and pushed him off it:

'Gull, Gull, filled his skull
With too much pirate cock and bull.'

'It *was* a pirate ship,' he hissed. 'I saw it through Mr Hardcastle's telescope. A black flag and open gun-doors. Why did it turn away?'

Tamo snorted. '*Gull, Gull, filled his skull . . .* '

'Because it knows the ship, that's why. Because Captain Sheller is expected. He's making for Tamatave.'

'Who says?'

'I'll show you.' Nathan got to his feet and, with a furtive glance over his shoulder, linked arms with Tamo and led him aft to Charles Hardcastle's cabin.

The navigator was nowhere to be seen, but the chart still lay on the desk, their course plotted into the very harbour of Tamatave. 'What did I tell you?' hissed Nathan. 'He's a pirate himself!'

'No, he's not.'

'Of course he is! Oh, come on! Just because he's your . . . '

'He's not a pirate,' said Tamo, slowing to his own moment of realization. 'You're right. He is going to Tamatave. To trade with the crew. He's a supplier.' White abruptly put on a belligerent bluster. 'So? He never said he was a saint, did he? He never said he wasn't a trader?' But Nathan could tell he was angry—could tell it from the way Tamo gouged a hole in the chart with the point of a pair of compasses, twisted them round and round and round till the metal point squealed against the desktop.

'You checking out our route, boys? That's right. That's good practice for you.' Captain Sheller stood in the door of the cabin, smiling his King Cole smile. His great shovel of a hat cast a horned shadow across the chart.

'You're going to Tamatave, then?' said his ward, as if it was nothing to him.

'My duty, boy. My duty. Every trip, my duty to relieve those unredeemed sinners of their ill-gotten wealth. Let 'em know crime has its costs and taxes, same as any Christian has to pay. God's appointed revenue man, that's how I see myself.'

'Isn't it dangerous to go there?' asked Nathan, selfishly.

'I'm fearless in the Lord's work,' said the captain. ''Sides, they need me, don't they? Can't do without their necessaries. Or their vices.' He flourished his pipe stem towards the land. 'I quicken their downfall with the liquor that kills them. If they choose to poison themselves with drink and indulgence, it's God's work to help them do it! You lads care to stretch your legs ashore?'

'No!' Nathan felt his stomach cramp and his heart fill up. Go among the pirates? See pirates, in their natural habitat? They were the stuff of all his daydreams; they were the very people he had thought about all his dull childhood—the beacons that had lit his way through every bleak, grey day of his bleak, grey life. But did he want to meet any? Did he really want to see the genuine item? No, he did not, no. Out there, he would be Nathaniel Gull among the world's hooligans, not a hero, not a swashbuckler, not a pirate chief or fearless admiral—just Nathaniel Gull, schoolboy, with weak wrists and scabby grey knees. 'No, thank you, sir,' he told Sheller. 'I'll stay on board,' he said.

'I've no business to be in the place,' said Tamo White, picking threads from his sleeve with concentrated care. 'But I suppose I could always visit my father's grave.'

'The very thing it was in my mind to suggest,' said Sheller, clapping his hands together. 'You two run ashore, while I do my painful, Christian duty.' He turned to go.

'I'll need to apply to my sea-chest . . . ' Tamo said suddenly.

'Nonsense, nonsense. I'll give you each a guinea out of my own purse to spend. But really, what could you possibly want to buy from these have-nothings?'

'It's not money I need from it. It's a charm. Something my mother gave me,' Tamo insisted. 'I'd like to put it on my father's grave.'

'Ah.' Captain Sheller looked mildly embarrassed, and fumbled beneath his big stomach for the key to his cabin. 'Thought those Christian schoolmasters would have careened you of all that native nonsense. But if you must . . . Come, and I'll let you into my cabin.' At the door, he paused, with an extra word for Nathan. 'You'd best tell that pretty sister of yours to stay safe aboard, mind, Master Gull. This is no place for a lass. Tell her to sit tight in my cabin till we sail.'

'Yes. Yes, yes, sir! Yes, I will, yes!'

All this while, the green arms of a Madagascan bay closed the ship tighter and tighter in its embrace. The leadsman at the ship's prow plumbed shallower and shallower depths, until the hiss of the shelly sea-bed could be heard distinctly through the bare boards of the ship, and men's voices came across the water.

The ships in the harbour were the strangest Nathan had ever seen. From a long way off, they reeked of pitch, and their ropes lay about like dishevelled hair. The sails were patchworks of mending, and the hulls listed alarmingly. Planks were sprung loose from the sides, and the iron monkey-brackets on deck, mostly empty of cannonballs, were red with rust. One vessel had the odd, pot-bellied shape of an Indian merchantman, but though it had been grand once, with gilded decorations to the bowsprit and gundoors, it was falling into melancholy disrepair, like a fairground booth in winter.

There was a skeleton of a jetty, only the barest bones hanging together, and the wood, like the fascias of the hillsides' huts, was bleached by the sun to a bone white. Only the vegetation looked entirely, breathlessly new, as if the palm trees had geysered out of the earth that very morning. A pall of smoke hung over the distant greenness, where patches of jungle were being cleared for planting.

As the *Tenderness* made fast, more and more people drifted down to the waterfront. The children ran, not troubling to stop at the water's edge but splashing out into surf. Native women in dazzling cloth wrappers glided serenely into the gaps between the huts, looking out from beneath their hands.

Then the men came, hunching their shoulders into jackets, though the noonday sun was overhead, and it was ferociously hot. Waistcoats and jackets and hats, tall sea boots, and cummerbunds bulging with pistols. They looked filthy and moth-eaten, and puce with the heat, and they shambled belligerently down to the quay as if supply ships disturbed them from their rest every day of the year. A member of Captain Sheller's crew manned the cannon on deck.

'Good health to you, gentlemen!' Sheller bellowed. 'How agreeable to renew acquaintance with you!'

'I thought you said you dropped the charm your mother gave you,' said Nathan, waiting for the gang-plank to stop bouncing under Tamo's weight.

'Never mind what I said,' hissed White. 'And keep your mouth shut, will you?'

Nathan wondered if the unpleasantness of the place was infectious, if he was leaving civilization on board and entering barbarian territory. 'At least you might see your mother, now,' he suggested eagerly.

'I told you, didn't I? She wouldn't stay with this kind. Not once the old man was dead.'

They walked on through the village, and Nathan scrupulously watched the ground, terrified to look anyone in the face for fear of having his throat cut. Small pigs dashed urgently across their path. Bullocks stood in the shade of trees, their horns twisted into weird, unnatural shapes. A strange, black-and-white animal ran up and down a cage outside a wattle house. A dog chased its tail in never-ending circles.

As the noises of the village closed round him, Nathan turned and walked backwards, trying to keep the ship in sight. What if it were to sail away and maroon him here . . . 'He doesn't sound as if he hates them, your guardian. He's being very friendly with them.'

Tamo spat—a refined, Graylake spit. 'Does a shark hate meat? They've made him rich, haven't they? Richer than any of them, I expect.'

They passed between fields of water, walls of mud where, in England, hedges would have stood. A boy was kicking a hole in one wall to take water from the next paddy. A group of women were mending another with handfuls of slimy mud.

'Does the captain mean to take us further on? Somewhere else? Somewhere better than this?' asked Nathan.

'I'm like a son to him. He swore an oath to my father. He won't cheat me.' But Tamo's voice was high and tinny with uncertainty.

Suddenly they came upon a compound—it looked

like a village in its own right—a village of carved poles or doorways of cane; archways to nowhere, little rectangles of sky. It was the graveyard. Personal belongings of the dead were strung from the poles—bowls and kettles, clothes, chairs, baskets and necklaces. They moved all the time in the breeze, knocking and tinkling like the top-hamper of a ship.

Nathan managed a generous surge of pity for the innocent ignorance of these savages. 'I suppose they believe people need these things for the after-life,' he said.

'Don't be ridiculous. They're polluted. They've been in contact with a dead body, haven't they—no use to anyone else, except for decoration.' He began to tug at his hair, running his fingers agitatedly through his fringe as he lunged this way and that among the graves. Nathan hung back at the perimeter fence, whispering the Lord's Prayer, his Catechism, his Creed and finally even nursery rhymes and pieces of Latin verse: anything, so long as it fended off the whispering of the breeze through dead men's belts and children's carved toys . . .

Clearly, Tamo White, for all his searching, could not find his father's grave, and though Nathan wanted to help, the more he peered among the strung belongings, the more he saw that he did not want to see—a wicker chair, a child's sandal, a rower's paddle. And there were so many! What had at first seemed a handful of graves, in fact numbered dozens, scores.

A woman came by, carrying a gigantic pile of palm leaves on her head, the green leathery tongues dipping fore and aft as she walked.

'Tamo White? Capito Tamo White?' said Tamo, and the woman pointed a languid arm in the direction of the jungle. It was the first time Nathan had realized that the pirate's son bore the same name as his father; it was just that the islanders said Tamo for Thomas. He, Nathaniel Gull, was on Madagascar with Thomas White!

At last, together, they found it. The old pirate had been given a Christian burial, of course, in a pleasant woodland clearing. The grave was surrounded by a picket fence, to keep the wild hogs from rootling, and had a cross at the head, with the name crudely carved: Cpt. Tomas Wyte. The plot had been planted out with watermelons, and the small, unswelled fruit lay about like cannonballs in a twining of blown flowers.

Nathan respectfully took off his cap (though Tamo did not). Here lay the celebrated pirate whose household name Nathan had read off the printed page, trembling with excitement. Now he lay at their feet in the tropical sunshine. He tried to recall everything he had read. It poured out of him in a nervous, confused babble. 'He was a gentleman, really, wasn't he? I read how, if it wasn't for being marooned that time, and picked up by mutineers and such, he'd never have been a pirate at all. I read how, when he took that ship, and there were two children on board and the two children were crying and he said, "Why are they crying?" and they said he'd taken their silver teaspoons and those teaspoons were all they had in the world, and he gave the teaspoons back and took up a collection and gave the orphans a whole fortune to live on . . . So he must've been kind, your father. He must've been . . . different, your father. Well, he must have! To send you to school, the way he did! Not like the others . . . '

The pirate's son stood looking at the grave, his face expressing nothing. 'He was just like the others,' he said, coldly. '*Nathan Gull filled his skull, With too much pirate cock-and- . . .* Teaspoons be damned. I've been clothed and fed and shipped away and educated on teaspoons, haven't I, one way and another? Children's teaspoons, ladies' wedding rings, brides' dowries. Shouldn't believe what you read in books. He was a thug and a drunk. When he was drunk he was like a mad pig. My poor mother—'

He broke off at the sound of choking, and turned to see Nathaniel Gull, shirtsleeves flapping as he lifted his hands again and again in an inarticulate, helpless grief. His shoulders shook, his face streamed with tears, and his mouth shaped itself into a kind of howl.

'Mine wasn't! Mine wasn't like anybody!' he called up into the sunny treetops, and the raucous birdsong was quelled for a moment. 'Mine was better than anybody else's! And I didn't even stay to see him buried! And I loved him, and I should've hit Thrussell when he said those things, and I didn't! And here you are, and here's—' He flapped his cuffs at the watermelon patch, laid his head back and howled like a wolf. 'And here's me and *what am I doing here*?'

In two strides, Tamo White leapt across the grave and collided so hard with Nathan that the younger boy thought he was being attacked and put up his fists. But the pirate's son only sank to the ground, grabbed up two clods of dry soil and smashed them against his own head.

'And I can't dance with mine!' he roared, tugging Nathan down beside him. 'We dance with our dead here! We raise them up and dance with them! But they've given him a Christian burial! He may have been a swine, but did they have to give him a Christian burial? Now I can't even dance with him! He hasn't been buried the right way!'

'Owow! That's terrible!' howled Nathan, not understanding in the least. 'I'm so, so sorry!'

Their hands on each other's elbows, their heads on each other's shoulders, they sobbed unrestrainedly, grieving for their lost fathers, sorrowing over what might have been. They cried, and all around them unseen creatures hooted and gibbered and sobbed too, and the flies keened and the tortoises plodded inexorably on, weighed down with their own burden of hard, heavy, green grief.

Then, for a long while, the boys sat in silence, but for their sniffing, and the heat bored into them, and the brightness of the sunlight half closed their eyes.

'Graylake boys don't cry,' said Nathan at last.

'Then aren't you glad you're not one?' said the pirate's son. Later, he told Nathan about painting the slogan along the chapel wall. As he did so, Nathan's mouth dropped wider and wider open, in spellbound horror.

'He'll think I did it!' he gasped. 'Thrussell will think I painted it!' And then realizing that Thrussell and everything he stood for had shrunk to the importance of a pin-head, he began to laugh. Tamo laughed, too, and they laughed for as long as they had cried, and the sun beat down impartially. A yellow tortoise, patterned with sunbursts of black, moved among the watermelons. As beautifully patterned as the fruit, it pushed on through life, regardless.

'Will Sheller really take us on down the coast?' Nathan asked at last.

'I don't think he means to. I think he means to set sail without us and keep the money that's in my sea-chest.'

'No!'

'Which is why I made an excuse to get to my sea-chest.' When Tamo tugged at his shirtfront, something impressively large jingled inside. 'I'm sure he loves me like his own son, but I don't believe I shall trust him better than a cat in an aviary. No one trusts a supplier.'

They began to walk back towards the harbour. Here and there, paths struck off the main track towards solitary huts hidden among the trees. A notice hung from a tree, which said OUT. Thorns and sharp stones had been embedded point-uppermost in the pathways, and jagged pieces of metal dangled from the boughs, so that a man might lose his ears who approached the hut after dark.

'This is what I remember,' said Tamo. 'The traps and the snares. No one went about the village at night. It was too dangerous. Everyone's great aim was to bury themselves in a jungle where they couldn't be reached. Fortresses, they built. Little fortresses.'

'Fortresses? What against? Against what? Crocodiles?' Nathan's voice was reedy with alarm.

'Against each other, of course!'

Nathan shook his head, appalled.

'Whyever would you want to come back to a place like that?'

'I didn't, did I? Not here. Not to Tamatave. I hate this place. There's nothing here for me. Here I'm just Captain Thomas's mulatto brat.'

Back on the waterfront, the crew were all redder in the face than ever. The prices Sheller was charging them for the most basic commodities of life were rocking them on their heels. Three pounds for a gallon of rum worth two shillings! Three hundred pounds for a pipe of Madeira wine which could only have cost him twenty in New York. Eighty pounds for a few carpenters' tools and a bag of nails. A hundred for three barrels of gunpowder.

Native women, whose menfolk were sick, shrieked shrill Malagasy swearwords at Sheller, gesturing wildly that they needed the medicine in his hand, needed it, must have it. And yet the little bottles of mercury or quinine, which Sheller carried in a pouch by his side, never changed hands for less than fifty gold pieces.

The smile never left his face, either, the tender sympathy never left his eye. But there were, as he explained, costs, insurances, shortages, bribes to pay, wheels to oil. The pirates called him a zooful of names. They wished on him a hospital of diseases. They damned his soul to all the seven depths of Hell, and laded his ship with curses. But Sheller continued to smile beatifically down on them, like a pastor from a pulpit, saying, 'The market, the market, dearhearts!' in answer to every curse.

They did not all pay with money, either, but in goods and valuables, booty from ships they had plundered. In exchange for rum and gunpowder, they offered gold pocket-watches, pairs of boots, women's bracelets and uncut gemstones, bolts of gorgeous Indian silk, and silver cutlery. Sheller rubbed the silk between finger and thumb and jutted his lower lip. 'Poor stuff, poor stuff,' he sighed. 'I sympathize with you, friend. For top grade I could have credited you three shillings a bale. But this is only worth one.'

'One!?'

Nathan and Tamo watched from the shade of the trees. The pirate's son seemed unmoved, as if he had seen it all a hundred times before. Nathan was besieged by a dozen different emotions. 'I was here! I saw it! I can write this down, like Exquemelin! Wait till I tell . . . !' But write where? Tell whom? He was as much a prisoner of Madagascar as the pirates. What had they done, these men, to get hold of those pewter tankards, that box of linen? Perhaps the captain was right to take their booty away from them, but was it godly to fill his ship with pirate plunder for less than the cost of a cargo of coal?

Captain Sheller knew several of the men by name, and the rest by their nationality—never guessed wrongly where a man came from. 'You! Newfoundland!' he called out to a knot of pinch-faced, undersized men. 'Saw seven of you fish-gutters hung out to dry like sardines on execution dock! Seven in one morning! You could smell fish all the way to Rotherhithe. You! Portugal! Heard a storm off Finisterre sank four Oporto ships with one wave, no word of a lie!'

At last, when he had grieved and discomfited them, prised more money from them than they had ever thought to part with, Sheller gave them joy. He had saved it up, so that they would remember, feel endebted to him as he sailed away over the horizon. 'Tell me, dearhearts, what is it you men are always in need of? What is it you feel daily as lacking from your lives? You never see me but you say what you could do, but for want of . . . an *artist*. Well, I've brought you an artist, and they don't come better!'

'An artist?' said Nathan. 'Why would they want . . . ?' Beside him, Tamo White went rigid, like a cat catching the scent of a dog.

It took four men to carry Charles Hardcastle up out of the after-hold of the *Tenderness*, even though he was bound hand and foot. His face was bruised, his jacket torn, and there was the print of a boot-sole on his back. Nathan took a step forward, but Tamo pulled him back among the trees and clapped a hand over his mouth.

Meanwhile, Captain Sheller's voice rang out, clear and jolly. 'He's thoroughbred horseflesh, all right! Ten years with the East India Company. I'll vouch for his art and pedigree, and—look—I'll even throw in his sextant, for good measure!'

By rubbing his face along the ground, Hardcastle worked the gag free of his mouth and spat out a ball of gun-cotton. 'You devil, Sheller! You can't sell your fellow man! You can't sell a ship's officer! Think what you're doing, for the love of God! Have you got no spark of conscience in you, man? Have you got no shame?' A sailor off the supply ship kicked Hardcastle to silence him.

'No, no, dearheart, don't damage the goods,' said Sheller reprovingly. 'Now, what am I bid for a first-rate artist? He'll take you about the seas as sure as Moses guided the Israelites safe through the wilderness!'

Nathan punched and kicked at Tamo White, but the older boy was too strong for him. He forced Nathan to the ground, bent his arm behind his back and pressed his face against the sand, kneeling on him to hold him still—*'Listen, you baby! There's nothing you can do!'*—while Sheller auctioned away his navigator.

Four crew had made their permanent base in Tamatave. There was no shortage of captains, for pirate captains either bullied their way into power, or were chosen by their crew as the easiest to bully. Navigators were different, however. Navigators were skilled, educated men, with home lives worth leading, a decent wage and more to lose than most by taking to crime. They lacked the desperation which made a poor man turn to piracy. So navigators had to be captured, like butterflies in a net, and like butterflies, they too often died in the netting.

Consequently, Charles Hardcastle fetched a very good price—a king's ransom. The sum they paid for him—now there was a thing to tell his pretty wife and newly born child. Except that now, of course, he would never be able to return home, never be able to recount his adventures to his wife and child, for he would be a pirate, and pirates do not go home.

The captain who bought him—a short, scabby man in a turban and curl-toed slippers who called himself 'King Samson'—was unmoved by news of Hardcastle's wife and baby. 'I had a wife once, somewhere,' he said, looking down at his expensive, unwilling purchase. 'They're easy come by. And your missus can find herself another husband sooner than I can find myself another artist. You're one of us now, sirrah. Make the best of it.' He did not stoop to untie the man, or set him on his feet, but left Hardcastle bound, lying in the sun. 'You stay just there, till Noah Sheller's done and gone, and there's no ship for you to jump aboard.'

' . . . And now!' said Sheller, blotting his brow with a lace handkerchief. 'Even now I've saved you the best till last, dearhearts! Some man's going to his bed happy tonight!'

The crew, who had thought the auction over and had begun to move away, looked back over their shoulders. More? There was more?

'What have I brought you, you say? What? I'll tell you! Nay, I'll *show* you! A little wife just the shade and colour to remind you of home! Not above thirteen, if she's a day, and white as the snow on Dover's cliffs. Fetch her out, quartermaster! Fetch out Miss Maud for the gentlemen to see!'

5

Miss Maud

When the light from the window of the captain's cabin suddenly decreased, Maud looked up from her knitting. She was already rigid with fright at the thought of the ship lying docked in a pirate stronghold. When she saw a figure spread-eagled across the lattice casement, she gave a sob of terror and clutched her head to her knees. The pirates were coming aboard!

'Miss Maud! Miss Maud!' hissed the silhouette. 'Do exactly as I say, and do it now. Get out on to the deck. Above here. Above me.' Fingers came through the lattice, gripping it. She thought of stabbing them with her knitting needles, but did not dare. 'Maud! It's I! It's Tamo White!'

'Master White?'

'Be quick. You're not safe there!'

She laid down her knitting and, as she did so, dropped a stitch and hovered over it, not wanting to let the work unravel. 'Maud!' the sharpness in his voice made her snatch in her hands against her skirts, and the knitting fell to the floor with a plinking of needles. She ran to the door, thinking to call the captain. But the door was bolted on the outside.

'What are you waiting for, girl?'

'The door! It's locked! He's locked me in!'

'All right. All right. Let me think—Yes. Get into my sea-chest. You hear? Get inside my sea-chest. Just there.'

She did as she was told straight away this time. But so much had to be pulled out before she could climb in—so much to be bundled out of sight. She could hear Sheller's voice loud on the quayside, agreeing the price of something—a harpist or a carpet, it sounded like—as she bundled her skirt round her calves and squirmed down into the chest. The lid did not quite close. She pulled down on a nail in the iron banding with her fingertips until she had shut out the daylight.

She was kneeling on something knobbly, and it hurt. So she swept her hand around the base of the chest and laid hold on one of Tamo's pistols. Then she dared not let go, for fear it shoot her point blank. She could not have been more afraid to have sat on a ferret.

One hand on the gun, one hand holding the lid shut, she heard the bolt rattle on the captain's cabin: in thumped the quartermaster. Maud had the strangest impression, also, of hearing her name shouted somewhere off the boat—'Fetch out Miss Maud . . . !'

The quartermaster was standing so close to the chest when he swore that Maud started and let the nail slip out of her fingers so that the lid sprang open—just a crack, but it seemed a blind man must see it. No . . . The man shook the captain's hammock, and some of the books she had off-loaded into it flopped to the floor with an explosive bang.

Then he was gone, shouting along the length of the ship, 'Where, captain? She's not in your cabin. Where did you say?'

Maud lifted the sea-chest lid and stood up. There was no silhouette beyond the lattice. 'Master White?'

A pair of feet crashed against the lattice as Tamo swung back into view; Maud recoiled with fright and fell out of the box.

'Give me a bar, a rod, a bar—something!' said White.

She looked around her. A clutter of swords stood propped in a tub-barrel, presumably to arm the crew in a fight. She pulled one out, and tried to poke it through the lattice to him. The hand-guard was too big.

'Try to . . . with the point. With the blade. Try to . . . '

Maud understood: she was supposed to prise apart the trellis-work of wooden slats—to make a hole large enough to escape through. She wedged the blade in and pulled. The blade bent in a great arc, then snapped, and the broken tip went wanging outwards, striking Tamo just below the eye. He gave a small cry, and dropped entirely out of sight.

So horrified was Maud at what she had done that she gathered up her skirt and, still clutching the broken hilt, ran to the door. The quartermaster had not shot the bolt on his way out.

Turning back at the door, she took a last look round the room, and grabbed up her knitting needles. The sea-chest lid still hung open. She lifted out the horrible pistol, tucked that too into her waistband, then she was outside in the companionway and running. Her chief thought was to find out if she had killed Tamo White with the sword-tip.

'What d'you mean, she's not there? Of course she's there! I locked her in myself!' Sheller hissed, like something venomous, not moving his lips.

'But I looked . . . '

'She's hiding, you fool! Asleep somewhere! Or hiding! Fool. Winkle her out.' He did not want any flaw in the smooth running of the auction. Selling things to men like these was all a matter of creating an atmosphere in which the desire to buy outweighed all considerations of cost.

'Where is she, Sheller?' whooped the pirates. *'Bring her out! Show us the goods!'*

As Maud went over the ship's aft rail, her skirt snagged in a carpenter's join. Not all her tugging or wrenching or devout, Church-of-England prayers would free it. So she unfastened it and left it there, hanging like a butterfly's empty chrysalis. The pistol slid down into the leg of her drawers as she climbed down—down the captain's lattice window, down the log-line and into the water, where her brother and his friend stood on the half-submerged ruins of the broken-down jetty.

She hated heights. She could not swim. She had never climbed down a rope in thirteen years of life. But she did it, even so, simply by saying one word. It filled up her head. It occupied her mouth. It deafened her to the thud of men's feet running on the deck above. It obliterated anything the boys said as she climbed. It was not a comfort. It was not magic. But she said it over and over, on and on, like a magical incantation: *sharks, sharks, sharks, sharks, sharks.* And because her brother was up to his chest in water, and because the green transparent water was filled with dark and unidentifiable shapes, she was quick and nimble, chanting as she went, on and on: *sharks, sharks, sharks, sharks, sharks.*

Her petticoat spread like a waterlily on the surface of the sea, and the water (which she had expected to be cold) closed tepid around her legs and body and arms. *Sharks, sharks, sharks, sharks, sharks.* Her tidy bun collapsed and her hair turned dark on the water round her. Tamo White took hold of her shoulders, towed her to the wreck of the jetty and pushed her hands up against the timber joists:

'Make for the shore, but keep under the jetty all the way; keep out of sight,' he said. There was a cut the shape of an arrowhead below his eye, and it was oozing blood. *Sharks, sharks, sharks, sharks, sharks.* Maud did exactly as she was told: her whole childhood had prepared her for this perfect obedience.

They crept ashore in the pitch black shadow of the jetty, and, by scooping away sand from under the bulwark, were able to crawl under the hull of a whaler lying upturned on the beach nearby. Ten yards long and stinking of fish, it was as hot as an oven, and the whole inside was aswarm with tiny crabs. Scuttling, scratching, moving, colliding, they rattled their tiny bodies by the thousand over and around the dripping, clammy, hidden children. *Sharks, sharks, sharks, sharks, sharks.*

The auction broke up bad-temperedly, as the pirates drifted home, angry, disappointed, trying to deduce what trick Captain Sheller had been playing on them: talking of a girl for sale when there was no girl.

Sunset comes quickly in the tropics. The sun rests, like a preposterous orange pumpkin, on the sea, then suddenly sinks, with a flash of green, plunging the land into darkness, the sea into starlit luminescence. Sheller knew it was unsafe to moor in the harbour. His disgruntled customers might come looking to recoup their plunder after dark, or take reprisals for his overcharging. So, despite his raging frustration, he was obliged to slip his moorings and move the *Tenderness* off-shore, posting look-outs from stem to stern.

From their hiding place beneath the beached boat, the children did not hear what Sheller said when he found Maud's skirt hanging from the ship's rail. They did not hear how he felt about Tamo's failure to return to the ship, or whether he missed the boy like a son. They did not hear what he said when he went rifling White's sea-chest for his money, and found only primers, commonplace books, one pistol, and a fur waistcoat.

Up in the village, the men were drinking their new supplies of rum, singing, quarrelling, lumbering about like the last dinosaurs trying to blind themselves to the closeness of extinction. A man screamed. A woman laughed. A baby whooped small, feeble, unanswered cries. And the forests threw up a great wall of nocturnal noise, as high as the sky.

Meanwhile, Tamo, Nathan, and Maud said not one word, made not a sound, clutching their bent legs to their chests, pressing their knees into the sockets of their eyes, while the crabs swarmed around them.

At midnight a noise came up the beach towards them. A thump, a hiss of sand, and a grunt. Thump, hiss, grunt. When it touched against the hull with a hollow scraping, Maud let fly a banshee wail. Like a rabbit digging under a fence, she squirmed out from under the boat, filling her mouth with sand as she went.

The snapped-off sword was in her hand, and her eyes were clenched shut. 'Get off! Get away! Go away! I'm warning you!' She held the swordhilt in two hands and offered its broken blade to whoever was there.

When she opened her eyes, she saw, by moonlight, a bald, shrivelled head, toothless gums and long, wrinkled neck. The beaky face weaved to left and right, while the huge feet scuffed at the sand. It was a rock with legs. It was a sea monster one thousand years old and clad in armour. It was a turtle, and in the world she came from, such things did not even exist.

Maud fainted clean away. When she came to, the boys had overturned the whaler, put her aboard it, dragged it into the sea and were rowing—or at least riding the current—south towards the constellation of the Whale.

'It was just a turtle,' her brother explained airily. But he only knew because Tamo had told him.

'Why did we have to leave the ship?' Maud asked at last. There had been no chance to ask earlier.

'Because Sheller was planning to . . .'

'I don't think Miss Maud really wants to know that,' Tamo interrupted.

'Whyever not?' said Nathan, and continued. 'Captain Sheller was planning to sell you to a pirate for a wife, you see. He sold Mr Hardcastle to them for a navigator. Poor Hardcastle! Now he can't ever—'

Maud gave a strange, subhuman yelp and curled herself up in a tight ball, her wet shoes squelching together, her hair dragged forward over her face. She rocked and sobbed and cried and shrieked, all the way from Tamatave to Zaotralana.

'I told you she didn't want to know,' said the pirate's son patiently.

Zaotralana was a fishing village. It was not as far from Tamatave as Tamo could have wished—only fifty miles down the coast—but it seemed untouched by piracy—no fortifications, no cannon, no traps or snares, no white faces. A steeply shelving cove cradled three big out-rigger sailing-canoes. Nearby, children were gathering shellfish, prising them off the rocks, washing them in the surf. Small fish hung on a rack to dry, like beads on an abacus. The dense, dark green of the rain forest spilled, in bounding profusion, the trees strung together with lacy creepers, the ground between confettied with a thousand colours of flowers. Golden clumps of bamboo made blond tufts in the green mane of vegetation, and here and there terraces of glinting water and white, bark-walled houses threw back shards of sunlight into their eyes as they came ashore.

They climbed the steep path to the village. On the trees hung breadfruit, figs, and bananas, and melons lay about like cannon-balls in the aftermath of a battle. Except that war had never touched Zaotralana. Zaotralana was peopled by exquisite, graceful women, Biblical and surreally tall with their slender earthenware vessels balanced on their heads; Zaotralana, with its glistening rice paddies and groves of rosewood, had seen nothing but peace since the world's beginning, or so it seemed to Nathan and Maud.

Tamo disabused them. Their white faces drew stares, but did not amaze. So white faces had been there before. Though a canoe put out to sea that morning, there were gaps among the rowers. Many of the women wore their beautiful hair loose to their waist, but when Maud admired it he said, 'They only wear their hair so when they have . . . lost someone.'

Slavers had come raiding—a neighbouring tribe turning a feud to profit by selling their prisoners to some passing slave-ship. Some of Sheller's provisions had probably been paid for in slaves from Zaotralana who were now on their way to the plantations of the Caribbean. They might as well be dead, for all their friends would ever see of them again, and the women left behind wore their hair loose in mourning.

One thing it did mean. Houses had been left unoccupied—not burned as they might have been had the owners died on the floor inside—but left forlorn and empty except for the wildlife which had crept inside to scavenge or nest. Not that these were much like anything Nathan thought of as a house—just hovels, really. A few thick poles stuck up out of the ground and, between them, strips of overlapping, whitening bark were lashed into place with ropes of creeper, to serve as walls. The roofs were a clutter of branches and leaves, and various props were wedged up against the houses to keep them from falling down.

The one Tamo found empty faced south-east so that from its door the sea was just visible through the bamboo and trees.

'Wait here,' he said. 'I'm going to take advice.' He stuck the broken sword and pistol into his belt, then thought better of going armed, and threw them aside.

He made himself known to the village chief, the old women, the brooding, muscular adolescents—anyone who might resent newcomers to the village. He asked their help and advice. He praised the beauty of Zaotralana and the magnificence of their cattle. He admired their gardens, the craftsmanship of their canoes, and the rice they served him on plates of ravenala leaf. He never mentioned his father's name. He never mentioned Tamatave or the ship which had brought him, nor where he had come from. He simply asked if he might live out his life under their baobab trees, on their picturesque doorstep to the sea.

They smiled and gave him food. They smiled and gave him beer. They smiled and introduced to him their daughters, their granddaughters—even took him to the graveyard and introduced their ancestors. They smiled if he talked and they smiled if he kept silent.

And when he got up to leave, they gave him advice. Advice on planting and pest-control, advice on fishing grounds and the weather, advice on local magic.

Meanwhile, Nathan and Maud waited in front of the hut. A woman came by with a baby tied to her back within her raffia sarong; a man leading a goat. They stared and smiled, smiled and stared, and Maud would have blushed except that her cheeks were already red with sunburn. When the sun overhead grew overwhelming, the two ducked inside the black shade of the hut. They could see nothing, but there was a great commotion which made them crash into each other and get stuck in the doorway, in their haste to get out again. As their eyes adjusted to the dark, however, they could see the shape of the creature they had surprised. Its shining, saucer-round eyes blinked at them, the only visible feature of its jet-black face. Its long-fingered hands fumbled with remnants of food from a spilled basket. They thought at first that it had been tied up, then realized that its long, prehensile tail was clinging on to a roof-prop, to help it balance.

'So beautiful,' breathed Maud. She wanted to touch the dense, white, glistening fur of its body, cradle the nerve-twitched animal. She took a step towards it—and the creature was gone—over her head, using all four feet and its tail to swing from pole to pole. Launching itself through the open door, it ran off, knuckles to the ground, hind legs pumping. Seeing Tamo coming up the slope, it veered away into the trees and climbed one, as easily as a fly might climb a window pane.

Tamo had a live chicken in each hand, and a bowl upside down on his head. There was a piece of raffia cloth draped over one shoulder, and he teetered a little as he walked. He stopped short as the black-and-white creature ran across his path, and watched it run into the trees. Then he stepped over the garden fence and set down the chickens which settled to pecking at the weeds.

'We can stay! We can use the house! Look what they gave me! Everywhere I went, people gave me things. In England no one would give a poor man the fur off his egg. My oath, it's good to be home!' He was drunk with triumph. He was also slightly drunk on local beer. 'We're here! What are you waiting for! Let's eat—I have some rice here, somewhere. Let's sweep out the house! Let's sing! You're back in Paradise now, Adam and Eve! All you have to do here is be happy!' He flung himself down in the sun; brother and sister sat down gingerly opposite him, inspecting the ground first for ants. Looking around them, they tried to imagine a lifetime of Madagascar.

'Is it really Paradise?' asked Maud.

Tamo flung his arms about in gestures of rapturous well-being. 'Food on the trees, water in the streams, fish in the sea. The sun shines, and everyone dances! Of course it's Paradise!'

A group of young men, who had heard news of Maud's underwear, came by to look at it. 'She's mine, she's mine,' Tamo told them matter-of-factly, and they shrugged and went away.

When Maud dared to look up from the ground, she found she was almost as frightened of Tamo as she was of the village boys.

'I'm glad he's dead,' said Tamo, glancing briefly towards the trees. He began throwing single grains of uncooked rice to the chickens.

'Who?'

'The man who lived here. Better to be dead than a slave. I'd sooner be dead.'

'Is he dead, then? How do you know?'

'He went by me. Didn't you scare him out of the house?'

Maud began to laugh. 'Gracious, Master White, I believe you need spec—'

'No! No more White, you hear? I've done with White. It's Tamo now. Just Tamo.'

'I was just going to say, Master Tamo,' said Maud (to whom informality, even in her underwear, came extremely hard), 'that was a monkey you saw running out of the house.'

'No, it wasn't,' said Tamo, trying to play jacks with a handful of rice. 'It was an indri. The souls of the dead live on in them. Don't you know anything?'

Nathan exchanged glances with his sister, then looked out past the bamboo thickets and rushy roofs, towards the green-caped hinterland and the never-ending miles of luxuriant forest. Where was the church spire and the granite chapel? Where was the market cross and the cathedral close? Where was he supposed to take Communion, in a land with no bread and no priests? Where was Sunday, here where the days all had different names? Where was God, that no one here paid Him the smallest attention?

'Tomorrow I'll find a fortune-teller,' Tamo was saying contentedly, as the chickens challenged him for the rice. 'We'll all visit a fortune-teller. Then we'll see. Then we'll see . . . '

The sunlight sat on Tamo's shoulder, warm and white as an indri. This might be Paradise they were in. Unfortunately, it belonged to someone else's god.

6

Fortune

The morning began with the hoots of a hundred indris whose eery, plaintive voices carried for miles. The tumbling notes were so peculiarly haunting that the children woke with the sense of having been summoned. The ringing cries of coua birds joined in the chorus.

A pink mist resting over the rain forests gradually dissolved, like a sugar confection, as the gold circle of the sun rose up, fresh washed, out of the sea. By the time Maud stepped outside, the garden was full of butterflies feeding on the orchids and melon flowers. Their huge paper wings buffeted her face.

Inevitably, some woman would be already pounding rice, banging her giant pestle down into the hollow mortar, pounding the grains, a drumbeat percussion to accompany the hooting of the indris. A cock would crow, a donkey bray, an axe strike a tree a mile away. The whole world was renewed and sweet and ripe. It said, *'Take. Eat. This is my plenty, which was given for you.'*

The water in the local river was red—dyed to the colour of blood by the red topsoil. It looked like Moses' plague which turned the Nile to blood. But it tasted like nectar, and was clear in her cupped hands. *'Take. Drink,'* it seemed to say.

While the boys slept on, under their raffia mosquito nets, Maud dug up sweet potatoes, sown by the woman who had planted the garden. She hoed the weeds, disturbing sometimes a vivid green lizard with red spots, sometimes a blind snake. Like Ireland after Saint Patrick, or Eden before Satan, there were no dangerous snakes in this Paradise: giant snakes, blind snakes, digging snakes who gardened for frogs, but nothing of any danger to people. Sometimes her hoe uncovered tiny gilded frogs, like ingots of gold carelessly flung down by drunken pirates. And a scarlet fody would perch on the fence and cock its head at her in interest, a rockthrush would savage a snail. Overhead, in a lake-blue sky, a male kestrel searched for lizards to carry home to its mate.

At home, there had been a cat, a rectory cat, a mousecatcher with a nasty temperament. Maud had trailed patiently after it, hoping to be allowed to stroke it, to take it on her lap. Here, she had only to put out banana skins and melon pips for animals to come flocking. They were so strange, they terrified her, but their beauty and oddness mesmerized her, too—porcupines and tortoises, lemurs, and skinks. The animals outnumbered people as she herself was outnumbered by the Malagasies.

There was guinea-fowl to eat, when Tamo managed to trap or buy one, and manioc and shellfish and bread fruit. But where were the tradesmen to pay? It troubled Maud. Her father (despite getting two terms' free education for his son) had often liked to say, 'You get nothing free in this life, my child, only by hard work.'

And so Maud worked—hoeing, cleaning, cooking—as if the bounty of the place had to be paid for. And just when it seemed she might settle the account, some other good fortune would pitch her back into debt. She knew just how her father must have felt, working to repay that impossible loan.

With so many villagers taken by the slavers, there were hardly enough hands to tend the paddy fields.

Because Tamo had arrived on the auspicious red Friday, he and his 'household' were invited to share in the labour and produce of the harvest, and to feed from the banana trees. Or did the invitation come because the people were naturally generous? Or because Tamo put a gold piece into the pocket of a village elder? How should Maud know? Everything that went on in the village was a mystery to her.

It was bewildering not to understand, never to understand. The language sounded like water glugging from a bottle: words went on and on, piling syllable on syllable, and there were no books to help her study it. She picked up a word or two—*vary* for rice, *vola* for money—but even then there were a dozen other words for rice, depending on how, and how much, it had been cooked.

And language was not the worst. It is true she had only Nathan and Tamo to talk to, but then formerly she had had only her father and the disgruntled tradesmen. No, worst was not understanding the rest: the hidden rules, the traditions, the way life worked. Tamo, because he had grown up in a Malagasy village, had ingested all the rules without realizing it. He could not explain to them why he always walked clockwise round a house to reach its door (even if it meant virtually circling the building). He just knew to do it—'not to go against *vintana,*' he would say, but could not say what *vintana* was. All life had its rules, its auspicious times, its unlucky sites. Days of the week had colours; times of day had different magics. There was a right corner of the house for flowers, a right direction for beds.

For a time, Tamo said no more about consulting a fortune-teller, and Maud was relieved. She knew that she and Nathan would have to talk him out of it. Use witchcraft? Necromancy? It was wicked and heathen! In England, the Church had burned all the witches, and set their souls hurrying back to Hell. And here was Tamo White considering visiting a fortune-teller! Maud shuddered at the very thought.

Her hoeing took her to the far side of the house, the east side. To her surprise, she suddenly noticed a second door boarded up with lathes of bark. The battens were rotten and pulled away easily; the door beyond was only propped in place. She gave it a push, and it fell inwards with a thud. A much brighter, easterly light penetrated the hut—a runner of sunlight directly across the centre of the hut.

'Tay be!' Tamo leapt out of his bed like a rabbit, eyes bulging, mouth rigid. He was out of the hut before Maud had even stepped over the threshold: *'Tay be!* What's happened? Is somebody dead?'

'I just opened the door,' said a piping voice from inside.

'But that's the *east* door! That's the spirit door. That's . . . *masina*!'

Maud whimpered. 'I'm sorry. I'm dreadfully sorry. I didn't know.' She had her hands pressed over her eyes, not just because of the tears starting there, but because Tamo was standing in the garden stark naked.

'That door's never opened except when someone dies!'

'I'll shut it again. Nat will shut it again, won't you, Nat? Only do come in, Master Tamo. Someone might see you.' Maud's hands stayed tight over her eyes; whoever did see Tamo in his nakedness, it was not going to be her.

Nathan looked around blearily. 'Who let that in? Maud, is that another one of your beasts?' He was looking at a creature caught in the sudden shaft of sunlight, surprised into total stillness. Only its eyes, mounted on volcano-shaped sockets, swivelled and blinked in alarm.

It was a hump-backed lizard, about the size of a small cat, and even as they looked, its black-brown body began to flush yellow, like the flask of an hour-glass filling with sand. It was changing colour to match the sandy floor.

Maud got down on her hands and knees to gaze at the chameleon, while Nathan (who was not so very fond of strange animals as his sister) furtively tiptoed out of the spirit door, wrapped in his mosquito net. He said, in parting, 'Now do be careful, Maud. It might be dangerous. You never know.'

Clearly Tamo thought it was dangerous. Nathan found him outside the garden, his fists gripping the fence and his whole body a-judder with fear. That, in turn, frightened Nathan. 'Maud, I think you'd better get out of there,' he called to his sister. 'What is it, Tamo? What's the matter?' He could hardly believe that this was the pirate's son who had stood, *en garde,* at the foot of Graylake's staircase with a drawn sword.

Maud had no intention of going outside until Tamo had his breeches on, but she decided she should put the creature out-of-doors. So she threw her own mosquito net over it, thinking to bundle it out through the spirit door.

The chameleon had other ideas, however, and scuttled away, inside the folds of orange cloth, into one corner of the house. It was the corner where Tamo liked her to put flowers. Within its raffia robe, the chameleon began to smoulder orange. Maud appreciated its anxiety not to be seen: she only wished Tamo White felt the same, and would put his trousers on.

When he got up close to his friend, Nathan could hear Tamo's teeth chattering with fright. 'For Heaven's sake, Maud! Just get out of there, will you?' Nathan shook the other boy. 'Will it bite her? Sting her? Is it poisonous? What is it?'

Tamo turned and stared at him with round, native eyes. His breath did not come and go at his command. It took him some effort to make the words audible: *'It's my father,'* he said.

Despite his terror, he could not keep away from the door of the hut; he had to see the object of his fear. 'He must have come in through the spirit door,' he said.

'No, I'm sure . . . ' Maud began, but Tamo could not hear her. His eyes, once he had dared to look at the chameleon, could not look away again.

'See how he goes to the ancestors' corner? It's my father, for sure. He was buried alone. He was buried wrong. His spirit's not peaceful,'

'Your father was a Christian,' Maud said crisply. 'He was buried just right, for a Christian.'

'Anyway—that was miles away!' said Nathan, pointing up country.

But Tamo was in the thrall of those swivelling, prehistoric eyes. 'I must find the *ombiasy.* I must.' He dashed as far as his bed, skirting as far round the chameleon as possible, snatched up the bag of money from under his pillow, and ran off, vaulting over the fence and running as though all the witches of Hallowe'en were on his heels.

'I hope he won't burn the house down,' said Nathan, watching his fellow Graylake scholar pelt naked between the baobab trees. And when he turned, Maud was carrying the chameleon out through the other door, wrapped in an orange cloth, like a baby in swaddling clothes.

* * *

The *ombiasy* said it was getting late for divination. Dawn was the best time, and the sun was already well up. Tamo had paid a handful of sovereigns for a zebu bull, with a massive hump and prodigious horns. Six young men led it up through the village by six hemp ropes looped round its bulging throat. Its horns had been trained, as they grew, like espaliered orange trees or a vine. They whorled and curled, casting fantastic shadows over Tamo and the *ombiasy.* Maud gave a peevish sigh and fetched Tamo's breeches out to him, thrusting them at him, to the great amusement of the gathering crowd.

The *ombiasy* was a dark-skinned, thick-lipped man with blazing eyes and flattened nostrils as wide as his mouth. There was a white circle painted on his forehead, between two clumps of excitable hair which fell forwards each time he looked down. His chest was cluttered with things strung on to cords and threads and ribbons—nuts, pods and leaves, bullets, pieces of hide and tree bark, purses stuffed with herbs, lumps of charcoal and brittle resin. For the *ombiasy* was doctor as well as fortune-teller, and carried his medicine chest strung about his neck.

The zebu's huge hump twitched, to dislodge flies and mosquitoes. It chewed the cud, and its stomach gurgled.

'Tamo, don't do this,' Nathan was saying. 'This is all wrong. You'll go to Hell, if you do this. It's one of the worst sins, you know? The worst. My father told me. It's devil worship.' But he could see that his words were falling useless to the ground. 'I mean, sirrah, consider!' he heard himself saying, in imitation of his father in the pulpit. 'This is just not how Christian folk behave! Didn't you learn anything at Graylake?'

At Graylake, Tamo had learned Latin and Greek, algebra and arithmetic. He had learned English history and how to drink coffee and bet on horses on race days. He had been the admiration of the boys and the pride of the masters. He was clever and quick to learn. But Tamo was not in England any longer. He was swimming away on a flood of strange superstitions, stranding his friends on their little island of Christianity. Maud took her brother's hand.

Poor little Maud, he thought. I brought her here, and she will never get over it. Her nerves will go all to pieces.

The *ombiasy* sat down on the ground, and Tamo sat opposite. The *ombiasy* took a sip from a bowl of something white, and began to utter a high-pitched whistling sound, which silenced all the morning birds. He asked Tamo a question, and Tamo shrugged. The *ombiasy* glared at him, and asked again. Large tears brimmed in Tamo's eyes, and his lips quivered. *'Tsy misy,'* he said. *'Tsy misy.'*

Maud pulled her hand free of Nathan's, and crouched down beside Tamo. 'What's the matter?' she said, as if to a little boy.

'He wants to know when I was born! What day. What hour. I don't know. I don't recall. I can't find out!'

'Good. Good,' said Nathan, smartly. 'That's the end of that, then. Now, can we stop all this?' He was horrified. An Old Testament world had come to life in front of him, full of Baal-worshippers and demons. He wanted to give the *ombiasy* a kick, but thought the outraged villagers might cut his throat with that long, thick-bladed knife lying on the ground.

The *ombiasy,* meanwhile, had decided to do without the details of Tamo's birth and was emptying into his hands a bag of glossy seeds. He took them back, one by one, out of Tamo's cupped palms, and laid them on the ground in rows, as if for a game of draughts, whistling and mumbling and rocking on his heels, to and fro, to and fro.

The clumps of hair swept sweat off his forehead on to the seeds, the mosaic pattern which Tamo saw as his stepping stones to the Truth.

'Toakagasy!' blared the *ombiasy* all of a sudden, in a coarse, aggressive bellow, and Tamo scrambled to his feet and pressed a coin into a woman's hand, begging her to fetch the man a drink. In due course, the rum came.

'Toakagasy. Maka! Take it!'

The *ombiasy* drank the rum, his head tipped back, his Adam's apple bobbing.

'What a sot. What a rogue,' muttered Nathan, and turned his back in disgust.

Then the *ombiasy* began to speak. It was not wild or hysterical, but pitched far higher than his natural voice—a keening such as women make over their husband's coffins. Then there was another bubbling out of words. Tamo, his face as rigid as a wooden mask, bit his lip, peered into the doctor's unfocused eyes. 'Is that true?' he said, shaking his head in denial.

The *ombiasy*'s long, spatulate fingers went on pushing the counters around in threes and fives.

'He doesn't understand you, Tamo,' said Maud, still crouching beside him.

Tamo struggled back into his own language—*'Marina ve? Marina ve?'*—and went on shaking his head, on and on, until he must have been dizzy. The *ombiasy* nodded.

Nathan, meanwhile, felt the whole weight of Christianity bear down on his shoulders—as if he were carrying his father on his back. Only he could stop this damnable sacrilege. Only he could save Tamo from damning himself with magic. Nathan drew a deep breath, shut his eyes and stamped one reckless foot down on the sikidy seeds: the *ombiasy* withdrew his fingers only just in time. The details of Tamo's fortune scattered to right and left.

The crowd gasped. The *ombiasy* glared, crooned and rocked, his fingers against his lips.

But Tamo, far from shouting at Nathan, looked up at him and said, 'Thank you. But you're too late. You won't alter the future like that.' (Maud, ever afraid of unpleasantnesses, began to gather up the scattered seeds with quick, deft fingers.) 'He says I shall follow in the footsteps of my father,' said Tamo, desolate and bleak. 'He says I shall do as my father did, and be what my father was. He doesn't know . . . ' The fig tree that Christ cursed could not have looked more blighted than Tamo was by the words of the fortune-teller.

Maud tried politely to pour the seeds back into the hands of the *ombiasy,* but at the last moment, he parted his palms and the black discs fell back on to the ground. The pale tips of his fingers came down on them. *'Iza? Vadiko?'* he said to Tamo.

The boy was stunned, preoccupied. He waved a vague hand at Maud and Nathan. *'Anadahy—anabavy. Izy no Maud.'*

'Volondavenona.'

'He says you are the colour of ash.'

And all of a sudden, the *ombiasy* was reading Maud's fortune off the sikidy seeds:

'Tsara—mahery—feno—faly—tena faly—afaka.'

The words sang out of him, mystical, musical, while the seeds lined up in columns and rows.

'What is he saying?'

'Maud!' Nathan tried to intervene, but the villagers had somehow jostled in front of him, edged him to the back. He jumped up high, but he could not see what was happening. 'Maud, come away this instant!'

'He says you will be strong—full—clever—no, I don't know: "can do"—able, yes, able. And happy, he says. Very happy.' Tamo, though he translated the words, was barely interested in the content of Maud's horoscope. The shadow of his own lay over him, darker than the shadow of the tethered zebu.

'Anadahyny?' asked the *ombiasy*, tossing his locks of hair towards the crowd. As if by magic, the villagers stepped away to left and right, opening up a clear space between Nathan and the sikidy seeds. Hands plucked at him, smiling faces encouraged him. The *ombiasy* was offering to tell his fortune, too! Hurry, hurry! Pick up the seeds! Don't keep the doctor waiting!

Nathan took two steps back, his shoulders slumping forwards, his fingertips feeling for the shirtcuffs which no longer dangled over his knuckles. He shook his head, and they laughed, thinking he was shy, thinking he was scared.

'No,' said Nathan. 'It's wicked. It's wrong. Don't you understand anything? It's witchcraft! It's sinful! It's a sin. Don't you want to go to Heaven, any of you?'

They listened attentively, those smiling people bound for damnation with their big white grins and gentle eyes. Then, believing that he was too shy to accept the honour offered him, they closed ranks once more, and put him to the back of the crowd, to the back of their minds.

Once again, the *ombiasy* began to whistle, and when he spoke again, it was in his normal, deep, unexcitable voice. His eyes came to rest on the bowl of rum, and he asked if he had drunk any, while he had been with the spirits. Told that he had, he reached into a purse and scrupulously paid for his drink. Then he stood up, complaining that his hips hurt him. He gave Tamo an amulet, from around his neck.

It was a coua bird, which eats chameleons.

To Maud, he held out the likeness of a zebu, and when she did not immediately take it, pressed it into her hand and folded her fingers shut over it. She stared down at her little white hand folded inside his two huge black ones—then at the zebu, shaggy, smelly, fly stormed, holy. It looked back at her with moist brown eyes. A woman gave her a sip of rum, thinking she looked unwell. The viscous liquor slid down her throat and seemed to kindle directly below her sternum. For all of a sudden, Maud's heart expanded, like the cloud of smoke above a fire.

How she loved these animals, she thought, these trees, these birds, the warmth, the fur, the colour, the smell. A long-tailed dove dived through her path of vision. A blue pigeon crooned on a roof. The barbet birds were small specks of bright colour exploding at the edge of her sight. Strong, happy, capable, full . . .

Tamo was speaking to it. He was speaking to the zebu. For one moment, Nathan, straining to understand, believed he must have broken the code, and begun to understand Malagasy. Then he realized Tamo was speaking in Greek. One hand on his hip and the other spread across his breastbone, he was delivering one of the orations he had learned in Classics at Graylake School. He had always done well in Declamation, the pirate's son.

The *ombiasy* was impressed. The people murmured and nodded at the flowing musicality of the faultless, foreign speech. They lunged forward and pressed little coins into the pockets of his breeches. Maud admired it, too. It was appropriate: Maud could see that, if her brother could not: an ancient dead language being used to address the ancient dead. For Tamo was speaking to his ancestors—she instinctively knew it—giving the zebu a message to carry to his father, in the spirit world . . .

'NO!' cried Maud, realizing, in an instant, what was about to happen.

But she was too late to stop the *ombiasy* slitting the zebu's throat. She leapt forwards only in time to be splashed from head to foot by the warm, spurting blood. She flung her arms round the gigantic head, and felt the long lashes, stiff as bristle, flicker under her hands. The *ombiasy* had to pull her away, for fear the huge beast fell on top of her. But he did so with gentle, unreproachful arms, not as if she had defiled his ceremony, but as if she had done something quite natural, something quite within her rights.

Maud did not cry. Even while the sacrificial beast lay twitching and dying in the dirt, she did not cry. Its blood flowed over and around the sikidy seeds, overtaking a colony of ants, steaming, soaking into the ground. She knew the precise moment at which the animal died. Of course she did. She was wearing its blood.

When she finally looked up from the dead zebu, she saw her brother Nathan looking at her, his face full of accusation and rage. He must think she had *asked* or wanted the magic-man to tell her fortune, and she had done nothing of the kind. Such a hateful look! It would normally have reduced her to tears. But the smell of the zebu's sweat and blood were on her, and zebus are strong, tearless.

The blood was warm against her skin. The flies laid siege to her. So she went to wash in the river. But the river, too, was red. So that even when she was washed clean, she felt that the colour crimson clung to her. Scarlet. The colour of Friday. The day for strength.

7
The Magic Finger

Maud took up crocheting. She crocheted raffia and wool, and experimented with coir, hessian, and the strands from bamboo stalks. Every item they owned soon had its own mat to stand on. The shelves she insisted upon having were edged with crochet, and there were lacy collars for the boys to wear on Sundays.

The boys took a dim view of these raffia cobwebs, but the villagers of Zaotralana appreciated Maud's skill and came visiting, to admire the handiwork. Maud taught the women to crochet, and in return they showed her how to winnow rice, and cook sheep's guts congealed in fat. The dead zebu's horns lay in the sacred north-east corner of the hut, along with scrolls of sacred writing which the *ombiasy* had written to repulse the spirit of Thomas White.

Nevertheless, for hours, Tamo sat brooding over the prediction that he would follow in his father's footsteps. Nathan badgered him—'God gave us self-will! To do as we see fit!' But Tamo took no notice. He did not garden or plant. He did not mend the holes in the hut or gather firewood for the fire. He just brooded, and cleaned his pistol, which was full of sea salt. He barely spoke a word.

For a time, Nathan considered not speaking to his sister, because she had had her fortune told. But when Maud did not take up chanting or dancing or making sacrifice, or drinking strong liquor, he decided she had been more sinned against than sinning. He merely insisted on her burning the clothes stained by the zebu's blood.

As a result, Maud took to wearing the Malagasy *lamba*, though she wore it like a Roman toga, having no bust to hold it up. After the business of the fortune-telling, she did *sing* rather more than Nathan had remembered. But she sang hymns, so he did not deter her. She must be keeping up her spirits, he thought, in the face of all this barbarity. In fact he took some comfort from singing, himself, particularly John Bunyan's stirring stuff, and brother and sister could be heard roaming around the coconut plantations.

'He who would valiant be
'Gainst all disaster,
Let him in constancy
Follow the Master!'

The moist, ceaseless heat grew, day by day, more oppressive. Mosquitoes the size of bumble bees blackened the air over any and every puddle of still water. The paddy fields dried up and crazed into mosaics of red tile. Plants shrivelled and died. Then the rains came.

The rainclouds piled up, fold upon fold, in beetling cliffs of black vapour. Then they broke, with a clap of thunder like Judgement Day. The temperature dropped ten degrees, the forests fell silent. All sound was blotted out by the universal hiss of falling rain. The trees steamed. The houses steamed. The cattle standing in the lanes steamed, and their flanks twitched under the goading cold of the tropical downpour. A charcoal burner's mound miraculously kept burning at its heart, the last fire it seemed, anywhere on Earth.

Everyone came out of doors and stood face-up to the rain, eyes shut, mouths open, while, behind them, all manner of small creatures and large insects crept into the huts to keep dry. Half the night Tamo was up, evicting rats and beetles and snakes. The sea seemed to have disappeared, for not only was the rain too dense to see through, it also flattened the surf, and obliterated the sound of breaking waves.

Overnight, it masked another sound, too: that of a ship beaching itself on the high tide.

The red earth began to move. It reconstituted from powder into clay, and by morning whole tracts of the settlement were a slurry of crimson mud. Without discussion, the people abandoned routine and headed for the paddy fields.

'What's happening?' asked Nathan, peering out of the door. It was like trying to see through a waterfall.

'Ploughing,' said Tamo, without getting up.

'No, no. People are rounding up the cows. They're driving them out of the village. There's going to be a flood, I know it.' He weighed up his chances of building a second Ark: Nathan's Ark: the chances were not good.

'They use the animals to make mud,' said Tamo.

'They?' said Maud sharply. 'Is it "they" now?'

In England when it rained, nobody went out. Here everybody was out-of-doors, and though they looked compressed, somehow—their hair plastered down, their clothes clinging—they were in a frenzy of joy. Hooting with laughter, wagging bamboo poles, they drove their sacred cattle in a bellowing, blundering procession.

'I want to see,' said Maud.

'Yes. Come on, Tamo, let's go,' said Nathan.

'Do as you like. I'd sooner stay dry,' said the pirate's son petulantly.

So brother and sister took a deep breath, like coral divers, and plunged into the rain. It struck cold at first, chilled their skin, then felt warm and soothing, as it ran down outside and inside their clothing. The soil yielded under their feet and oozed between their toes; every footstep slipped. Birds sat open-winged on the ground, jarred by the size of the raindrops and yet singing with ecstasy of the wet. A pitcher flower brimmed with water. The river was thick with stirred up mud.

Mud! It was as fertile and alive as volcanic tilth, and the object was to plough it and plant it as quickly as possible with first-rice. There were no ploughshares, no horses or harrows or spades. So the people drove the cattle into the paddyfields and chased them up and down, whistling, yelping, and singing. And the cattle weltered in the mire, trampling the red earth into a deeper and deeper tide slurry till they could hardly lift their hooves clear of the cresting mud.

Tamo, whatever he said, could no more stay indoors than the rest. He felt desiccated, like some cracked brown seed waiting trapped in a fissure of earth and he needed to soak in the rain. But instead of following the others up to the paddies, he went the opposite way, down to the beach. He wanted to be on his own. The rain would wash out of him all the dust, dead insects and blown rice husks of the dry season. He would stand thigh-deep in the sea and spear fish with a sharpened bamboo, and let the rain wash away the dark thoughts.

But someone had reached the beach ahead of him. A ship lay on its side, as big-bellied as a stranded whale. It was being careened, its hull scraped of weed and barnacles and parasitic snails. A sea salmon coming home to its native river never carries as many lice as a ship's hull plying the Indian Ocean.

All the cannon, all the small arms, all the ammunition had been off-loaded on to the beach, and the whole bay fortified against attack. For sailors deprived of their ship feel vulnerable, suspicious of the dry land, the hanging forests, the unpredictable savages inshore. The sailors had turned three turtles on their backs: fresh supplies of meat. The animals lay helpless, belly-up, looking at a sky they had never contemplated before, waving stumpy, feeble legs.

Tamo froze. The rain veiled out all detail of the ship, and since the mast-top was now resting on the sand, no flags were hoisted either. The crew moved like ghosts through the downpour, any sound their tools made was smothered by the hiss of rain. If they spoke, their words were carried away in rivulets down to the shoreline. A carpenter soundlessly sawed a plank.

Once an area of the hull had been cleaned, the object was to lard it with tallow and pitch, to make it watertight. But all efforts to melt the solid tallow had failed utterly. There was no dry kindling. A man came and swore at the waterlogged bonfires, kicking them apart; a man in a red jacket and huge tricorn hat the crown of which kept filling with rain and emptying when he dipped his head.

It was Sheller.

He must have spent the intervening weeks sailing round Madagascar, visiting the various pirate strongholds, slaving, dealing. He must have crossed to the African mainland, too, to off-load his cargo, for there were no slaves and little cargo on the beach. Tamo watched through the veiling rain: his father's friend, his guardian, the man who sold men and girls.

A ship needs careening every two or three months;

Sheller's visit might last no longer than it took to renovate the ship. But what when the careening operation was finished? He would send men inshore for fresh provisions, make a quick, greedy foray to seize more slaves. It seemed to Tamo no accident, no accident at all, that his guardian should have stumbled on Zaotralana. It was all part of Tamo's oppressive Fate . . .

Tamo shook himself. The villagers must be warned. It was not right that his bad Fate should fetch down any more misfortunes on them. They must melt away into the forest—hide until Sheller had stolen what he wanted from the village and put out to sea again.

Tamo moved away backwards, unwilling to turn his back on the beached ship and its swarm of crew. His bamboo spear caught in a rock crevice and sprang out of his hand, bounding end-over-end down the beach path. But the crew saw neither spear nor boy. The whole seaward wall of vegetation was soughing in the rain, twigs and dead leaves washing down from it like straws from a man's hair.

Because of the ploughing, the village was deserted but for one old lady minding a handful of very small children. All well and good. Even the cattle might be saved—led away into the bush, and saved from the quartermaster's need for fresh meat. Tamo skidded and slithered up lanes of red mud. From some distance, loud singing broke through the rain. In among the Malagasy clapping music he could hear strange echoes of Graylake School:

'We plough the fields and scatter
The good seed on the land!
But it is fed and watered . . .'

Tamo, when he reached the paddy fields, could not make himself heard at first. His voice was swallowed up by the bellow of the bulls, the squelching mud and the singing. He slipped, and plunged face-first into the mud. But everyone there had already done the same, more than once. When he pulled himself upright again, he was plastered from head to foot, surrounded by men and women and children similarly smothered. Their faces were caked with mud, their arms and legs and bodies redded with clay. They looked like terracotta statues wading to and fro, the tops of their heads washed clean by the rain but the rest of them clarted inches thick.

'*Mpanompo!* Slavers!' he shouted, plucking at the nearest shirt. When the face turned towards him, its eyes were blue, and the mouth was singing,

' . . . the snow in winter,
And warmth to swell the grain!'

'Will you listen?'

'No? No snow? No, I suppose not.

He sends monsoons in winter
And mud to swell the grain . . . '

For the first time in his life, Nathan was glorying in getting filthy.

'Gull! Listen! In the bay! It's Sheller!'

'Sheller?'

A cow banged into Tamo's back and knocked him over. Nathan dredged him up again. 'Sheller's come here?'

A terracotta woman stopped and stared at them. Tamo realized from the colour of the top of her hair that it must be Maud. 'What do we do?' she said.

'Run. Hide. Lie low. If he's after slaves, he won't find any here.'

'Then he'll take what he can find.'

'Things,' said Tamo disdainfully.

'And go on somewhere else. To the next village.'

'Right.' Tamo pecked and lunged his way through

the mud, shouting into every Malagasy ear. *Mpanompo!* pointing towards the bay. The brown eyes widened, the whites of eyes showed in fear. The noise subsided, as the ploughers, soul by soul, came to a standstill.

They began to move away, like spirits scenting the dawn, towards the forest. Women who had left their small children in the village wanted to go back for them; some did, and some their husbands drew away moaning and keening, gazing back towards the roofs showing above the bamboo groves. The mud on their faces turned to a paler pink, drying. The rain was slacking.

'He'll loot the village,' said Maud indignantly. 'He may go into our house.'

'He may burn the village; he's that kind of a man,' Tamo agreed.

'Burn our house?' Maud would not budge. More and more of her pale hair emerged.

'What, you think we ought to fight them? Fish-spears against swords and muskets?'

'In Bermuda they drove them off with cows,' said Nathan moonishly. 'I read it.'

'Your trouble is, you want them to burn it down,' said Maud and pursed her lips.

'They started a stampede,' said Nathan, watching the cattle begin to follow the villagers.

'*Want* them to? Why would I *want* them to? Don't talk folly, madam.'

'Don't call me madam because you think I'm a fool!' retorted Maud. 'And I'll tell you why! Because you can't remember how to be a Malagasy!'

Nathan stirred out of his reverie to find the two of them at war. 'Stop it! They're coming,' he said.

'On the contrary,' said Tamo, in his superior, Graylake prefect's drawl. 'I expect they are sailing away even now. Even as we speak. I expect they only beached the ship to careen her. They probably won't come up here at all.'

'Then why did the birds just fly up out of the trees. Someone's on the cliff path.'

'Tay be! Let's hide! If Sheller sees us . . . '

They scowled at him, two terracotta gargoyles.

'You think I'm scared? You think I'm a coward. But if Sheller sees us here, he'll take out his spite on the village. Now, will you hide?'

'There are little children down there.'

'He won't take little ones for slaves: they'd die on the voyage.'

'If he looks in the huts, he'll find your pistol. It has your name burned on the stock.'

Tamo's mouth dropped open. He had not thought Maud noticed such things. But she was right about the pistol.

'In the Carribees . . . ' said Nathan doubtfully.

'Well?' demanded Tamo.

'Well, what?'

'Well, *what did they do in the Carribees?'*

'Oh.' He had not expected to be asked. Nathan held two fingers together, for a pretend pistol. 'Bang,' he said genteely. The others stared at him.

Then, all of a sudden, Nathan wielded his bamboo goad and ran at the cattle, which were bunched uncertainly in one corner of the paddy. He lashed and yelped and fell headlong in the mire, picked himself up and went on yip-yipping like a sheepdog. Maud joined in, clacking together two sticks of wood and yelping.

The cattle moved idly out of the paddy and began trotting back towards the village.

Tamo ran to where the charcoal-burner's tumulus of wood and turf still smoked, defying the rain, and began kicking it apart, laying bare the red hot heart. As the cattle came lumbering past him at a slow, sedate amble, Tamo pulled out a burning stick and lashed at the backsides of the sacred beasts.

The hindmost zebu, feeling a burn to its rump, jumped forwards, banging into the cow in front. The charcoal burner's children came running from their shack to shout at Tamo for destroying their father's mound. They added to the din. The zebu took off at an awkward, knock-kneed run, cannoning into each other and into the corner of a house. Palm leaves slid down from the roof on to the cows, and they lumbered forwards faster than ever, bellowing. The old woman minding the little children snatched as many as possible into her arms, and called to the others to scatter. As the cattle stampeded by, the look on her face was purest fright.

At last the zebu outran Nathan and Maud, who were already exhausted. They outran Tamo, too, galloped through three gardens and knocked over the winnowing pots outside the longhouse. They were heading for the sea.

Captain Sheller, intent on righting his ship, looked back at the precipitous greenery of the cliff and saw a disturbance. He had sent men to forage for fresh fruit, poultry, and a few slaves.

But now he saw his party of shoremen starting back down the track, yelping and pointing and running for their lives. The path was awash with rain, and disintegrated under them, spilling them down the slope like coal down a chute.

'To the guns, men!' ordered Sheller, but the wadding in one cannon was sodden and the touch-hole of another brimmed with water. The third recoiled into the surf as it fired, and the ball hit the cliff-face. Three palm trees fell over like skittles, and brought down a fourth and fifth: they toppled end-over-end on to the beach, sending Sheller and his careeners skipping into the ocean.

Uncertain of the nature of the attack, Sheller withdrew. He boarded his ship, left a longboat for the shore party, and retreated to deep water, abandoning two cannon and two barrels of tallow as he did so. Along the skyline, all that his telescope could discern were the weirdly buckled horns of cattle tossing among the bamboo. One animal came over the brink, carrying away with it two crewmen as it plunged feet-upmost on to the beach. Another hurtled, like a missile from a siege engine, over the cliff edge, snapping branches as it fell. All over the cliff, petrified crewmen who had expected no more than the easy abduction of a few natives, slithered down the bitter fronds of aloe trees or tore their snagged clothing off the prickly milkweed.

As the stampede faltered, native figures appeared among the zebu—Sheller saw them through his telescope. Their faces were plastered in red mud and their hair stood out in mud-caked spikes. He saw savages, because that was what he expected to see. And Maud, realizing how completely she was masked by the mud, stood in plain sight, glorying in her disguise. It was almost like being someone else.

Beside her, Nathan squared his shoulders and made a defiant fist.

It was a wrong move. It was not appreciated. The villagers, emerging from their hiding places, did not see what purpose had been served by stampeding their cattle. They might have remained invisible in the forest until Sheller had given up and left: what need for a fight? Some of the young men liked the daring of it, the drama. But their mothers soon slapped the grins off their faces. Little children had been endangered. A house and gardens had been destroyed. Worst of all, two sacred cattle had fallen to their deaths over the cliff. It was as though, in washing off the red mud, the villagers of Zoatralana washed off their smiles. The friendly faces were gone which had welcomed the strangers.

Together, Nathan, Tamo, and the young men salvaged Sheller's two cannon from the beach and, with infinite sweat and toil, mounted them on the cliff path. But while they did it, no one spoke, no one laughed.

'This is how they used to look at my father,' said Tamo bleakly.

But then the aye-aye died.

One night, sitting in the garden, eating crayfish and rice, Tamo and Maud and Nathan watched the glow of other fires, and the black constellation of bats eclipsing the moon. The elevated position of their hut gave them a clear, panoramic view over the mosaic of houses and gardens.

'They don't want us here,' said Nathan. 'Even I can tell that.'

Maud looked up from her dinner, to see if Tamo White would contradict him, but no.

'I don't belong anywhere now,' he said self-pityingly. 'Not England. Not Madagasikara. Perhaps I never did.'

'Did you see that?'

'What?'

'Down there. Somebody threw their rubbish into the next-door garden. They did, honestly. Look—the woman in the doorway has seen it! How funny!'

The outraged housewife gave a shriek of horror and called her husband to come. He came out and threw the thing back again over the fence along with a colourful curse.

'It's not rubbish,' said Tamo darkly.

'No, it's a dead animal!' said Nathan, as the little silvery carcass flew back over the fence. 'A monkey or something.'

'It's an aye-aye,' said Tamo.

Almost at once, the body flew over the fence on the other side, into an area used by the women for winnowing. It lay slumped and shapeless, between two mortars.

A woman, her hand covered in cloth, dashed out of one of the houses, picked up the corpse and threw it haphazardly into the central clearing.

'Poor little thing,' said Maud, trying to make out the nature of the animal. 'I'd love to see it.' She got up and took their leaf-plates from them, as if she might wash them up.

'Why don't they cook it?' said her brother. 'They cook everything else.'

For a time, it lay outside a hut undisturbed, until a busybody neighbour rattled at the door and alerted the people inside. An old lady, tottery with sleep, blinked out at the dead animal. Neither was willing to touch it. Busybody and old lady clung to each other, making shooing gestures with their hands, which the dead creature ignored. Then the busybody pointed in the direction of Tamo's hut.

Tamo crouched up on his heels. 'They'd better not

bring it here,' he said, reaching indoors for his pistol. 'They'd better not try.'

'Why? What is it? Did it die of something horrible? Is it infected, or what?' asked Nathan.

'Aye-aye,' said Tamo disgustedly. 'The magic finger. It's good luck when it's alive, but dead it's bad-luck-in-a-skin. If they bring it here, I'll . . . ' Tamo began to prime his pistol, even though he had no powder to load in it. He might just deter the villagers from dumping bad luck over his garden picket.

Just then, another figure appeared in the village street. It was Maud. The boys had not noticed her leave, but her curiosity to see the dead animal had taken her down the hill. The villagers eyed her morosely, made no greeting, and backed away leaving her closest to the dead aye-aye. Maud looked down at it.

Its face was delicate and, like a bush-baby's, had been almost entirely taken up with eyes. Its fur stirred in the breeze, giving the illusion of life. Its hands, frail and furless, had one elongated middle finger with which it seemed, even in death, to be pointing at Maud.

Maud spoke to it soothingly. It was nothing new for her, to speak to a dead thing. Daily, throughout her lonely life, she had carried on conversations with the chairs as she polished them, with the brushes which stood straight-backed in the scullery, the dead birds brought in by the cat. Such an extraordinary animal. Sad to think that she had missed seeing it alive, Maud picked it up and cradled it in her arms.

The villagers stared, their eyes as round as the aye-aye's had once been.

At the top of the rise, Maud's brother fell into step with her. 'What are you going to do with it?' he asked.

'Bury it under the orchids.'

'Around here, people think it's the worst kind of bad luck.'

'Ah. That explains it,' she said.

'Tamo thinks so, too,' said Nathan pointedly.

'Oh. All right. I understand.'

Maud veered away and, instead of climbing to the house, pattered softly away among the boabab trees, where she planted the dead aye-aye inside a hollow trunk and covered it over with ferns.

The next day, the village could talk of nothing else—how the white girl had carried the aye-aye out of Zaotralana, taken all the bad luck on herself, for the sake of her neighbours.

They were in awe of her. They would not shake hands with her—not till the bad magic had washed off—but they were as grateful to her as if she had rescued them from fire or pirates. She was a heroine.

Tamo called it bad luck, but Maud did not feel any clammy foreboding. In fact, if this was bad luck, it seemed to her the most fortuitous piece of bad luck to fall on them all since they had first arrived.

8

Haunted

Nathan considered how to get home. He realized now that he had only come on vacation to these foreign parts. He did not belong. It was beautiful, but incomprehensible. It was paradise, but somebody else's. When they got out their dead, that was the last straw.

'You put someone in the ground. You leave them there. They get up on Judgement Day,' he told Tamo categorically. 'What you're telling me—that's vile. It's disgusting. The only people who dig up bodies are witches and body-snatchers.'

'In England,' said Tamo.

Nathan went to find Maud. 'Now, Maud dear, you must be very brave,' he said, trying as hard as possible to sound like his father. 'Something perfectly dreadful is going to happen, but you and I shall keep quite out of the way.' His dry lips crimped tight in front of his teeth. He placed a brotherly arm around her shoulders. Behind his sunburn, he had turned a nasty green.

'Are you making a fuss again, Nat?' said Maud. She was trying to pollinate the orchids in the garden. Around her, a raft of hutches and nesting boxes rustled with small animals. A lemur was cradled in her lap, as she squatted over the flowers. The creature was a present from one of her many girlfriends in the village.

'They are going to dig up the corpses of their ancestors,' said Nathan.

'Tay be!'

'Maud!'

'I beg your pardon, brother.' She bowed her head penitently, but was in fact rather surprised at Nathan knowing what it meant. He did not show much aptitude at learning the language. '*Why* are they going to dig them up?'

'To dance with them.'

Maud gave him a long, old-fashioned look. 'Nathan. You've misunderstood again,' she said.

'As God's my witness! They're going to dance with the corpses! Ask Tamo! Ask him!'

Maud shuddered.

'Isn't that disgusting? Isn't it?'

Maud's face set like a plastercast. Her eyes remained on Nathan's grimacing mouth, but in truth she was somewhere else, seeing someone else. She was standing in her father's bedroom, a tray of morning tea in her hands, trying to wake him. He would not wake up. There was no blood: only the brown tea gleaming amid the broken shards of the teapot at her feet. Only the spilt milk.

Later, as the bailiffs plundered the room, and the church parochials argued shrilly on the stairs, she had bent to kiss him on the cheek. The flesh was so cold that she snatched her head away and recoiled. She pulled away—just as everyone else had drawn back from him at the end of his benighted, unfortunate life. So unexpected, that coldness. So unlike the warmth of a living thing.

Maud clutched the lemur close, for the sake of its warmth.

Later, she had gone to see her father buried—in the pauper's lot. And all she remembered was the stench, the overpowering stink of the place.

Nathan had thought his sister would be impressed

by his piece of news. But he had not expected her to be suddenly sick at his feet. 'Perhaps I shouldn't have told you,' he said weakly.

Brother and sister shut themselves away in their hut on the day of the *famadihana.* The prospect of the festival plunged Tamo White deeper than ever into depression, thinking how his father had been denied it all. 'I suppose it will be the same for me,' he moped. 'No proper grave. No *famadihana.*' He got no sympathy at all from the others, who were lying on their beds with their eyes firmly shut. 'Are you ill, or what?' he demanded, and slammed out-of-doors.

Nathan made a peculiar snuffling sound, which he disguised with a cough. Maud lifted herself on one elbow to look at him. 'What's the matter?'

Nathan drew his legs up to his chest. 'He seemed so brave, back at school . . . I only came here because I thought . . . I thought he would take care of us . . . you. But now we're here, he seems as big a coward as . . . as . . . '

' . . . as me,' said Maud, generously.

'Right. Yes. Scared as a girl.'

'I know. It's like going somewhere with a grown-up, then finding out that the grown-up's only a child dressed up,' said Maud.

'Exactly!'

Maud allowed a while to pass in silence. 'I remember, mind. Father said once: grown-ups are only children in bigger clothes. Pretending to know better.'

'When did he say that?'

'The day the bailiffs came to take away the piano.'

They half-expected slow drum beats and tolling bells. They half-expected satanic chanting and the cackle of grisly witches. What they did not expect was a village fête. As the sun's strength grew, and the heat leaned against the closed hut, like a herd of zebu, the noises that came up from the village were of a party. Children were laughing, musicians in several different places were playing different tunes on their bamboo *valihas*. The women were making their clapping music, ten rhythms overlapping, all perfectly syncopated. All the cooking fires were lit, and there was a smell, not of graveyards, but of roast meat, and of nuts cooking on a brazier. Orators were making speeches. Storytellers were exaggerating. The villagers must be steeling themselves to the horrible task.

Suddenly the hut door opened and a girl stuck her head into the hut. It was Maud's friend, Noro, who had given her the lemur. *'Oh! Ianao marary?'* she asked. No, Maud said, they were not ill. *'Avia bampahalalako ny renibeko!'*

'What does she want?' asked Nathan.

'I think she wants us to visit her grandmother.'

Noro stood grinning in the doorway, breathless from the climb. Her hands were full of toasted coconut flesh. She threw some to Nathan, and said that he was not invited, only Maud.

Maud could find no polite way of refusing. The rituals did not seem to have begun yet, and it felt foolish to be found in bed in the middle of the day.

'You're not going?' demanded Nathan as she stood up. 'Well, on your own head be it!' Only after she had gone did it occur to Nathan that the villagers wanted his sister for a human sacrifice. Fortunately, even he did not quite believe that.

Maud walked with Noro up to the north-west meadow beyond the village, where the river ran between the graveyard and a pleasant, grassy place.

They laughed all the way, though they barely understood one another—perhaps *because* they barely understood one another.

'Your grandmother . . . she's visiting?' Maud asked, knowing she would not be understood.

'Ho tianao ny renibeko,' said Noro, knowing it just as well. Neither minded. All in good time, it would get easier. All in good time.

The meadow was a beautiful spot. Portions of meat were laid out on a cloth on the ground—to be sure of everyone getting a share of the cow sacrificed that morning. The dogs tied to the doorposts down in the village were barking themselves off their legs at the smell of all that meat.

A group of little children gasped with amazement at something the storyteller said. Lemurs had come out of the trees and were prancing up and down, at a distance, on their hind legs, curious to see what was going on. Banana skins lay just where the children had dropped them. The families sat about in little picnic groups, everyone talking at once. They were all wearing white—like children at First Communion—and had all brought white tablecloths with them.

'I could make *sheets* with tablecloths like that,' was Maud's first thought. Most people in *England* did not have sheets.

But before she could ask Noro where to buy such luxurious cloth, Noro's family caught sight of her and beckoned Maud over excitedly. 'Come and meet grandmother!' they were saying, wagging their great brown hands. Several old ladies—forty, say, or fifty—bared their toothless gums at Maud, and she curtsied to them respectfully. But none of them was Noro's grandmother.

She was lying on the ground, being fanned with a giant leaf, while her shins were washed in a bowlful of river water. Painstakingly reconstructed, bone by bone, her skeleton lay listening to the latest family news, while her foot bones were washed and re-assembled. ' . . . And this is the girl who took the bad luck off us all, the night the aye-aye died,' they explained. 'Such a good girl. From over the sea, grandmother.'

Maud understood quite well the gist of what they were saying, but not what to do. The ghastly skull gaped at her, its jaw at a crazy angle to the cranium. There was no smell at all: only a corpse, with air where her sinews had once twisted, sunlight where her skin had once stretched.

In England they carved heads like that on sepulchres to say, 'Life is fleeting. Death is certain', and to frighten men into being good. They were a warning against enjoying life too much. And yet these people had lost their grandmother to this . . . this *horror*, and they did not even mind.

What should Maud do? What would Nathan have done? Pointed out to them the error of their ways; that is what Nathan would have done. The skeleton grinned at her, as happy as the rest. 'Who's the outsider here? You or me?' it seemed to say, through its no lips.

Summoning all her courage, Maud said, 'Your grandmother is with God,' picking out the words in careful Malagasy.

'Yes, yes, that's right!' they agreed. 'And now she's here, God is here too!' And they laughed and offered her a mango, because she was such a clever little girl.

The white sheeting was not a tablecloth at all, but a new shroud. Every one of the white tablecloths was a new shroud for the disinterred dead. All over the meadow, the same rite was in progress: the bones of dead friends and relations were washed then re-wrapped tenderly in the clean cloth, bound round with cords, and lifted shoulder-high to begin the dancing. Noro's family began to gather together the washed bones, to make a compact parcel. Still Maud stood at the end where the feet had lain.

She could feel the tray of tea things in her empty hands.

'Wait,' she said, and the relations looked up, startled. Maud walked round their squatting picnic group, to grandmother's head. She bent down and touched the skull's cheek with her fingertips. To her astonishment, it was warm and smooth, and a little dry, like an old person's skin. 'I'm sorry I pulled my face away, Papa,' she said. Then she stood up and curtsied respectfully to Noro's ancestor.

Noro took her elbow. She was not giggling any more. She was well aware that her friend came from a different land with different customs. *'Tena sahy ianao,'* she said. *You are brave.*

And Maud thought, It's true, I would not have done that in England. I could not have done that in England. She did not tell Nathan anything of what she had seen or done.

Brave, strong, and what? had the *ombiasy* said?

By nightfall, all the bodies had been put back to rest in their Village of the Dead—each under a little palm roof, each little house renovated with flowers and white banners. A wind was getting up, and soon afterwards, the cut flowerheads came bowling through the lanes and lodged in crevices, tree roots, and spiders' webs.

Overnight, the forest began to move, like a great choir swaying to its own song. Whole tiers of greenery darkened and grew light again as the wind turned each leaf. Whole acres of woodland seethed, as though the forest were coming to the boil. The leaves on the baobabs trembled expectantly.

'More rain,' said Nathan, feeling expert by now on the tropical monsoon. But the raindrops on his skin tasted salt. They had blown in off the sea.

The wind had a voice—a groan and moan rising to a roar; the sea sounded like sheet metal being shaken. The animals in Maud's pens grew agitated, and gibbered, teeth bared. Three brothers asked Tamo and Nathan to help them move their canoe. Nathan thought they meant to move it above the high water mark but apparently they wanted it fetched right up the cliff path. It was all the boys could do to lift the outrigger, let alone the canoe itself, and they broke the two apart, then sweated and strained till their hands were full of splinters, and still got only as far as the foot of the cliff.

Nathan was standing with the boat over his head, when something struck the hull right alongside his ear—a tree branch snapped off by the wind. 'That could have knocked out my brains!' he protested. But no one heard him. A litter of cones, coconuts, twigs, and stones were bombarding the canoe. The boys threw it aside and ran. The sea came after them, grey, like the lash of a whip.

In fact, by the time Nathan emerged from under the canoe, the whole landscape had changed colour. It was as if the wind had stripped away all the greens, crimsons, and aquamarine, and left a uniform grey. The sky had subsided to just above their head. The wind off the sea pushed Nathan bodily up the path, bullied and bludgeoned him up against trunks, and hit him with a free-rolling bush. When he looked back, the sea was haunted.

Tall figures stood among the waves—grey twists of movement running towards the land, dancing on the surf—sailors and fishermen disinterred from the seabed to dance. Ghosts.

He grabbed hold of Tamo, but could not make himself heard over the noise of the storm, until they got back to the hut. All Maud's pens and nestboxes were overturned, and she was struggling to free the animals from inside.

Nathan began to shout in Tamo's ear: 'God's angry! God's going to destroy you all for digging up the dead! I knew He would! I knew it! He's going to wipe you out, like Sodom and Gomorrah! Maybe it's even the end of the World! There's the sea giving up its dead and everything! Didn't you *see*? *Ghosts walking on the sea!'*

Tamo was anxious to wedge the eastern door shut with a plank of wood. He looked round. Morose, gloomy, craven, superstitious Tamo looked round . . . and laughed—so suddenly that it took even him by surprise and started him coughing. Then he coughed and he laughed and he laughed and he coughed till he was lying on his back, kicking his feet in the air.

'You superstitious little savage, Gull! Ghosts? *Ghosts?!* Shame on you. Ghosts! They're waterspouts, Gull! Did you never see a cyclone before?'

'A cyclone?' said Maud, crawling indoors with a lemur in one arm.

'You mean it's all right? We'll be all right?' said Nathan.

At that moment, an entire aloe tree impaled the roof of the hut like the thrust of a giant's sword—*Fee fie foe fum*—searching for English bones to grind.

'Oh, I wouldn't say that, exactly,' said Tamo. 'We might all be killed . . . But all said, it's only a cyclone. They come every year.'

9

Cyclone

The outrigger canoe they had tried to save was picked up by the wind and thrown fifty yards in the air. It sailed out its life on the oceanic green of the tossing forest, high in the branches of a tambourissa tree.

Ropes and hanks of seaweed, fences and crates, hurtled about, as if the world had stopped spinning with such suddenness that everything on it had broken loose. Gravity had lost its grip on solid matter. Flying debris demolished anything held fast at the roots. Bamboo, like thrown spears, flew lethally sharp over the roofs of Zaotralana—such roofs as were left, that is, for one by one the skilled work of months was torn apart in minutes. Palm leaves sharp as scimitars sliced at anyone, body and limb, who found themselves in the open. Salt sea rain sluiced, not in drops but in cataracts, over the village and forest. Dogs and chickens were picked up and pitched about.

Maud's hutches and pens bounced end-over-end in among the baobabs, and smashed to matchwood. The charcoal burner's hut, having no post sunk into the ground, simply rolled away, the family inside it squealing like those pigs rolled downhill in barrels on fair days.

Darkness closed in—a lumpy aggregate of cloud, litter, rain, and sand, which flayed the fruit from the trees, the young rice plants from the paddies, the coir shag from the coconut palms. The river moved backwards up its watercourse, flowing uphill, defying Nature. There seemed to be no air to breathe, only a vacuum left in the wake of the wind rushing inland.

The sea tried to fill the void. Waves lost all rhythmic patience, and rushed ashore, rolling up within the seventh wave all the previous six. Waves as high as London buildings shunted ashore tons of pebble and rock, whole shoals of sand. Shoals of fish hung in those blue-glass walls of moving water—shark and turtles, suspended in the hectic stillness of unbreaking waves, hurtled ashore into a strange environment of submerged mangroves and drowned trees. The ocean itself, inflated by wind and a billion gallons of rain, swelled and filled, till it seemed that all Madagascar would be overwhelmed or dashed against the coast of Africa in a continental shipwreck.

Inside the hut, the children lay flat on the ground, hard up against the walls, their blankets over them, hiding from the malice of the wind, while the cyclone tried to break into their home. It clawed away the bark boards. It turned the aloe tree in the roof like a corkscrew, until tree, roof, and all were wrenched away. After that, the cyclone was both indoors and out, gouging out the doors, stoving in the very ribs of the building with great welting kicks.

Nathan, his blanket over his head, was filled with thoughts as wild and irrational as the weather. He bitterly resented the damage to the shelves he had put up as, one by one, they fell on him like blows. In reaching to dislodge one from his back, his fingers closed around a piece of Maud's crocheting which at once fell apart. *'I'm sorry, Maud! I'm sorry!'* he yelled. But the hurricane would not even let him repent, for it drowned all sound but its own. He could not make her hear.

Suddenly, he was inside his school chest once more,

being banged down the stairs at Graylake, while his treasured possessions were torn apart page by page. All that awaited him outside was a thrashing by a bully—though this time the bully was twelve storeys high and armed with uprooted trees.

Either this memory, or the suffocating lack of air, made Nathan throw off his blanket. At once he was dowsed with sea-rain and confronted with the sky—a purple and yellow bruise, rather, where the sky had previously hung. The house was disintegrating around him. It offered not shelter any more but imminent physical danger, as piece by piece of the wall broke free of its twine lashings. Tamo was lying hard up against the base of the west wall, his blanket over him as protection. He did not see, therefore—as Nathan did—when the rotten north-east corner-post, in rocking to and fro, snapped off at the base, leaving the whole hut wall snaking free. The zebu horns enshrined there were sent corkscrewing across the ground, lethal as a harrow broken free of the horse. They struck the wooden door prop and were deflected into the air, where the wind took hold and spun them before driving one sharp horn's point through Tamo's blanket and what lay beneath it.

Nathan stared. The wind pushed and barged him about in teetering little steps, but he did not even notice. For the massive twisted spike of polished horn had pierced the very outline of Tamo's head. He heard Tamo cry out—even above the sound of the wind. Now there was no more sound.

Maud, losing hold of her blanket, had it whisked away and saw it flap into the sky like a giant manta ray swimming. She also saw her brother standing up, being whirled around like a whipped top. *'Get down!'* she screamed at him. *'Nat, get down!'*

'It's Tamo!' was all he said. *'He's dead. He's dead. He's dead!'* Though he tried to point, his arms were forced back down by the wind. Maud crawled across what had once been a room and, grabbing Nathan's belt, hung on it until she brought him down on top of her. *'He's dead! He's dead!'* he kept saying as he fell.

Keeping low, they were able to worm their way under the rushing weather and reach Tamo. They could even hear each other, with their heads so close together.

'I did nothing! I just stood by!' Nathan kept repeating. 'I saw it moving and I watched it. I did nothing! I just let it stick him!'

'What could you have done?' said Maud briskly. 'Silly boy. Bear up. Be brave.' But she shut her own eyes as she pulled the blanket away from Tamo's face.

'You see? He's dead! And I just stood by!'

The pirate's son was quite a vivid blue. It was true, he did look dead. But where was the blood? Where was the gash that had left him this deathly colour? The zebu's horn, though it appeared to have passed clean through his neck, had actually passed hard by it, although one of the elaborate twists must have struck him a blow on the forehead; there was already a swelling. 'Nat! Help me!'

'I jumped out of the way, you see!' Nathan confessed, stupefied with guilt.

'It's pressing on his windpipe, Nat! The horn is pressing on his windpipe! He's not breathing!' Maud made the mistake of kneeling up too high, and the wind took her by the hair and threw her to the ground. When she got up again, Nathan was already wrestling with the weird, contorted length of horn, like Jacob wrestling with the Angel, trying to pull it out of the ground, trying to lever it away from Tamo's throat. The pinned blanket flapped round him, and the cyclone pelted him with dust and rain.

When it came free, Nathan picked up the pair of horns in both hands, lifted it over his head, and pitched it away from him. He grabbed Tamo by the shirtfront and, in his eagerness to make him be alive, pulled him half-way to his feet. The wind blew directly into Tamo's face—forced its way into his mouth and nose (along with a fistful of grit) and made him cough. Then both boys were overbalanced again by the howling wind.

Just then, a party of young men—an expeditionary force from the village—crawled up the hillside. From the shelter of the elder's big hut, they had seen the shack on the hilltop blown away piece by piece, and had come to see if anyone was left alive. They came lashed together by comradeship, their arms round each other's shoulders, bending into the blast.

The line parted to take in first Maud, then Nathan and Tamo, dragging, carrying, supporting them and each other back down the hillside. Maud, with her arms round the shoulders of two men, hung clear of the ground, and her feet swung to and fro, like the clapper of a bell. A wind-tossed chicken struck the man alongside her in the chest, and he roared with laughter and spat out feathers. She began to laugh, too, and felt the laugh snatched off her face, out of her mouth, as if the spirits were hungry for laughter . . .

Entering the large, dark, substantial house of the elder (where most of the village had now gathered), the sudden stop to the pressure of the wind made her ears ring. For the first time, Maud was properly able to see that Tamo was recovered. He mimed, for the benefit of the crowd, how something—something heavy—had fallen on him, knocked him half insensible, fallen across his throat, so! to choke him. Nathan had pulled it off him, pulled it off his windpipe, saved his life—no, don't deny it!

Her brother was looking sheepish, embarrassed by all the attention, but pleased too. He turned rose-red as the village girls began to kiss him and stroke his hair, making much of him. Along with these excitable girls and the more stoical village matrons, Maud too kissed her brother in congratulations at having saved Tamo's life. But she whispered in his ear as she did so: 'Don't say what it was that spiked him.'

She saw the meaning sink home behind his sore eyes, and he began to blink rapidly: lying came hard to Nathan.

'What was it, Gull? What hit me? What did you pull off me?' Tamo was elated. Just being alive outweighed all that he had lost in the storm.

Nathan blew through his lips. 'Just a branch. Just a big old branch,' he said. For he, like Maud, saw that it would not do for Tamo to know otherwise—to think his ancestors had come after him, out of their ancestral corner, malevolent and murderous, going for his throat. And that was just how he would see it if he knew. After all, that was just how it had seemed.

Hard to believe, having lived through it, but the heart of the cyclone did not strike directly at Zaotralana. If it had, there would have been far more to show for it next day than a lost fishing boat, and a few dozen roofs to renovate. The eye of the storm had lighted further north. There, the forest would have been crushed flat like a field of wheat—long corridors of devastation cut through the trackless wilderness, whole villages disappearing overnight. As the cyclone subsided to a storm, the storm to a downpour, the downpour to steamy sunlight, Zaotralana emerged from its ordeal with only superficial wounds. The forest had been gleaned of all its deadwood. Wasps still clung together in emerald, urn-shaped societies of thousands. Pollen still clung to the stamens of the tiger-lilies.

But the sea was blood red. The rivers, like severed veins, were issuing their red sediment into the bay, turning the very sink of the sea a bloody crimson.

'It always happens—after any big storm,' said Tamo, wanting to get on with the rebuilding.

'Doesn't it frighten you, though?' said Maud, gazing down at the sea from the clifftop. 'It looks so . . . ominous.'

'Like the land bleeding,' said Nathan.

But Tamo could not see it. He had spent his boyhood in this land of blood-red rivers, not in the English countryside where the trout streams flowed into slow, placid waterways. 'The fishing will be good while the sea-bed's stirred up,' was all he had to say. 'You want to fish?' He turned his back on the sea.

Maud reached out to stop him leaving; her fingertips bit deep into his arms.

Sailing down from the north, seven whaling canoes were just rounding the headland. Each boat was crammed with men, each boat linked by a rope to the prow of the dilapidated sailing hulk they were towing. Though not a silk sail remained to it, and its three masts leaned at three different drunken angles, although the cyclone had sand-blasted its tarred sides to a paler colour, Nathan recognized it at once. He had seen it moored in Tamatave harbour.

The pirates of Tamatave crossed the bar, and entered the blood-red bay. It was 'King Samson' decamping. The cyclone had demolished his kingdom, fouled the harbour with sunken ships, and killed a dozen crew. His men did not relish the work of rebuilding, but preferred to find somewhere that had fared better than Tamatave in the cyclone. And so, as rowing had brought Tamo and Nathan overnight to Zaotralana, so it had brought King Samson, his queen, and his court of pirates, looking for a new kingdom.

'The cannon!' said Tamo, and the three set off to run.

The cliff-side path barely existed any longer. Debris hung in the trees like flocks of dead birds, and loose sand had reshaped the face of the cliff. They had to clamber from tree to tree, scramble over tree roots laid newly bare, find new passageways among the maze of mangroves, before they reached the projection of rock where the first cannon had been mounted.

Not only was the cannon gone, but the rock had gone too, carried away. They scrabbled on towards the other gun.

'You won't kill them, will you?' panted Maud. 'There's women out there, too! I can see them!'

Tamo snorted at the mere possibility of hitting the distant rowing boat with an uncalibrated cannon. He did not choose to admit that he had never fired a cannon in his life before. 'If we can just let go a shot, they'll think the place is already fortified by another crew, and push on past,' he said.

'Push on past, yes!' said Nathan, his hand against his chest to suppress the rising fright.

'It's still there!' exclaimed Maud, catching sight of the cannon.

Overhung with fallen ivy, the second gun stood rock-solid where it had been installed by so much hard labour. Even the balls, though their pyramid had collapsed, had rolled only a few yards, not plummeted down on to the beach.

'How do we light it? How do we fire it! We forgot a light!' wailed Nathan, jumping from foot to foot in agitation.

'Peace! I can use the flash from my pan,' said Tamo. To their astonishment, he pulled his pistol from under his jacket. How long had he been carrying a loaded pistol in his belt? Oh, but of course. Where else had he to stow it since the cyclone? He showed them how he would use the flash of sparks from his pistol's firing pan to ignite the gunpowder in the cannon's touch-hole. They had left the gun primed and loaded, but Tamo emptied the last of his powder over the damp charge in the touchhole, even so, to give it a better chance of catching. 'I'll just check that a bird hasn't nested . . . ' said Nathan vaguely, to himself, and clambered out alongside the gun.

'Be careful! Don't fall!' Maud scolded him.

'Get back! Leave it! You're in the way! I'm going to fire!'

'NO!'

Tamo clenched his fists in frustration and again tried to gesture Nathan out of the path of fire.

Nathan folded his shoulder forward, hollowed his chest, and felt reflexly for his shirt cuffs.

'DON'T! Or you'll blow us all up. It's BLOCKED!' he bawled.

The barrel of the cannon was more than blocked. It was packed, from breach to mouth, with wet sand driven home by the cyclone. Like a stoppered bottle, its mouth had been sealed tight. It was powerless to utter a single sound of protest at the noisy arrival of King Samson far below. He and his pirates were even now leaping over the gunwales to wade ashore through the blood-red surf.

10

The Excellent Exquemelin

'Listen,' said Tamo. 'Before they get here. I'm Thomas White's son, and we came here for a roving life.'

They struggled back along the cliff-face, the chant loud beneath them of men pulling the heavy row-boats up the beach.

'What does he mean?' Maud asked her brother.

'We have to pretend to be pirates,' said Nathan. He did not sound nearly as appalled as he should.

The hulk of King Samson's sailing ship slumped unhappily in the bay, anchored in water deep enough to float in, but shallow enough to leave her masts above water if she sank overnight.

'You, Maud, you're my wife,' said Tamo.

'Don't be ridiculous. I'm thirteen.'

'Unless you'd prefer King Samson to take you,' said Tamo.

'I'm your wife,' said Maud.

'And we are here waiting the chance of a fresh ship. These types, they see a weak thing and they crush it. They see a strong thing and they step back. Understand?'

'They'll never believe us,' said Maud.

'Make them. If they think we're honest—if they think we'd sell them for a bounty, anyway—they'll kill us straight out.' He turned and glared at Nathan. 'None of your Graylake principles and preaching, you hear?' Nathan spread his hands innocently.

'Why don't we just hide till they're gone?' whispered Maud, unwilling to climb the last few yards, as if it might bring her face-to-face with a pirate.

'Because they won't go. They're here to settle. They'll make Zaotralana theirs.'

'Well, we did,' said his wife meekly.

'No!' He reached down a hand, impatient for her to keep up. 'No, no, no. We live here. These types, they take places like they take ships, cargo and crew. They think they can own a place like this.'

Maud thought of Noro and her parents and aunties, about the work they had put into beginning the new hut, and the others who had helped. She did not want their lives overrun by these brutish criminals. They deserved her help. Clearly her brother had found some secret reserve of courage, for he was standing straight-backed against the skyline, one foot raised on higher ground, one hand on his hip. He cut quite a gallant figure, thought Maud, with a twinge of family pride.

Gallant did not describe King Samson. He was small and bald, with a wig which he tied round his neck by its pigtails, and eczema which he picked. A big jewelled cross hung round his neck, along with a carved tusk of some kind, an oriental dagger in a velour sheath, and a big, tin spoon. The toe caps of his boots flapped loose from the soles, and the leather cuffs, which sagged round his ankles, had caught so many scraps of food as he ate that they were alive with cockroaches and earwigs. His neck was goitred, and bulged like a bullfrog's, and his teeth were a thing only of memory; he had left them with a dentist in Accra so as not to be troubled by toothache.

His courtiers were mostly Newfoundland slitters,

their new life chosen in preference to gutting fish on frozen quaysides in an arctic winter. Their early years had been spent eating fish-heads and cutting off their own fingers by mistake, and time had turned them into thin, grey, small-eyed men like maimed sharks. One had a P branded on his forehead, witnessing some capture and conviction for piracy.

Leaving his queen and quartermaster, goods and a rearguard on the beach, King Samson climbed to Zaotralana and, finding the place strangely quiet, thought he must have scared away the inhabitants. But a solitary boy with a European look stood outside the door of the big hut in the centre of the village. 'You are King Samson,' the boy informed him. 'The wind blew you here from Tamatave Bay. Welcome to the stronghold of Captain Thomas White.'

King Samson was taken aback. His eyes flickered behind dropped lids. Both forefingers twitched on the triggers of the pistols he held. Suddenly he snorted, so that his short, pig-like nose spattered Nathan with moisture.

'The stronghold of Thomas White? You his ghost, are you? Thomas White? Found the fountain of youth, did you? Thomas White? He was dead before you were born, runt. I've pissed on his grave, me! Damn me, I even took his . . .'

'You mistake, sir,' said the boy in the refined voice of an English choirboy. 'I am merely quartermaster to Captain White. And I refer not to Captain Thomas White of Tamatave but to his esteemed son, Thomas White, esquire, lately of Suffolk, now of Zaotralana.'

Samson stepped forward into the hut. Its sudden dark blinded him after the brilliant sunshine outside. A young man in a white shirt, tailored breeches, pistol and sash (seemingly of lace) was facing him, long, combed black hair tied loosely in the nape of his neck and a lacy stock frothy beneath his chin. He alone was standing, while the entire room glimmered with the eyes of people seated on the floor. They were looking not at Samson but at the young man—clearly a figure of authority or fear.

'My father sent me to England,' said the youth, with the same precise diction as the choirboy outside. 'But now I am returned. To take up his calling. To take up, as it were, the family business. Won't you partake of some refreshment, sir, after your arduous voyage? We share a profession; shall we not share a drink of liquor, too?'

King Samson snorted again and wiped his nose on his sleeve. He hurried forward, toe-caps flapping, pointing his pistol at Tamo's stomach. When the barrels jabbed into Tamo's sash, Samson looked down: he had forgotten he was holding them, and promptly stuffed both pistols into his sash. Then he grabbed Tamo's hands in his dry, flaky paws, and pumped them up and down. 'An honour to meet you, sir. An honour! Thomas White's boy? 'Pon my word! 'Pon my—damn me! Thomas White's son! And there's me married to . . . ' Then, with a suddenness which took even Tamo by surprise, he sat down on the floor. The tightness of his trousers forbade a measured descent.

Now Nathaniel Gull knew all about pirates. Never at school had anyone asked him about anything he knew. They had asked him about things he ought to have known and didn't. They had asked him questions and he had guessed wildly at the answers. But never had anyone asked him about pirates, and he knew about pirates. The excellent Exquemelin had told him, in lurid detail, every aspect of their colourful lives. After years of reading *Bucaniers of America* every night, Nathan felt he knew the very colour of their coat linings, the very shape of their souls.

He knew, for instance, what they ate. So that is what he told Maud to fetch.

'Are you quite sure about this?' she said.

Nathan was. Absolutely certain.

'You say you lost your ship in the cyclone?' said King Samson, unfastening his trousers to make room for his dinner.

'Yes. A three-mast Indiaman with four demi-cannon,' said Tamo. 'Out there in the bay. And I'd not had her above a month. It was a great setback to my plans.'

Nathan embellished the story. 'Of course, we first took the ship bringing us here—out of England—but she just wasn't yare for roving, so we set about the Indiaman, and took that instead. Best cedarwood she was. Better looking than a woman.'

'That's a blow. That's a blow,' said Samson, deeply affected. 'Well, you can join up with us, if you've a mind. If you can stand the stink of slitters. It's fair shares on all takings—'cepting captain's share's fairer than most, naturally.'

'That's a fine gentlemanly offer, sir,' said Tamo graciously. 'But I fear I've grown fond of the power of command. Also, having a horror of wet feet, I like a vessel that's seaworthy. Pray don't take this amiss, sir, but your ship looks past her best. You'll need to make repairs. We shall assist you.'

Maud, as she prepared the meal, watched Tamo White with new eyes. He was stylish, he was convincing; he had panache. With her crocheting round his waist and bunched under his chin, he looked, frankly, debonair. A sharp excitement filled Maud's throat, almost a pain. As for her brother—she barely recognized him.

'And how long have you been on the account, sir?' asked Nathan.

'On the . . . ?' said King Samson.

'Account. At the seas. A corsair. A privateer. Do you carry letters of marque?'

'It was like this,' said King Samson, feeling himself out of his depth. 'I was saw-ripper on a whale-ship. One day the captain hit me. I hit him back. He died. I was a pir—corsair.' (He liked the word almost as much as Nathan, and resolved to be a corsair in future, rather than a pirate.)

The 'wife' of Thomas White put down a serving of food in front of King Samson, in a broken shard of terracotta pot. It looked like something for caulking a leaking hull, except that it steamed a little. No one else was offered any; it seemed he was being especially honoured with a local delicacy. When he lifted it close to his nose, it smelled . . . indescribable. With his spoon still strung round his neck, he scooped the jelly into his mouth and swallowed.

'The favourite meal of any buccaneer!' said Nathan proudly. 'The warm marrow of a freshly slaughtered beast!' (Though he did not admit that the beast had had to be a goat.)

Silent and demure, Maud stirred the meat of the goat in the longhut's large, communal cooking cauldron. It smelled delicious.

'Give me some of that!' said Samson, pushing his head into the tasty steam. 'Quick! Quick! Does she understand me? Give me some of that to kill the taste!'

'It won't be properly cooked for an hour or more,' said Maud, in her correct, rectory English. But Samson took some anyway, to rid his mouth of the taste of marrowbone jelly. Suddenly catching the scent of Maud herself, he put an arm round her knees and pressed his face against her lap, breathing deeply in. 'A white girl! Where did you get her? Oh, just smell her! The smell of her!'

Maud went rigid. She could see the Newfoundland slitters, still on their feet by the door, were all looking at her now, their faces expressionless, moulded by the weather and by hardship into deadpan masks.

'My wife, you mean?' said Tamo. 'I brought her here from England. Sadly she contracted leprosy on the voyage. But her conversation is still fair, and her cooking.'

Maud felt her legs suddenly released, and moved away silent, wraithlike, to fetch drinks.

'Me, I have a wife!' declared King Samson, and he laughed until he choked. 'Queen Delilah! Good Christian girl. Says her prayers reg'lar.' He seemed only now to realize that she was not with him. King Samson's memory was not good. ''Pon my soul! Damn me, but I forgot her! Left her on the beach with the baggage! Fetch her up. Let's surprise the captain!' He flagged his hands at the Newfoundlanders, and four slipped away to fetch Queen Delilah and the baggage.

'So how d'you mean to lay hold on another ship?' asked the king.

Tamo fixed the pirate with his dark eyes—a calm, level gaze which impressed upon him that he was in the company of Captain White's son and heir. 'Ways and means, sir. Ways and means. We are young, and life is sweet here. There is no hasty need.'

It was preposterous. Three children without a home, let alone a ship, and yet King Samson nodded and beamed. Why not child pirates, after all? he was thinking. There are women ones.

'And these are your crew, are they?' he nodded towards the villagers of Zaotralana who were so patiently co-operating with his deception. 'Give me slitters any day. Can't trust these savages . . . What's your ship's articles?'

For the first time, Tamo blinked rapidly and examined the roofbeams of the hut. He had no idea what Samson meant.

But Nathan, his hand shaking only a little as he poured drink into two calabashes, said swiftly, 'Nothing out of the ordinary. *Every man shall drink as much as he wants. No women on board. No smoking below decks. Hundred pounds for a leg lost. Hundred for an arm. And fifty pounds to the widow of any man killed.*'

The king scratched ferociously at his elbows and head. He glanced warily at his henchmen and gave a nervous giggle. 'What d'you want to go saying that for in front of them? You trying to tempt them away from me?' And he scratched his back against a supporting pillar of the hut. 'You offer articles like that to a bunch of savages?' Then he realized that he was talking to a boy half-Malagasy, and stared down into his drink, embarrassed.

'A toast, sir,' proposed Nathan. 'An oath of friendship sworn by the sea. What do you say, captain?'

'Peace on earth. Good will to all men,' said King Samson, which was the only toast he ever remembered drinking. In England once, at Christmas.

Tamo looked up at his 'quartermaster', awaiting a suggestion.

'In the words of Blackbeard, *Come let us make a Hell of our own!*' declared Nathan.

King Samson beamed and tossed back his drink, as

he had been longing to do. He was expecting it to be arrack or beer—perhaps even wine. Inside the calabash, he could not even see what colour it was. But he swallowed it down at a gulp.

'What was it?' asked Maud later, as they listened to King Samson being violently sick behind the hut.

'Don't ask me. I didn't drink any,' said Tamo.

'Nathan . . . ' said Maud accusingly.

'It's traditional,' her brother said defensively. 'For an oath of friendship. Pirates always use it when they're making alliances: a glass of saltwater mixed with gunpowder. Exquemelin says . . . '

Tamo raised his calabash, as if for a toast. 'To the excellent Exquemelin, and all the nonsense he ever invented!' he proposed. The others took up the toast—'The excellent Exquemelin!'—and Tamo emptied his calabash out on the floor, rather than drink the grey liquid inside. More of a libation than a toast.

Thanks to the marrow jelly, the saltpetre-water and the raw goat, King Samson was still vomiting in the long grass, watched by his Newfoundlanders, when Queen Delilah arrived from the beach.

She was a woman of about forty, muscular and broad-beamed—a great Madagascan beauty grown fat, her silk, embroidered clothing stained by the sea voyage, her face lined by the sun. Her hat was a man's tricorn adorned with long streamer-feathers bedraggled now and sticking to her dress. But most remarkable of all was the array of jewels she wore—so many that she seemed to have stepped from under a shower of rain and still to be glistening. There were jewels in her earlobes, on her hands, sewn to her clothes and gummed in her hair. The sunlight refracting from her threw tiny fragments of rainbow in through the door of the hut.

Tamo, seeing her shape dark against the doorway,

got up and went to greet her. Strangely, however, they looked at one another—Malagasy at Malagasy—and spoke not a word, before Tamo brushed past her and walked away. Nathan and Maud were left entirely alone with her.

With no translator to help them, they stood smiling gauchely at the woman. Maud did not feel that any of her meagre vocabulary equipped her to address a pirate queen. In any case, the woman only stared after Tamo, her lips clenched between her teeth, her long jewelled hands opening and closing.

Queen Delilah was accompanied by the 'king's' quartermaster, a lean bristle-haired man with a scar beside his mouth. He looked around him with quick, suspicious eyes. Both his pistols were drawn. When he found his captain heaving up, behind the longhut, he cocked both guns and pointed one directly at Nathan's head.

'Did you poison him? Will he die?'

Maud wiped her face of sweat, stepped forward in the small, timid steps of a vicar's daughter, and bobbed a polite curtsy. 'Begging your pardon, sir . . . ' Her hands took hold of the quartermaster's pistols and lowered them to point at the ground. 'The gentleman ate some undercooked goat's meat. It disagreed with him,' she said.

The quartermaster curled his lip in contempt, but this time at King Samson.

With Tamo gone, the villagers disbursed out of the longhut and went to their own homes. They looked uneasily at the pirates, knowing that their lives would be radically altered by these newcomers. Several asked Maud where Tamo had gone, but she could only shrug and busy herself feeding goat stew to the Newfoundlanders and the queen.

Tamo came back at sunset, looking as if he had drunk several glasses of saltwater and gunpowder.

'What's the matter? Where did you go? We needed you! What's wrong?' said Nathan.

'He's been with his ancestors,' said Maud with uncharacteristic malice. 'I know the look.'

Tamo gave a wry, sad smile. 'Yes. In a manner of speaking I have,' he said, in a voice thick with tears. 'Where's the queen? Where's the royal Delilah, then? Where have you stowed her for the night, my mother?'

11

The Pirate's Doxy

Nathan ought to have known, from reading Exquemelin, that the quartermaster was the real ruler of Samson's little kingdom. A pirate crew is democratic: it elects its captain. It elects the man it can bend and mould, the one it can tame and master, one who will not dare withhold a man's rightful shares, who in no way resembles the tyrannical sea captains who drove men to piracy in the first place. The quartermaster is different. He rules by brute strength. No one dares dispute his rank or disobey his orders. He has to be clever and resourceful to survive the hatred he arouses. Captains rule by his permission.

King Samson's quartermaster was known simply by his rank. Marooned for mutiny by the British navy, he had been picked up by Samson and had quickly taken on, unasked, the role of quartermaster. He seemed to have left his real name behind on the island. Though first appearances suggested that Samson was monarch over his subjects, it soon became plain that Quartermaster was the true despot.

It was he who billeted the crew around the village, placing at least one Newfoundlander in every hut so that village resentment had nowhere to foment into insurrection. He commandeered the large hut for the king, queen, himself, and all stores of powder. He set quotas of fish to be caught each day to feed the increased population of Zaotralana, threatening the fishermen with death if they returned before their quota was filled. And to ensure that they returned at all, he made hostages of their children, mothers, wives.

King Samson ordered the construction of an open sedan chair—a throne on poles—so that he could be carried by four men and never set foot on the ground.

Meanwhile Quartermaster ordered the cutting of stone slabs to fortify the village against attack.

King Samson, finding the elder's ceremonial bath in the hut, ordered it to be filled with beer daily by the villagers, as a tribute to his royal personage.

Meanwhile, Quartermaster set about burning the jungle back a hundred yards, to prevent the approach of an enemy from the interior. He peppered the ground around the large hut with poisoned thorns, so as to deter night assassins.

King Samson produced a Bible and commanded every villager in Zaotralana to kiss it, saying, 'Look! I've converted them all, already!'

Quartermaster meanwhile sent teams of carpenters out to Samson's ship to see if she could be saved. He did not ask Tamo's help.

Quartermaster assembled the entire village and redivided the population, separating men and women into different living quarters. 'One wrong step, tell them, and the women and children burn,' he told Maud, for the purpose of translation. Strangely, he left the three European children as they were, camping uncomfortably in their part-rebuilt hilltop hut.

King Samson assembled the village to hear Queen Delilah recite the Lord's Prayer and twenty-third Psalm from memory. She stood on an upturned mortar, strands of grey hair blowing loose round her hairline, and her arms glinting with gold bangles, and she shouted the words, without punctuation or pause. The villagers looked puzzled but, assuming it to be some foreign feat of oratory, nodded their approval.

The calamity which had overtaken them they accepted as they had accepted the cyclone. It had happened to other villagers before now, and it would happen again. The pirates would stay or go, as Fate decreed. The Malagasies wore their misery and fear with patience and dignity.

As for Tamo, he stood and watched his mother recite the Bible, like a man holding his hand over a candle-flame, to prove the pain can be borne. His face was a picture of contempt, his loathing fed and increased by every garbled line she spoke.

'He leadeth minto grinpastors
Mysoley duth ristorygin . . . '

'Perhaps she had no choice,' whispered Maud soothingly. 'Perhaps Samson forced her to marry him.'

Tamo covered his head with one arm to shut out the suggestion. After a while he burst out, 'She's the daughter of a chief! He married her to Thomas White! After she was free of him, she could have gone back to her village. Sooner than this! Look at him. Smell him. Marry another sea-rat? She likes 'em. That's the only reason to do it. She likes their kind. She's a doxy. No more virtue than a bitch on heat.'

Maud was horrified by the change in Tamo. She needed him to tell her what to do next, how he intended to save the village from becoming a pirate stronghold. But he was thinking only about his mother, burying himself in mounds of resentment and spleen. He was barely aware of Nathan and Maud, so great was his passion of hatred against his mother. 'The doxy. The whore. Shaming herself. Shaming her ancestors for a few gems and baubles. Bitch. Goat.'

Delilah, reciting her verses, searched the crowd for a

sight of her son. But she no sooner caught a glimpse of him than he turned and walked away. She tried to see which way he went and, in doing so, omitted one of the Ten Commandments (the one about bearing false witness). King Samson punched her in the ribs, then sent her to fill him a pipe. The crowd disbanded, murmuring in their own bubbling, fermenting language.

The half-built hut to which the three children returned after dark was no more than a tamped mud floor and a roof held up by cornerposts. But it was high up, and gave a clear overview of the village. They felt safer there—as if they were not quite a part of what was going on in the village below.

That night, Queen Delilah came looking for her son. Nathan stirred in his sleep and was confronted by her huge, handsome face, as long as a sheep's and framed with the white wool of her hair. It loomed over him as she straddled his body: she was attempting to crawl across the hut to where her son lay cocooned in his mosquito blanket.

Nathan's first thought was of wild animals, his next of pirates, and he gave a yelp of fright. Tamo woke from the shallowest sleep and rolled out of his blanket. It was slow to release him and, with a string of swear-words, he tore at it and stumbled away with it dragging from one foot.

'Zanaka! Zanaka!' Queen Delilah, still on hands and knees, reached out a hand towards her son, imploring a word with him. It seemed for a moment that he would grant it, too, for he turned. Then he spat into her outstretched hand and, kicking his foot free of the blanket, ran off into the darkness.

The native woman whimpered and let her big hips sag to the ground. They pinned Nathan's blanket so that he could not move; and when Maud stirred, she was just as equally pinioned by the woman's piercing eyes.

'You his wife?' Delilah demanded to know.

'Me? No! Who? Oh. Yes! His wife,' said Maud, realizing, in the nick of time, that the truth might find its way back to King Samson.

'You wife of my son. Real thing? So. You make him to come back here. You make him talk to me.' Delilah folded her legs in front of her and regained her composure. In the darkness only her eyes showed, and the related glimmer of moonlit tears on her cheeks. 'My boy,' she said proudly. 'He goodly boy, yes? Not like his father.'

Maud and Nathan shook their heads. No, not like his father, they said.

'English little gentleman. Clever, yes. Books. He is proud and haughty, yes?' She used the words as if well acquainted with them. Plainly King Samson liked to think of himself as . . .

'Proud and haughty, yes,' said Maud.

'A fine clever gentleman.'

'He was very good at Greek,' said Nathan, eager to please.

'A fine English gentleman,' said the queen with a massive sigh. A wealth of sadness glistened in her eyes.

Maud crawled closer. 'No, no. Not a whit. All Malagasy. He came back, didn't he?'

The woman seemed to be deflating in the darkness, like a tent without poles. 'To be pirate,' she said, and sighed again.

Nathan scowled at his sister, forbidding her to say any more. But he need not have worried. Maud's heart had already been hardened against this woman, bespangled with jewels, her head full of gibberish psalms and her purse full of ill-gotten gold. 'You are,' said Maud. 'You stayed with the pirates when you could have gone—after Thomas White died.'

Delilah shrugged. 'Must.' Suddenly she straightened her back and glared at Maud. 'You look at me like he looks. Why you look at me like that, white girl? I your mama.'

Maud drew back. She tried to imagine having this woman for a mother-in-law. She wanted only to say, '*I'm thirteen. I'm sorry.*' In point of fact, there was nothing she could say.

'You tell that boy. You tell my Tamo!' Delilah said in a loud, clear voice. 'He don't trust that pig Samson. No more Quartermaster. He worsen.' She got to her feet with great nimbleness for so big a woman, scrubbing the palm of her hand across her nose and cheeks as if to erase her tears. As she straightened her back, a wealth of grey hair came unfastened from a jewelled clasp in her hair and cascaded down, like water in the dark. She moved away from them, rolling her weight from one foot to the other.

The darkness had almost swallowed her when Maud called out impetuously, 'Why did you marry him, if he's such a pig?'

Delilah halted.

'That's what Tamo wants to know. Why did you marry another pirate when you could have stayed free?'

'You mean, after his wonderful father?' said the bitter voice out of the darkness.

'When you were rid of pirates. When you could have stayed free. He thinks you sold yourself again for gold and jewels.'

'Maud!' Nathan was deeply shocked.

The queen's laugh was like a man's, deep and

rasping. It was not a laugh at all, but the bark of a monkey surrounded by hunting dogs. Queen Delilah returned to squat in the garden and tell her story.

After the funeral of Thomas White, Princess Andriamahilala, his native wife, looked up from the grave to see the eyes of four ships' captains fixed on her. When she returned home to her hut, she discovered the meaning of the looks on their faces. For the house behind Tamatave, despite its thorn-paved lane full of snares and mantraps and boulder palisades, had been torn to pieces. The French furniture, plundered from the vessel of a Parisian ambassador, lay with its clawed feet in the air, smashed with axes. The bed where Thomas White had died had had both mattress and goose-down quilt slit and gutted of feathers. His sea-chest had been set alight for the sake of any precious metal or gems inside. But the vandalism had not stopped there. The roof, walls, floor, and half the garden had been destroyed by those searching for Thomas White's treasure. But having found nothing, the pirates looked to his wife to tell them where it lay hidden.

There was a Spaniard, a Dutchman, a Newfoundlander—and King Samson, only come to Tamatave that week. They offered to cut off her fingers one by one until she told them where Thomas White had kept his treasure. Then the 'king's' quartermaster, a grey, rat-like, scuttling man, whispered in Samson's ear. And Samson proposed marriage in return for her dead husband's treasure.

There he stood on the waterfront, awaiting her answer, this lice-infested barrel of tallow and greed; a man full of egotistical fantasies, holding himself all-powerful, like God, despite the quick-grey-eyed wickedness of the quartermaster lurking at his back. His ship was also well armed.

So Andriamahilala went and knelt at Samson's feet, and danced a dance for him, and accepted his offer in the English her husband had taught her.

Dutifully she delivered up the secrets of White's hiding places—told him of almost every treasure there had been. The others had to watch from a distance, snarling their disappointment. Only one secret the pirate's widow kept to herself as she settled back—as a rabbit sits quiet in a snare—into being a pirate's doxy again, a chattel, a piece of property somewhere between cargo and crew.

Her chief comfort lay in knowing that somewhere else her son was enjoying the liberty of a gentleman, an honourable heart in his Malagasy breast, full of tenderness towards the mother who had raised him to be so different from his filthy father or any of these other grubbing sea dogs . . .

Moving between the English language and Malagasy like a shark between sea-lanes, Queen Delilah told her story to the girl she supposed to be her daughter-in-law.

'I know he come back. I know. I know I see him with my eyes again. Pirate is not a good life. But . . .' She shrugged. Despite thinking that her son had returned to take up his father's disreputable trade, despite the honourable precepts she had taught him as a boy, here she was, scenting the air for the smell of him, caressing the air as though it hung softer where her son had slept. He was her son, and beyond that, nothing very much mattered.

'He really isn't . . .'

'Maud, be silent!' said her brother. But it was a

dilemma. How could they explain, apologize for Tamo's shunning of his mother without explaining that he was not a pirate at all?

'I understand,' said Delilah, seeing their confusion. 'A man do bad things and it's business. A woman do bad things and she a bad woman.'

'Oh, but . . . '

'Maud, be silent!' said her brother.

Tamo's mother narrowed her eyes at them, looking from one to the other. 'You are brother and sister. One face,' she said. Then she moved deliberately closer to Maud, choosing between them which was to be best trusted. 'You tell him, daughter. You tell my boy Tamo: I say those Lord God words, but they don't mean nothing. They's no magic in those words. Not how I say them. You tell him, I don't shame my dead. Don't want for him to think I shame my dead.'

'Oh, but Tamo's really a Chris—'

'Nat, be silent,' said his sister.

Delilah grunted with the exertion of climbing over the broken garden fence. 'You tell him this, also. One treasure I keep for him. I give him treasure. It was White's. Now it is his.'

'Really?' exclaimed Nathan.

'He doesn't deserve it . . . turning pirate, I mean,' said Maud.

Delilah opened her hands. 'He is my son. What can I do?' She began to pick her way over the heaps of building materials around the half-built house.

'Oh, but Mama . . . ' called Maud. Nathan hissed at her in vain. 'Mama, I'm not his wife. I'm only thirteen. I'm no one. He only said that to protect me from Samson. I'm no one.'

The woman smiled and nodded and said nothing in reply.

'Why did you tell her that? What did you want to tell her that for?' Nathan demanded.

'She gave us a secret. We had to give her one,' said Maud, unrepentant. 'Don't you understand anything? Secrets are what make people trust one another.' And she seemed so sure of this that Nathan took her word for it and retreated to the folds of his blanket. Besides, the mosquitoes were biting.

Maud could not wait to tell Tamo about the visit, and how his mother had only married Samson to stay alive and save the treasure for her son. She wanted to see his face when he realized that his mother was not the mercenary doxy he mistook her for. Together they would plan a rescue—an escape with Andriamahilala to Tamatave, to recover Thomas White's treasure. When they were rich, they would all laugh at the notion of Tamo being a pirate, or even wanting to be a pirate. Maud sat up all night waiting for him, but Tamo did not come back.

The possibility of seeing his mother was so repellent to him that he roamed about for hours on end, with only his thoughts for company. Night thoughts grow misshapen and huge. Only at dawn did he turn for home.

Home? A handful of logs and a heap of palm fronds? In England his apartment had been three times bigger. In England, his power and prestige over men had increased every time he opened his purse. And what had been in his purse? His father's money. Pirate money.

As he reached the bottom of the hill, Maud at the

top jumped up and began waving and beckoning. She looked absurdly cheerful. Perhaps she had found some new animals—new to her—unremarkable to him. She would tell him how beautiful it was, wasn't it marvellous? And he would not be able to see the beauty of it: Madagascar was crawling with animals. Even so, Tamo walked a little faster.

It was just as Maud leaned over the low branch of the tambourissa tree and began to say: 'Tamo, I've got something wonderful to—' that Samson's quartermaster appeared behind her. He had a marlin spike in one hand.

'Early abroad, Mister White?' he said, over Maud's shoulder. Maud started visibly. The man had crept up on her from nowhere.

'No earlier than you, sir, I see,' said Tamo.

'I don't sleep well with questions running loose around my head, like cargo broke loose.'

'And is it your belief I can secure you an answer to your question?' said Tamo, with Graylake niceness.

'Well, it is, I'd say. Yes.' Quartermaster tapped the marlin spike against his unshaven jaw. It was possible he had decided to eliminate from Zaotralana any possible rival to King Samson. And Tamo was not wearing his pistol.

'If it is in my power to help you, pray do not hesitate to enquire of me,' he told the pirate.

'Truth is,' said Quartermaster, putting one arm round Maud's waist and resting the marlin spike on her bare shoulder. 'Truth is, I was asking myself just how a young man like yourself was thinking of taking a ship, when he's got no ship to call his own. "Ways and means", you said to his majesty. I recall it. "Ways and means". But then I asked myself in what way you meant "way", and what you means by "means". If you understand me.'

Maud thought: We have been found out. He knows we aren't pirates and never were.

Nathan thought: So. *His* ship has finally sunk, has it? Samson is no more pirate than us now. No ship and no notion how to get another. But what could Tamo say, who had no plan, no ways or means, no intention of capturing ships? Whatever would he find to say?

Tamo said: 'The war canoes in these parts are big—bigger than whalers—big enough to take, say, twenty men close hidden. When a ship comes down the coast, in sight of land, the people hereabout row out to trade with it—fruit and cloth and so on. They're friendly. They're trusted. That's how to take a ship. Get close under pretence of trading. By canoe.'

Quartermaster scrutinized his face for lies, but found none. He had suspected the boy was a shipwrecked unfortunate, talking big because he felt small. Quartermaster had not believed their story of being boy-pirates. Now he was not so sure. It was a sound plan. The boy looked Malagasy; the villagers did as he told them. The canoe plan could work.

'Is there one of these canoes here?' said Quartermaster.

'There's one hidden. When you came, the warriors hid it up the creek, to keep it from falling into your hands.'

'Tamo, what are you doing!' cried Maud.

Quartermaster looked at them both and snorted his laughter. He had had the smell of virtue in his nostrils ever since arriving, and had thought it came from Tamo White. Now he saw the real source of it.

'What am I doing?' Tamo answered Maud, as the little grey ferret of a man scuttled back down the hill in the greyer morning light. 'I'm going the way of my father. I'm pursuing my destiny. All this time—all the time I was in England—I thought I took after my mother. But I've had time to think. Now I look at myself, I take after my father.'

He had had all night to think this out. All night he had writhed with disgust at the thought of being Delilah's son, the son of a pirate's doxy. Like a snake sloughing its skin, he had finally broken free. 'I'm a pirate, me,' he said. 'I always have been. I was born to it . . . What were you going to tell me?'

'It's of no consequence,' said Maud. 'It doesn't matter now.' And her brother said nothing of the treasure either.

12

On the Account

They put Delilah in the bow, so as to make the outrigger look harmless and welcoming. She cooked rice and sang. Her son sat in the stern, a pistol out of sight under his native skirt, a strip of cloth round his head to keep off the sun. Between them, hidden underneath a length of sailcloth, King Samson and his chosen raiding party lay sweltering, with pistols and knives, a loaded blunderbuss, and cutlasses so red with rust that they looked already bloody.

In among them was Nathan, for 'Captain White' would hardly leave his lieutenant on shore. Besides, Samson did not like anyone languishing outside his field of vision. If he knew where they were, he reasoned, he knew what they were thinking.

Sweating under the tarpaulin, Nathan hoped no one knew what he was thinking, for he was stupid with terror. At Graylake the assumption had always been that God, the Great Referee, was constantly looking on, making note in His Golden Book of those who did not flinch from danger. But the idea of God watching Nathan lie in wait to plunder innocent travellers was intolerable. Better that God should be asleep on the other side of the world, rather than here, watching this devious, dishonourable sneak-thieving. And if God was absent, where was the point in showing manly fortitude?

The pirate in front of him stretched a cramped leg and pushed his boot into Nathan's face. It was dark.

He needed daylight and fresh air. So he lifted his shoulders a little to raise the edge of the fish-reeking tarpaulin and let in a trickle of light and a breeze. And there, inches away from his own face was a face he knew.

'Mr Hardcastle, sir?'

Nathan had seen Sheller begin the sale of his navigator, but not stayed to see it through. The need had been too pressing to rescue Maud. Now he realized what the outcome of that sale had been. King Samson owned Charles Hardcastle.

'Mr Hardcastle? It's me.'

'Keep still, you scum!' King Samson reeled off a string of curses and kicked out in all directions, making the tarpaulin ruck and toss. Darkness settled over Nathan again. Hardcastle did not reply; it was almost as if Nathan had dreamt him. But reaching out a hand to where the face had been, Nathan ran his fingers over the unshaven jaw, the nose, the hairline, the ears. Hardcastle did not so much as pull away. His skin was oddly clammy.

'Mr Hardcastle?'

No reply.

The pirates' first take was so simple that Samson praised God for it, with a great many obscene oaths. A Moorish pilgrim ship—the *Ganesa*—with ninety women and children aboard, was bound for Zidon, manned by twenty sailors and defended with ten half-cannon. But so eager were the women to exchange blessings and buy the fresh fish and fragrant herbs from this peasant canoe, that they lined the rails, laughing and chattering, reaching down their brown arms bangled with gold, and begging their mariners to drop scaling nets.

When Samson threw off the tarpaulin and fired his blunderbuss into the rigging, the crew scattered to hide, while the girls screamed and wept and clutched one another and called on Allah for protection.

Allah, like God, seemed absent from the Indian Ocean that day.

The blunderbuss had been charged with rusty nails. During the next few moments, the nails trickled down through the rigging and tinkled on to the deck. Unused to this kind of attack, the pirates made a clumsy job of boarding, and once aboard began treading on the hot nails with their bare feet, and cursing. Nathan went last, his arms and legs rubbery with terror. Half-way up the ropes, he decided he could not reach the top and must drop back down into the canoe. But the canoe had drifted out from under him, and a green, welling sea came surging up over his feet, trying to wash him away.

Tamo, on the other hand, ran up the ship's side like a lizard up a tree. He screamed a continuous, howling shriek, never seeming to pause for breath, never looking behind him to see who else had got successfully aboard. He knocked seamen down, he shot bolts to trap them below decks. He pulled the fuses out of cannon and ropes out of cleats, so that the air overhead was filled with the rattle of loose canvas—a noise which heightened the universal panic. He hauled girls out of their hiding places and stripped their arms bare of gold ornaments. He pulled daughters apart from their mothers and sent the mothers below to fetch up the remains of their baggage.

Nathan, finally crawling aboard amid the bedlam, attached himself to Charles Hardcastle, and clung as close to the man as his own shadow, trying all the while to explain he was not there by choice, trying to apologize, trying to express his regret at the terrible perfidy of Sheller who sold navigators like kegs of rum. Hardcastle said nothing.

Once Samson's men started to see booty—silks and purses, skirts sewn with mirrors, little coffers of spice—a frenzy of looting set in. They snatched greedily at inlaid combs, silver fasteners, leather panniers, and lacquer trinket boxes. Valuable cartons of saffron were scattered in favour of worthless baubles, staining clothes and faces and hands a bright, jaundice yellow.

Eagle-eyed, Samson stood on the rails, crooked his arm through the ratlines and supervised the pillage. A woman with a baby pulled her headcovering forwards so as to envelope the child in diaphanous shadow and shut out the noise, holding the child's gaze, creating a place of safety the two of them could share.

'Like lambs to the shearing,' said Samson, shaking his head in wonderment. Even he was amazed at the ease of the thing. 'No more'n they deserve, setting their womenfolk on the seas all alone.' To him, any wrong had already been transferred to the shoulders of the husbands and fathers who had let their wives and children go unaccompanied on pilgrimage.

His quartermaster bared little yellow teeth in a rat-like grin. 'It's a holy journey. If they die, they'll die in Allah,' he pointed out derisively.

Reminded he was in the presence of heathens, Samson spat. 'Get them off my ship,' he said. 'Won't have women on my ship. S'no luck in a ship with women on it. 'Specially not heathen women.'

So the prisoners, once they had been robbed of their possessions, were transferred to the *Ganesa*'s jolly-boat and to the canoe which had ambushed them. Six strong men hauled up Queen Delilah who, alone among women, was not considered unlucky by the pirate chief.

'Mr Hardcastle? Mr Hardcastle, sir? I never realized it was Samson who bought . . . '

Hardcastle said nothing. He neither answered nor acknowledged Nat's presence, as with dogged obedience to orders, he went from fo'c'sle to afterpeak, searching for valuables below deck. He would fire a warning shot into each dark recess and, as the crew hiding there crawled, abject and gibbering, into the open, he would bend and pick up the belongings and weapons they strewed at his feet: a pair of compasses, a penknife, a music pipe, a tinderbox, a cook's cleaver.

'What are you going to do? How do you plan to get away? What's he going to do with the prisoners?' Nathan yapped on and on at Hardcastle's heels. Now that Tamo was a pirate, Nathan needed a friend, and the navigator had been a good friend to him on the long voyage out of England.

But Hardcastle had changed. He was different. He was empty. Even when Nathan grabbed him by the arm and shook him, he was so empty that he did not make a sound.

'What about your wife? What about your baby?' Nathan found himself picking up the mariners' belongings, so as to be of help, carrying Hardcastle's loot for him. But the navigator's expression did not even change for an instant. He was a blank.

'Shan't we take them back, for to save their souls from perdition, captain?' It was Quartermaster who first put the thought into Samson's head. 'Shan't we take the pretty ladies home with us and have a Christian wedding or two?'

It was a wicked thought, a barbarous thought. Only Quartermaster could have inserted it so sweetly into Samson's head and locked it there with talk of a Christian wedding party. Ninety women and girls forced into slavery and debauched by a rabble of vicious drunkards. Needless to say, Samson's pirates caught on to the idea like dogs picking up a smell. They rushed aft, to point down into the little boats and leer and say, 'I'll take that one.'

'I'll have the one with the hair down to her feet.'

'I'll take the one on her mother's lap. They're easier trained up while they're young.'

The pilgrims looked up, their liquid brown eyes as large as the eyes of sacrificial zebu. They were just as silent. The woman with the baby rocked forward and back, forward and back. The two ropes running between ship and jolly-boat, ship and outrigger, pulled taut and trembled. King Samson was going to tow the prisoners home as entertainment for his men.

'Mr Hardcastle, do something!' said Nathan. He thought of appealing to Tamo for help, but Tamo was Thomas White's son now, and a pirate. Right and wrong did not fall within his province. 'Mr Hardcastle, please! What if one of those ladies was your wife!'

Hardcastle had been given the task of looting the map-cuddy, seizing whatever charts the Moors had which might update Samson's. While he searched, Nathan buzzed about him like a fly, begging him to think, to apply his educated, adult brain to saving the women. But Charles Hardcastle wore the look of a man who has visited the *ombiasy,* learned his fate, and accepted it. He, too, was a pirate now. He had lived with pirates, done and seen things which the old Hardcastle could never have stomached. He had surrendered to his fate.

Above their heads, up on deck, Samson was shouting commands for various sails to be raised. The ship caught wind and began to move. The ropes twanged taut between the ship and the boatfuls of women it was towing.

The map-room lay at the stern of the *Ganesa*. Through the casement, Nathan could look directly down the ropes and into the boats. His guts surged with indignation and revulsion: that Tamo should have made him party to this!

He realized that his arms were full of booty—all the things he had picked up as Hardcastle robbed and disarmed the crew. He emptied everything, in disgust, across the charts Hardcastle was studying. In among them was the cook's little meat cleaver. Suddenly Nathan picked it up again, clambered up into the casement alcove, and opened the port.

The ship was picking up way, and a hissing white foam frothed in the wake of its broad, clumsy hull, breaking over the prows of the towed boats so that the women clung to the thwarts and to each other. The beautiful colours of their flapping clothes overlapped, mixed, like the colours in an artist's palette. They seemed all to be looking up at him, every last face, looking up at Nathan and his little meat cleaver.

He climbed on to the outside of the casement and up it, towards the tiller post to which the tow-ropes were tied. He took a swing at one rope, but his whole hand just bounced away from the impact, and he thought he would drop the axe. He was balancing precariously against the casement, his feet through the latticework, his knees braced. He only kept his balance because he was holding on to the rope as he cut it. When it broke, he would fall for sure, down into the boiling wake.

'Boy!' said Hardcastle's voice from inside the map-room. 'Boy! Do you want to kill yourself, like your father did?'

Hardcastle leaned out and passed him a Turkish scimitar. His arm encircled Nathan's legs and held him steady. One slash, and the ropes were cut through, all but a few tenuous strands. Nathan crouched gingerly down and slithered back in at the open port.

'Boy! Boy!' said Hardcastle, helping him down. 'What did you think you were doing?'

With a soft twanging, and a small cry of alarm from the women, the two towing ropes fell away into the sea. The jolly-boat and the outrigger dropped away to stern, heeling and rocking, the women screaming. Samson swore and from somewhere he bellowed, *'What happened?'*

'Ropes broke,' came a reply from directly above.

It was as if something, too, had broken inside Charles Hardcastle—some rein which had held him in check. 'There's no going back, child,' he said to Nathan. 'Not ever. Sheller has posted me for a pirate in England. If I go home, it's only to hang in chains. He did for me. And your friend White has done the same for you. We're pirates, boy. It's no good thinking we're any different from them.' But he took Nathan's hand between his two, and squeezed it in a gesture which was more father than buccaneer.

'Put about and grapple them boats!' bellowed Samson above deck. *'I want those women!'*

But there was a stiff breeze, and a strong current running, and it would have taken considerable seaman-ship to manoeuvre in an unfamiliar, Moorish ship.

'What'll become of them?' said Nathan, watching the two small boats fall further and further behind, bright and small as flowerheads on the water.

'Maybe get ashore. Maybe get picked up out on the sea-lanes,' said Hardcastle.

'Or drown,' said Nathan. 'Or die of thirst. Because *I* cut them loose.'

Hardcastle rolled up three charts and shoved them inside his jacket. 'That would be their preference, boy. It's what they would choose. Sooner than be taken by rovers and Christians.'

Nathan took heart. Hardcastle was his friend again, and with Tamo turned pirate, he was sorely in need of a friend.

Tamo thrust ten gold and silver bracelets at Maud—his share of the voyage's takings. She recoiled as if he had offered her scorpions and slugs.

'You needn't think I shall wear . . . '

'It's the safest place,' said Tamo sharply. 'If they can see my share on you, they won't trouble to break in here and dig up the floor when we go out. You want the place dug up?'

Maud pursed her lips and looked to Nathan, who nodded feebly, as if to say, 'Wear them. Do as he says.'

They lay down on their mattresses, but the soft darkness outside was ragged now with pirate fires, the night noises of animals and birds suppressed by the noise of men getting drunk.

'What happened to the crew?' Nathan wondered aloud. 'What happened to the Moors?'

But Tamo did not reply. He appeared to be already asleep. 'You can see nothing rests too heavy on *his* conscience,' he said to his sister.

She did not reply either, but he knew she was not asleep. He could see the glimmer of her eyes in the darkness and hear the *tink-tink* of the bracelets on her arms. Somewhere a mosquito was droning round the dark hut, like a pirate roaming the black ocean of air, in search of flesh to plunder, blood to drink.

It was all so easy, once King Samson had a ship again. His kingdom extended to the uttermost horizon. He considered every sailor, every passenger, every ship's officer, every ship's rat his rightful subject. Their belongings and cargoes were merely tributes owing to him. The *Ganesa* proved the ideal ship to have taken; she was not fast or yare, but she did let Samson get close in to Moorish vessels, because they mistook her for a pilgrim ship and hastened to put alongside. Before they could realize their mistake, Samson's cannon were blasting into them, broadside, and Quartermaster's grappling hooks were clawing them close, like the talons of a vulture. Moorish crew rarely fought back. As Samson's pirates stormed aboard to the din of drums and rattles and clashing cymbals, the Moors rushed below decks to fetch up their cargoes with eager, imploring hands, asking only their lives in exchange for carpets, gold dust, gems, spices, bullion—cargoes so absurdly exotic that Nathan could barely credit them. What persuaded men to entrust such unimaginable wealth to a cradle of wood, and send it out across the Indian Ocean, a prey to typhoons, reefs, ship's worm, mutiny . . . pirates. Each vessel was a treasure cave worthy of a fairy tale, and at first the glitter dazzled Nathan.

'One handful would have paid off father's debts,' he told his sister, returning after one particularly successful sortie.

'No. He would never have taken it,' said Maud crushingly.

Even so, she was dressed now in Indian silk—blue

shot with turquoise—and small gold coins circled her forehead. The floor of the hut was bright with thick plush Arabian carpet, and bolster cushions slouched up against one another in every corner but one.

Maud kept accounts. She wrote down every item and coin paid them as their share in the roving—as if she might one day repay it. Her father had kept accounts—secret, desperate accounts where income never tallied with debts and never would. But his had never itemized a man among the debits:

'To the purchase of Mr Hardcastle .. .. .. 50 guineas.'

They had not acquired Charles Hardcastle outright; Samson would never have parted with his 'artist'. But for a few guineas, a sum of silver wire, and some moulded metal buttons, Nathan had managed to buy his friend the freedom to live in their hut while they were not at sea. He made a strange lodger—rarely spoke and seemed always to be asleep—taking refuge in sleep. Quartermaster's tyranny had accustomed him to doing exactly as he was told for fear of a kick or a punch, and he had virtually lost the power to act of his own volition. So instead, he slept. When Maud tried to wake him with food or the offer of a cushion for his head, Tamo snapped waspishly, 'Leave him be, madam! He's not one of your damned animals.'

The path outside was also spiny with long thorns and fragments of jagged tin. A wire at neck height was just visible by daylight, not at all by night. With stealing an accepted way of life, it was naturally accepted that the pirates would steal from each other at the first chance. Zaotralana had the look now of an entrenched battlefield. The animals rarely came near; the smells were too rank, Samson too partial to shooting small birds and livestock for the sport of it. Sometimes, in the morning, lemurs would be hanging snared in the wire. Then Maud would disentangle them and cradle them and talk to them, even though they were dead, and take them into the jungle to bury in the undergrowth.

The villagers cowered in abject, uncomprehending terror, amid this terrible occupation. They saw their sacred cattle slaughtered for roasting, their houses armoured and fortified until they were no more pleasant to live in than the pits hunters dig to trap animals. They went and whispered to their ancestors the strange sights they had seen—brocade, silver silk slippers, incense burners, a blunderbuss—but they did not raise up their dead to dance any more. Not with the barbarians polluting their village. Not with Zaotralana in the hands of demons.

'Why would we wake them up to show them what would break their hearts?' Noro told Maud. And so the dead stayed underground, prisoners, like the living, of King Samson and his bullies.

13

The Lie

Nathan knew what the books had to say about oaths and toasts and ship's articles. But Tamo White had a real instinct for the job—almost as if it ran in his blood. He knew where the Moors hid their valuables—in the ceilings and amid the ballast. He had an eye for a ship laden and empty, could read a flag at a mile's distance and recognize a captain from among a crew all dressed alike. He knew the value of the theatrical gesture, beating the drum, mounting the bowsprit when they rammed, and always first aboard, shrieking his banshee war-cry. Samson was impressed quite as much as the Moors.

But to Nathan Gull, it was as if Tamo were falling away from him—into the pages of Exquemelin—into the Graylake past when White had been the 'pirate's son', the boy in the class to whom he had hardly spoken, hardly dared speak.

The fairy-tale plunder—the diamonds, sequins, and lacquer furniture—one day quite suddenly lost its brilliance, as if Nathan had grown too old for fairy tales. The day they took a ship carrying cordage, chains, and bolts, there were wild celebrations, and men danced yoked together with yards of clanking chain, rejoicing in its usefulness. What good were diamonds in Zaotralana? Another trip out, it was sailcloth and coir. Another, it was butter, rice, and coarse osnaburg cloth.

A man does not have to hide butter or defend butter, fortify his treasure of butter or wake up with his throat cut for owning butter. He can simply cram it into his mouth, golden and starting to melt, and all that is left to show for it afterwards are a few more greasy stains on his gabardine jacket. Nathan ate his share of the butter as he walked home from the long-house where the takings were divided up. If he saved it till he got there, either Maud would shun it as stolen property or feed it to one of her damned animals.

But then the butter sat on his stomach—salty, oily, curdling in the rum Samson dispensed to his crew when they had done well. And Nathan remembered the taking of the butter.

The ship carrying it had been so small, the cargo so humdrum, that they had not expected a fight. But suddenly, at point blank range, the merchantman had fired a single cannon. The noise lagged behind the flash of fire at the gunmouth. The ball passed so close by Nathan that he felt the disturbance to the air. Then it struck a Newfoundlander, busy clashing the cymbals, and carried away his left leg, hurling him into the scuppers.

There was no going to help him, for the grappling hooks were already out, and the boarding under way. His screams were swallowed up by the crescendoing war-cry of men hurling themselves across the closing gap between the ships. The hulls rubbed together too hard, and a monkey-rack of cannon-balls were jarred loose; they rolled over the side, one after another. *Splash. Splash. Splash.* The water was no more than ten fathoms deep and so clear that the balls were still visible on the sea-bed: a flurry of sand and then clarity.

After the ship had been taken, all Nathan could think of was the Newfoundlander with one leg torn off. He did not want to see, did not want to look. But he need not have worried. As they transferred the butter and rice and osnaburg to the *Ganesa* and set the disabled ship and its crew adrift, Nathan asked after the missing man—Jan was he called?

'Fool,' said King Samson. 'Must've thrown himself overboard. For what? For a leg gone? He know'd I pay for a leg gone. A hundred pieces for a leg, he could've had. And him throwing himself over the side like that. Fool.'

Walking back to the hut, with a ladleful of butter on his stomach, Nathan felt his arms and legs grow deadly cold and his hands leak sweat and his face burn. He thought of the Newfoundlander standing on the bottom of the sea on his one leg, like a stork: a flurry of sand and then eternity. And Nathan started to be sick. He crouched in a huddle behind the hut, not wanting to be sick on the Arabian carpet, and he clutched his two legs as the tears rolled down his face.

'Maud!' he called feebly. But Maud was not indoors. Maud was out with her animals or with the Malagasy women. Tamo was still at the longhouse, being a pirate, drinking rum. Nathan crawled into the hut. The darkness felt so cold that he might have been crawling into the sea.

One day, perhaps, he would lose a leg or an arm or an eye. It was all part of roving. Every day of his life now consisted of being a rover. It would shape the rest of his life. It would shape his body, decide his death and his resting place. He tried to get up—to go and find Maud. But his legs seemed to have been carried away. What good are gold pieces to a man without legs?

Besides, Hardcastle had *seen* the Newfoundlander go overboard; he told Nathan about it in a whisper, after the sharing out of the butter. Samson, he said, had rolled the Newfoundlander under the rail with the toe of his boot, when he thought no one was looking. A hundred gold pieces saved. A hundred gold pieces, to a man like Samson, is a lot to part with, whatever promises a man has made to his crew.

Maud was with Delilah, washing shirts in the red river water, slapping pirate shirts against the rocks. The water made their hands red, but not as red as Maud's cheeks. The older woman could see the agitation in her face, but said nothing, waiting for Maud to find her voice.

'I have a great favour to ask,' said Maud.

'Ah!'

'It's a terrible, terrible thing. I don't . . . I wouldn't ask, if I could . . . I've got no right to ask you.'

'You wan' go,' said Delilah flatly. 'You wan' I help you go off home, yes? You wan' take my boy with you.'

'No! No, that's not it.' Maud was startled by the calm straightforwardness of the woman, those big muscular hands lifting and throwing, the rhythm of her movements not faltering as she spoke. Maud had been struggling with such complicated, convoluted plans that it threw her off her stride to hear anything so simply put.

'I got ship,' said Delilah breezily. 'I got big ship. But you not take my boy back in England.'

Maud was even more confused. 'You have a ship? Where? In Tamatave? A canoe, do you mean?'

'No! Big damn ship! Big like whale. By Jesus, I swear. Not here. Not Tamatave.' She rocked her head to and fro mysteriously and tapped her nose. 'Half-way. Din' I say I keep most big treasure of all? For Tamo? I keep iron ship.'

'Tay be!' said Maud involuntarily. 'An iron ship? Are you serious?'

'Yeah! Yeah! Iron ship. Damn strong. I remember. He lie on his back, Thomas White—he lie on his back in nights and look at sky and say, "I took her—iron ship." Number One treasure in all his life.'

'What then, can it keep out cannon-balls? And fire?'

Delilah wriggled her forefinger in front of Maud's face. 'Worm, child. Worm.'

Maud pulled her tangle of washing to the bank. Sleeves were knotted together, buttons snagged in loose threads, legs half inside-out like amputees. Thoughts whirled through her head. A ship? Hidden between Zaotralana and Tamatave? What did it signify: salvation or disaster? What if she told Tamo? He could no longer look at a ship and see a way of escaping: he would see a vessel to go roving in. And an armoured ship? It would make him the terror of the seas, the scourge of the shipping lanes.

No, amazing as the news was of Delilah's hidden ship, it did not help, as far as Maud could see. She still needed to ask her huge, her hopelessly huge favour of Queen Delilah, and Delilah, she was sure, would say no.

'Please don't be angry, princess. Please don't be offended.' (Ridiculous. How could she not be offended, thought Maud, and once more fell silent.)

'What you wan' ask me, daughter?' said Delilah, taking Maud's chin in her big wet hand. The fingers were as rough as pumice. The woman's hair smelt of palm oil. 'Ask. I not like, I say no.'

Maud closed her eyes, so as not to see the reaction to her wicked suggestion. 'It's like this. The *ombiasy* told Tamo he would follow in his father's ways. Now Tamo thinks it's his fate to be a pirate. He does what his father did. He does what he thinks he must, to be like Thomas White. If the *ombiasy* had said something different, Tamo would never have turned pirate—never!

But it's as if he's tied to a horse now, and he's got to go wherever the horse goes. He can't break free of the prophecy.'

Her fingers were as tangled as the washing at her feet, as she knotted and twisted them together. 'I don't want Tamo to be a pirate. If his father were to have been someone else . . . ' Queen Delilah looked blankly at her: the grammar was too difficult; she did not understand. Maud tossed her hair back off her face. 'I don't want Tamo to be a pirate,' she insisted. 'So I want you to tell Tamo that Thomas White was not his father. That you . . . That he . . . That someone else . . . '

Delilah gave such a roar that Maud overbalanced backwards, expecting to be slapped. There was even the noise of the slap landing. When she opened her eyes, the woman was smacking down a shirt—an arc of rainbow waterdrops still hung in the air from the overarm swing—and Delilah was whooping with laughter, snorting and yelping and rolling on the balls of her feet.

'Sure, I tell him! Praise the Lord and hallelujah! What joy you give me, child! *Tay be!* You grown woman! You understand plenty, Maud-woman! You understand good. I tell him!'

'You will?' Maud could hardly believe it. Suppose she had asked the dean's wife to publish abroad that her son was not the dean's at all, but the result of a love affair with the haberdasher? The clock would have thrown up its hands, the carpet shrivelled up with shame, the ceiling crumbled, the respectable ladies of town mobbed her like starlings.

'Who you wan'? Who? Who I sleep with to get my boy?'

'Who what?' Maud was confused by the wet hands patting at her, stroking and caressing her.

'Who you wan' for my lover? Who I sleep with to get my boy? Crocodile, maybe? Magic aye-aye?'

'No, I don't think . . . ' (Maud seriously doubted that Tamo, after a public school education, would believe he had been fathered by a crocodile.)

'Zanahary come down from the sky, yes!' Delilah was up on her feet now, dancing to a rhythm of her own making, drawing her wet hands up her great stomach as she envisaged mating with the god of the sky. When a still greater inspiration struck her, she thrust one hand in the air and crowed with delight. 'Yeah!'

Maud did not dare ask.

'Jesus Chris'!' yelled Delilah. 'My English gentleman Tamo, he like that! His daddy Jesus Chris'!'

Maud whimpered.

'Not Jesus Chris'?'

'I'd rather not, if it's all the same.'

'Who so? You choose! You choose man. Then I say, "Tamo-boy, I sleep with that man! That your father!"'

Maud racked her brains. She had thought her plan so hopeless that she had never got down to specifics. Who should she say? Someone who might have docked in Tamatave without necessarily being a pirate or a supplier. On the spur of the moment she said, 'A ship's doctor?'

All of a sudden, it seemed there was a third party present, for Delilah began shouting towards the blue-green canopy of the rain forest, haranguing someone a great way off. 'You hear, you bas'ard? You hear? I lie down with ship doctor! I make chil' with ship doctor! Good man! Gentle man! School man with brain in his head. He fine big lover, you hear? You hear me, bas'ard?'

Maud cowered by the waterside, trying to pretend she was somewhere else. Eventually, puffing and blowing, Delilah crouched down again between her huge thighs, balancing on her thick, splayed feet, and began to slap the washing on the rocks again, as if nothing had ever stopped her.

Timidly, with a demure primness she had last used in her back parlour talking to the bishop, Maud asked, 'Do I take it . . . possibly . . . that, perhaps you were not greatly . . . er . . . *fond* of your first husband, princess?'

The shirt in Delilah's hand was Samson's. Its threads began to part, its sleeves fell more and more feebly across the stone, fraying with every blow.

'Daughter, daughter,' said Delilah. 'One day you marry maybe. Then you know.'

She lapsed into Malagasy, and Maud could only filter, like sand from water, a blurred picture of the princess's marriage.

Sold to the pirate chief by her father, for prodigious sums of money and gems, she had accepted the brutality, the dissolute idleness, and long absences of Captain Thomas White—'white, like a thing from under stone,' she said of his unwashed, overfed, unhealthy English body. Once she had a child, she was content. The child was everything his father was not—handsome, dark, and innocent. The captain had fulfilled his part of the bargain; he had given her all she needed to be happy.

Delilah slapped down a shirt. 'Then he put my Tamo on ship. No word to me. Not one word. Send him in England. Send him for ever. My boy. My son. My Tamo. One day you have child, Maud-*ala*. Then you know. How I hate. How deep I hate that man. How I wan' crack his bone. Break his head.' Samson's shirt, still in her hands, fell apart strip by strip, and still she went on pounding it against the washing rock. 'I beg. I pray. I say, "Jus' one year, husband! Let me keep my boy one year!" But no. White send him in England.' Delilah nodded to herself sadly, nostalgically. She wiped her nose with the heel of her hand. 'That why I kill him.'

Maud felt her eyeballs dry in the parching heat, as she stared and stared at Princess Andriamahilala.

'You killed Tamo's father?'

'Day after ship go. I put bad stuff in food. Him dying two week, three week. Slow.'

Unabashed, she rescued out of the river the washing that Maud had left to drift downstream. 'All years, he steal things: ship, money, treasure. Me, I only steal his life.' She beamed suddenly at Maud. 'Now you, Maud-*ala,* you steal his son. Jus' like he do to me. Yeah, I tell Tamo! I tell everybody. Tamo father is handsome ship doctor! Tamo father never Thomas Almighty Captain White.'

Her gratitude swelled and overspilled in tears and laughter and clapping. She embraced Maud as fondly as any mother, and lifted her up into a dance of delight. She said that the iron ship was Maud's to do with as she liked, such was her gratitude to Maud for the blow she had struck to Thomas White's immortal spirit, such was the pain her clever lie would inflict on the dead.

'What do you mean, *not my father*?'

'I am only saying what was said at the washing place,' said Maud, lying with prim attention to the wording of the lie. 'Princess Andriamahilala says that your father was a ship's doctor called . . . er . . . I don't know what he was called.'

She would never have believed lying could be so easy. So simple in comparison with telling the truth!

What was she supposed to do with the knowledge that Delilah had murdered her husband? What was she supposed to think? Supposing the alderman's wife had confessed over coffee in the parlour to having poisoned her husband's steak-and-porter pie? Would Maud simply have patted the cooling coffee pot and suggested a second cup? Was this place robbing her of all moral fibre, like a shirt beaten too often on a rock?

Tamo knew nothing of her dilemma. He just kept asking over and over again if it was true. Was it true Captain Thomas White was not his real father?

'Absolutely,' said Maud, looking him in the eye. The sin of lying seemed to have shrunk a lot since morning.

At that moment they reached the hut. Tamo was so overwhelmed by Maud's news that he did not even observe *fady* and enter from the propitious side. In the darkness, Maud could hear a chattering, as of a mantis or cricket. Not until Tamo lit a stolen cabin-lamp did they see where the noise came from. It was Nathan's teeth chattering.

He lay curled tightly on his mattress—had pulled all the blankets off the three beds, and still he was shuddering with cold. When Maud touched him, his skin was hot and dry, like a shirt fresh from under the flat-iron, and his jaws clattered.

'It's a judgement from God,' said Maud.

But for what? Her lie, or for their crime of piracy?

'It's *tazo,*' said Tamo.

'What's that?'

'A disease. The flies bring it. To white men especially.'

'What do I do? Is it serious?' Maud crouched beside her brother, appalled, bereft.

'He must have quinine,' said Tamo. 'That's what the pirates use.'

'Where can I find some. I'll go,' she said. 'Tell me which plant.' She knew the plants, the trees, the flowers, the local herbs. He only had to tell her which to fetch.

But Tamo shook his head: 'There's none on Madagasikara,' and he ducked outside into the sunlight.

'Where are you going?'

Maud ran as far as the door. She saw Tamo pick his way among the traps and snares to reach the central hut. He was asking King Samson if he had any quinine; she saw him point back towards the hut. But nothing changed hands.

Queen Delilah came to the door of the long hut, shielding her eyes from the sunlight, indolent in her stance, her arms encrusted with jewellery. Maud could hear Tamo shouting at her: *'Marina ve? Marina ve?* Is it true?'

Delilah chewed on a straw and began to describe to him in infinite detail something, someone; since morning, the ship's doctor had become as large a part of her past life as Captain Thomas White had ever been. She had much to tell Tamo about. Like Zanahary the creator-god, she had fashioned a man out of nothing and given him life.

Delirious with fever, Nathan shouted out at some hallucinatory creature scuttling through his nightmares. Maud went and stroked his forehead, making soothing, encouraging noises. He opened his eyes and looked directly at her; she could see the pupils of his eyes shrink, then dilate. Then he shouted, *'I'm sorry, Mister Thrussell, sir, but I have to go. It's my father, sir. He's calling . . . '* Maud did not cry—crying would serve no purpose—but the wish inside her—to be dreaming, for this not to be true—was growing and swelling to the point where she thought her chest would burst.

When Tamo came back, he had no quinine. He was agitated, but not in despair. She knew that his head was full of the things Delilah had been telling him, whereas she cared about nothing but Nathan.

'Do people die of this *tazo*?' she said.

'He must sweat. He will. Soon he'll break into a great sweat, you'll see. If he doesn't . . .'

Maud did not want to hear what would happen if Nathan's fever rose and rose and he did not sweat. She tore back the blankets and looked at her brother's clothing. A wave of relief swept over her. 'There! There's sweat pouring down his jacket!'

Tamo bent and smelt the grease stains down Nathan's chest. 'That's butter,' he said, with appalling calm.

She pushed past him and ran down to the village herself. If Samson could not help, perhaps the Malagasies could—her friend Noro—Noro's kin, the elders, the old ladies. She wove between the huts, she gashed her skin on the pirate booby traps of dangling shrapnel. *'Milo dokotera ah!'* She shouldered by the few surviving cattle and called to the women in the rice paddies, *'Milo dokotera haingara aho!'* But they looked back at her with bleak, blank faces. They did not step towards her. They stepped back.

So. She had become one of the enemy. She was a white girl and therefore part of the evil which had overrun their lives. They were probably glad Nathan was sick. One less white face in Zaotralana. One less pirate. Even Noro, seeing her coming, drew back inside her hut.

Beside the door, Noro's mother sat on a little wicker chair, peeling sweet potatoes. Maud went and fell on her knees in front of the woman, breathless and panting. *'Anadahy . . . Tazo. Milo dokotera aho!'*

The woman looked back at her and nodded, then returned to preparing the food.

A hand gripped Maud's shoulder. It was Tamo. He put an arm round Maud's shoulders and looked into her face. The rum-blur had gone out of his eyes, the menacing hysteria from behind them.

'What happens if he doesn't sweat?' she asked. 'If he goes on getting hotter and hotter?'

'Nathan will be all right,' said Tamo. 'I won't let him come to harm. Do you think I brought him here to catch *tazo* and die? He won't. I won't let him.'

'Yes, but . . . '

At which Tamo squared his shoulders imperceptibly, tipped back his forehead and set his jaw. 'I am the son of a doctor, am I not?' he said.

14

The Price

Maud blamed herself. She thought of all the things she might have said, and she cursed herself for saying it: for saying to Delilah, 'ship's doctor'. Now her brother was gripped by some terrible tropical sickness, and his only physician was a pirate schoolboy who believed medicine was in his blood.

She could have corrected him, of course. A hundred times, as Nathan tossed and thrashed between them like a beached shark, it was on her lips to say, 'I made it up. I lied to stop you going at the seas—to stop you turning pirate.' But she stopped short. How could it help Nathan? And besides, Tamo was so altered by the news. He had come back, like a salmon from the sea into freshwater rivers. As the sea-lice drop off the salmon, the pirate weaponry had dropped from around Tamo's waist: the club, the pistols, the knives. He still would not speak a civil word about his mother, and yet Maud knew that he was grateful to her, grudgingly indebted to her for the change in his fate.

But if Nathan died, Maud knew it would be her fault. Tamo was not a doctor, and neither lying nor wishing would ever make him one—not even the son of a doctor.

Just before dawn, a tinkling rattle beyond the doorway announced the arrival of the *ombiasy*, and Maud burst into tears of relief. The villagers had not shunned her. Noro's mother had sent for the *ombiasy*, and the *ombiasy* had come—even though Nathan was white, even though he and his friends had brought all this misery to the village. Maud ran and took the man's hand, dragging him inside. The dozens of necklaces threaded with roots and charcoal, bark and dried meat, amulets and spices for burning chanked as he crouched down beside her brother.

But then Nathan opened his eyes.

'Devil! Witches! Avaunt thee, demon!' he screamed—and would not stop screaming till the *ombiasy* had returned into the sunshine.

Maud was glad the man could not understand the names he had been called. She ran after him to apologize, to cling to his hand, to beg forbearance from the tall cadaverous wizard loping off down the hill. Could he still do something, leave something to fight the *tazo*?

The *ombiasy* lifted the two clumps of hair from over his eyes, one with each hand, and looked at her with gentle, unoffended eyes. He was sorry, he said, to see the Englishman so ill. There was nothing he could do until the *tromba* spoke.

'The *tromba*? Who's the *tromba*?'

The *ombiasy* smiled his crooked smile at her lamentable ignorance and, leaning on his staff, loped away.

'Tamo! Tamo!' Maud scrambled, on hands and feet, up the slope to the hut. 'Tamo, who's the *tromba*? The *ombiasy* says the *tromba* must speak!'

'The *tromba* is the spirit of his sickness,' said Tamo soothingly. 'It won't leave him until it has spoken.'

'But he just now spoke! He called the *ombiasy* a demon and a devil!'

Tamo smiled and shook his head. 'That was Nathan, not the *tromba*,' he said, as if only a fool could not tell the difference. 'That was good Christian Nathan. You know how our Malagasy customs offend him.'

Once upon a time, Maud knew that she too would have scorned this talk of spirits as pagan gibberish. But what else was there? The world had shrunk to this single island floating in the oceans, ruled by customs and beliefs as old as the sea.

'But how will we know . . . ?' Maud began.

'The *tromba* is Malagasy, Maud-*ala*,' said Tamo, softly, patiently, patronizingly. 'It will speak in Malagasy, won't it?'

'But Nathan *never* speaks Malagasy!' Unlike Maud he had never troubled to learn it, like those travellers who do not unpack for fear they may have to settle in a place. How likely was it that he would open his mouth now, and speak in Malagasy? Maud wanted to believe in the *ombiasy*. She wanted to believe that his prophecies came true, that his magic worked. But after all, as Nathan had always maintained, he was a primitive heathen, an unbeliever, an idolater. She wanted to say her prayers and to trust in Jesus; if her father was there, that is what he would have told her to do. But prayers had not served when *he* was sick, when *he* was dying.

Once upon a time she would have sat passively by, her hands in her apron, and accepted God's will. But that was before the *ombiasy* had told her she would be strong and happy. Strong and fulfilled. Strong. Strong. Strong.

While they sat out that long night of Nathan's unbroken fever, keeping vigil, huge moths fumbled the cabin lamp, filling the hut with grotesque shadows. And Maud confided in Tamo-the-doctor's-son all the things she had felt unable to tell Tamo-the-pirate. She told him how his mother had been obliged to marry Samson as protection against all the other men covetous of Thomas White's treasure; how the princess had hated Thomas White for sending away her only child; how she hated Samson just as much.

He listened now, and wept at the thought of it, though Maud did not realize at first that he was crying. Tamo was not a western man: he did not contort his face into ugliness trying to hold back his tears, but let them flow readily down his cheeks.

Encouraged, Maud told Tamo the last of her secrets: how his mother had kept secret from Samson the greatest of White's treasures, the iron ship. 'An iron ship!' she repeated, when Tamo seemed insufficiently astonished. 'Could there truly be such a thing?'

'I remember,' he said distantly. 'I remember my fa—White talking of it. Iron cladding to keep out teredo worm . . . Where is it now?'

'Half-way between here and Tamatave! Andriamahilala says we may have it—er, I may have it. She doesn't want you to leave Madagasikara again. Oh, but we can take her with us! Get away from here! Start again! Go to Zanzibar, maybe—or Mafia!'

Her clamour failed to excite Tamo. His face was thoughtful, his eyes full of lamplight. Even when moths settled on his cheeks to lick the salt, he did not so much as brush them away.

When he saw her looking at him, urgently hopeful, he seemed to weigh up the confidences she had shared with him and decide to tell her something in return.

'Sheller is due on this coast,' he said. 'Samson told me earlier. This month. If Sheller comes, he may have quinine.'

'Buy from that man?' said Maud, but her heart had already leapt at the renewed possibility of medicine for her brother. 'Would he sell it to us. We made a fool of him. He hates us.'

'He's a man of business. Liking doesn't enter in.' Something in his voice did not sound perfectly certain. His fist closed over the coua-bird amulet the fortune-teller had given him. He knelt forward so that he was leaning over Nathan. *'Tromba? Inona no vaovao? Fiharabana. Mihaino oho.'*

For half an hour he shouted into Nathan's face, and when he tired, Maud took over from him.

'Tromba! What is it you want? What news? Won't you speak to us, *tromba*?'

After all, she told herself, Jesus Christ had cast out demons.

It seemed the only alternative to the evil of Sheller. Sheller might not come. Unless, by some fantastic coincidence he arrived that night, Sheller would come too late. He might have foundered, changed his routes, retired to spend the fortunes he had made. Or Sheller, when he came, might simply choose to empty his pistols into the three who had put him to such embarrassment and loss of profit in Tamatave. So, instead, they begged and pleaded with the spirit of malaria to speak and come out of Nathan Gull.

Towards morning, the sweat burst from Nathan's face, as though, like a swimmer, he had just broken surface. His hair went dark: in front of their very eyes it turned black with sweat and dripped salt tears on to his pillow. He fought off his blankets like a pack of pirates, and when Tamo heaped them back on top of him, opened his eyes to shout aloud in protest. Whether the word he spoke was in English or Malagasy, there was no knowing: names are not limited to a single language. But Nathan opened his eyes, saw the dark shape of Tamo's head looming over him, the lamplight distorting it into the shape of a shovel. And he said, *'Sheller!'*

* * *

'But now there's no need, surely!' said Maud, for the thousandth time, as Tamo raised the black flag to the top of the cliffside flagpole. 'Nathan is going to be all right! He'll be well again, soon! We can take the iron ship and sail away! We don't need Sheller any more!'

But Tamo only said that *tazo* did not leave a man like measles or an ague. Once *tazo* was in the blood, it returned like a ghost intent on haunting a house. And with each visit the ghost shook and weakened the fabric of the house a little more.

Even Nathan said they must not summon Sheller—should never have conceived such a crazy idea as summoning Sheller. But nothing seemed to deter Tamo from the plan, now that he had spoken it. He had asked King Samson's approval, and the pirate chief had agreed to the notion of hailing a supplier. In fact Samson liked the idea more and more, had thought of things he would like to buy. Finally, even if Tamo had begged and pleaded for the black flag to be lowered, Samson would not have permitted it. He, after all, had nothing to fear from Sheller.

'Perhaps it is for the best,' Tamo told Maud. 'Nat may sicken again soon, and his constitution is not strong. He needs quinine. Besides, some other supplier may come.' And yet Maud had the strangest feeling that Tamo *wanted* it to be Sheller who came.

It seemed a lifetime of waiting. Three, four, five weeks passed in wanting him to come, dreading him coming. The black flag hung limp on the flagpost, signalling the desire to trade. Perhaps another supplier would come. Perhaps a stranger would bring them their wine and tobacco and mercury and nails and Bibles. And quinine.

But Maud knew in her heart of hearts that it would be Sheller. There was a kind of *fady* in the coming of the man. Fate demanded that events be brought full circle. The whaling men of Zaotralana said they could smell whales long before they came into sight. Maud could almost smell Sheller: a rank, unwholesome something on the wind.

The third week in July he came. He dropped anchor in the bay and came ashore in a jolly-boat; he was easily recognizable. The red coat was new, with gold lace inserts between the flaps and round the cuffs. But his hat was the same old tricorn, buckled by damp salt air until he had the look of a zebu with twisted horns. A green velvet cummerbund bound a pair of pistols, back-to-back, on the crown of his stomach. His boots had preposterously wide cuffs, big as guttering, and he had acquired an Irish wolfhound half as big as a horse, to guard him against his customers.

King Samson greeted him—they greeted each other—with hugely mannered and exaggerated gestures of friendship as ritualized as any dance. He was decked out in cloth-of-gold turban and pantaloons, with a jacket tailored out of Arabian carpeting. Like peacocks in breeding fettle, or fat dowagers at a county ball, they were vying with one another to prove their status in society.

They had neither of them bargained for Tamo White.

He came to the sound of drumming—as pirates do when they take a ship. The drummers were not visible, but hidden among the trees—native Malagasies playing native drums. Maud had sewed him a panelled jacket of flame-coloured silk stained with the stamens of exotic lilies to produce large, intricate splashes of yellow. White lace frothed at cuffs and throat, and his long hair was tied back with a broad black bow whose ribbon-ends cracked out behind in the off-sea wind. Behind him, Maud, in a long shift of yellow silk, her hair fastened up on top of her head, wore nothing by way of adornment but a stolen bo'sun's whistle on which she blew, now, a long two-tone blast of the kind which welcomes aboard an admiral. The drums fell silent.

At the sight of Tamo and Maud, the smile froze on Sheller's face, and the pistol butts above his belly rolled a little as he clenched the muscles of his stomach and mastered his rage. 'So. The blossom of his family tree, eh? It serves to prove what I have always said: you cannot take a savage and turn him into a Christian gentleman.'

'Thomas White had few wits and no schooling, guardian,' Tamo replied. 'But he taught me the precise worth of a good Christian gentleman like yourself.'

Sheller's eyes were lost, as usual, in the shadow of his hat, but Maud could feel them watching her: the malevolence all but charred her dress. Her heart was thudding so hard that she could see the yellow silk jump with every beat. But she fixed her eyes on the wolfhound, and cultivated an air of vacant detachment, as if to say that these boys' games did not interest her.

'Where's the *other* schoolboy?' said Sheller sneeringly.

'My lieutenant died,' said Tamo.

King Samson no more than blinked with surprise. He had a long association with lying, and if a man wanted to lie to a supplier, there was probably a good reason for it. (Quartermaster grasped at once the reason for the lie: if Tamo let slip that his lieutenant's life depended on having quinine, the price of quinine would instantly double.)

Tamo was saying, 'Let us not rush needlessly into business, guardian. I'm sure King Samson's good lady has furnished hospitality for Captain Sheller and his crew. They must be in need of refreshment after an arduous voyage.'

'On the contrary!' declared Sheller, beaming with mirth, taking a grasp on proceedings. 'I never eat when I am about God's work. A man could die of such hospitality. Let us to business immediately! Have you prospered, Samson, since the hurricane unhoused you? Has the breaking of the Eighth Commandment brought you enough treasure to recompense you for your immortal soul?' He caught sight of Charles Hardcastle, his one-time navigator, and hailed him cheerfully. 'Never fear, Mr Hardcastle! I told the navy of your change of career, sir. They assure me there is no shortage of chains and tar waiting for you at Execution Dock if you ever touch ground in England. Should I call on your dear wife, perchance, next time I am there, and give her your blessing?'

Hardcastle gave a demented roar and rushed at Sheller, swearing to kill him. The dog leapt to the full extent of its choke-chain and filled the village with its barking. Quartermaster stepped smartly forward and tripped Hardcastle, so that he sprawled virtually into the dog's jaws, and it was only by curling himself up and rolling away into the darkness of the longhouse that Charles escaped unbitten. The dog went on and on barking.

A certain amount of loot was held 'in common', as King Samson liked to call it, for the purchase of necessaries. With it, the king now bought rum and ale to dispense to his subjects, and several pipes of fine wine for himself. The sun was hot. His men grew impatient. Their fingernails were dirty from grubbing up their own buried treasure, and now, like children holding pocket money, they were eager to buy.

Tamo let them all bid.

King Samson bought an etching of Windsor Castle: he was even pleased at the price. But little by little Sheller revealed the true cost of his services. The price of rum rose from two guineas a gallon to four, the Madeira to three hundred pounds a pipe. Mercury was six hundred pounds an ounce. A grindstone was traded for a service of silver plates. A bag of nails swapped for a bag of gems. The pirates brought out their treasure for Sheller to sneer at, and in the bright daylight the stolen jewellery even *looked* tawdry and cheap and valueless.

Time and again, Sheller looked towards Tamo to see if he would bid, but Tamo leaned against a palm tree as if the whole circus bored him and was beneath his dignity. It nettled and unsettled the supplier. Was there nothing the wretch wanted? In that case, Sheller would have to think of some other way to have his revenge. He could always name Tamo's life as the price of some vital commodity; the brat's severed head in exchange for a case of musket balls, perhaps? That would see God's work done in a twinkling of knives. But it was a dangerous manoeuvre. Sheller wanted his customers' minds on buying, not slaughter. You never knew where slaughter would end. Already the pirates of Zaotralana were cursing him and his inflated prices.

'Is there nothing the young Thomas White has a mind to buy?' said Sheller at last.

Tamo picked some grains of coconut off his tongue. 'I'll take quinine, if you have some,' he said casually. 'To safeguard my crew, you understand.'

Sheller chafed his fat legs together in a paroxysm of joy. His whole demeanour changed. He seemed to swell with triumph.

'Ah! Malaria, is it, dearheart? *"In his disease he sought not the Lord, but physicians."* Yes, I have quinine, if you have the price of it.'

Many of Samson's men were also suffering from malaria to some degree or other. They began to call out. 'I'll take some! How much?' But Sheller ignored them. His eyes stayed only on Tamo White. 'And what, pray, does Master White have to offer me for a pint of quinine?'

'And ivory ship's compass on gimbals,' said Tamo.

'I have a ship's compass. I want no ship's compass.'

'Seventy gold talents, then,' said Tamo.

'Seventy thousand, rather,' said Sheller.

A gasp went through the crowd. Most had not even realized, up until now, that Sheller and White knew each other. Now they saw that there was a score unsettled between the two.

'I want quinine, too!' one man called out plaintively. But no one paid him any heed.

'I have more goods than gold,' said Tamo. 'Perhaps we might reach a bargain more readily by barter.'

Sheller appeared to reflect on this. At length he said, 'You appreciate, Master White, that my price carries a certain *loading*—a purchase tax, as you might say. A penalty fee to cover earlier losses suffered at your hands.'

'I thought it might,' said Tamo. 'But, *enfin,* you are a business man, a man of business. I cannot think you will turn aside from profit for the sake of past disappointments long forgotten.'

'I have not forgotten,' said Sheller, and the dog beside him growled. The crowd stirred uneasily, too. They understood Sheller-the-Greedy, but they had never seen before Sheller-the-Vengeful.

'There is a certain debt outstanding between us,

dearheart,' said Sheller, in an excitable rush thinly disguised as a laugh. 'Settle that, and I'll make you a present of the quinine. There was a certain piece of merchandise I was minded to sell, up in Tamatave. Brought it all the way from England. But you stole that item from me, sir. At no small harm to my professional reputation. You *removed* that item from my ship.'

Maud took her eyes from the dog and looked directly at Sheller now.

'Give her back, and the quinine's yours. Come now. There's buyers in plenty here, sir, for the commodity I refer to. Buyers are always ready and waiting for a special purchase of that sort. What do you say, Master White? You just give me back Mistress Maud, and we'll call it a deal.'

Maud screamed, but the sound that came out was like the whistle of the bo'sun's pipe. Tamo grabbed hold of her wrist to stop her running away. His fingers made purple bruises on her forearm. She looked at him and realized that he had foreseen all along what Sheller would say, had foreseen it and was not horrified.

Well? His mother had been sold to pirates by her father, hadn't she? Malagasies were accustomed to such deals. Perhaps they all thought of women, ultimately, as things to be bought and sold.

Maud continued to struggle, trying to pull her wrist out of his hand. Tamo looked at her until, in struggling, she finally met his eyes. 'You knew he'd ask that!' she spat. 'You knew!'

'I knew he would ask that,' he said. 'But I know there's something he wants more. Trust me.'

Tamo adjusted the lace at the wrists of his flame-silk jacket, and stepped away from the tree. 'The lady is not, and never was, available for sale. But I believe

I may have merchandise that you will accept as of equal worth, Captain Sheller.'

Sheller's mouth was stiff with grinning. It slurred his speech. 'I doubt that, Master White. Little about you interests me more than an itch it might please me to scratch. Name your *merchandise.*'

Tamo breathed deep. 'A ship, Sheller. An iron-clad ship. The greatest treasure and most valuable prize of the late Captain Thomas White, and the most modern ship on any ocean. A ship, captain, proof against worm. And how much would any of us give for that, captain? To be proof against worm?'

15

The Iron Ship

'What are you thinking of? You had no right! It isn't yours to sell!' Maud slapped at Tamo's shoulders as he walked ahead of her. 'It was given to me, not you! Your mother gave it to me!'

'Hold your peace, girl,' said Tamo. 'Be still.'

'A ship for a pint of quinine? A ship we could have used to get away?'

He turned round so suddenly that she collided with him, her nose against his chin. 'And what makes you suppose I share your ambition to sail away to somewhere more "civilized"?'

'You should have asked!' she insisted, pushing him in the chest.

'Asked? *Asked?! Please may you pass the plum preserve, ma'am? Please may I have your ship?* What? Did you think to sail it on your own? Weigh anchor? Heave sail? Be captain, mate, and crew? Pray know your limits, Maud-*ala*. What? Is your brother's life worth a compass but not as much as a ship?'

'Oh!'

Tamo had meant to go alone with Sheller, up the coast in the *Tenderness*, and find the iron ship. There Sheller would split his crew and sail the iron ship on to Zanzibar to take on extra sailors, while the *Tenderness* carried Tamo back to Zaotralana. But then Sheller insisted that Maud and Hardcastle must come, too. And Tamo could not find a way of refusing.

Though Sheller made a great show of suspicion and scorn, he did believe in the iron ship. More, he *knew* the iron ship existed—remembered more clearly than Tamo the swaggering pride of Thomas White as he boasted of an iron-clad ship hidden at a secret mooring. Had White lived a month longer, he would have found a buyer for his cedarwood ship, and gone at the seas in his new iron marvel. As it was, shaken by the flux already, the man had become suddenly more sick immediately after putting his son aboard ship for England, taking to the grave with him (or so Sheller had thought) the secret of the iron ship. Sheller and a dozen other captains had scoured the coast to north and south of Tamatave looking for it, but with no success. The lush Malagasy terrain could conceal the Seven Wonders of the World in a single fold of its green skirts.

He suspected a trick. He suspected some childish attempt by Tamo to murder him. But Sheller considered himself a match for any half-breed savage. Also, he believed in the iron ship—had to have it, even though it meant feigning politeness towards the arrogant, conniving brat. Making the girl come too—that would draw his sting. Besides . . . the course of action that had been agreed between them was not necessarily the course of action Sheller intended to take.

King Samson felt left out. He had known nothing beforehand of the quarrel between Tamo White and the supplier. Tamo ought to have told him, he thought peevishly. He had known nothing about the iron ship. His wife ought to have told him about that. As he walked back into the dark of the longhut, he drew his sword with one hand and uncinched his sword belt with the other, letting his various weapons fall to the ground around him. His pantaloons drooped down round his hips. Delilah had kept secret from him the iron ship, but she had told her brat of a son. So that now Sheller would take the ship when, for seven years, he, Samson, should have been sailing her. The woman had to pay for that kind of unfaithfulness, that kind of betrayal. She might pray the Lord's Prayer and invoke all the prophets by name: nothing would save her now. He had beaten her before. This time he would finish her, for robbing him of White's iron ship.

But Delilah was not in the hut. Though he lunged with his sword and lashed with his belt, Delilah was in none of the shadowy corners. Piles of copper vases and pots clattered out at his feet, but his wife was not there. She must be washing clothes or pounding rice, or picking sweet potatoes. He could wait. She would come back. And when she did . . .

As he poured himself a cup of wine, Quartermaster came softly in, eyes glimmering in the dark. 'Have you seen the queen, Quartermaster?'

'No, Majesty.'

'This ship—I didn't know of it.'

'Nor I, Majesty.'

'I don't like that.'

'It was *lèse majesté,'* said Quartermaster.

'Was it? What?'

'It showed a lack of respect for your royal supremacy, Majesty.'

'Ah! Just! Yeah! Quite. Very.'

'Besides. The iron ship is yours, Majesty. By right of marriage.'

'Yes!' said Samson. 'I know!' He flung aside the turban and scrubbed at his itching scalp. But he still had no idea how to get back his stolen property. 'I've been thinking how best to put matters right, Quartermaster . . .'

'Why not send an ambassador to observe and act on your behalf,' suggested Quartermaster.

'Yeah! Yes, you go! You sail up there with 'em. See what can be done.'

'Very good, Majesty. An excellent idea.'

'Oh, and Quartermaster . . .'

'Yes, Majesty.'

'Slit a few throats on my behalf.'

'Your servant, Majesty.'

Left alone once more, the pirate chief brooded on the unpleasant nature of his fellows. Untrustworthy, greedy, self-serving. It sorrowed Samson. A cauldron was bubbling in the centre of the hut—a concoction of beef-strips, manioc, and beer, made for Sheller and his crew. The churl had even spurned Samson's hospitality, he thought morosely. The king picked up a bowl made from half a gourd and scooped out a serving. Eating the meat strips with his fingers, he poured the broth down his throat, spilling runnels down his cloth-of-gold. Delilah's treachery, Tamo's deceit, Sheller's overcharging. They depressed him unutterably, and he always ate when he was depressed. And drank. Samson ate another bowlful and opened another pipe of wine. Thank God for Quartermaster, that was all he could say.

Nathan shivered. He felt the malaria in his blood, like spawn in a stream waiting to hatch. 'All this is happening because of me, and I have to stay here?' he said, attempting to understand.

'Sheller thinks you're dead.'

'He has the same in mind for you, Tamo. One league off shore and he'll blow out your brains.'

'Then he won't find his precious ship.'

'Nor will you. You don't know where to look!'

'My mother has described the place to me. She described it as White described it to her. Of course, if Sheller could lay hands on my mother, then he'd have no need of me. That's why I told her to go. To hide.'

'Yes, but just a description! And it's been seven years!' Nathan protested. 'The coastline will be all changed! Hurricanes! Tidal waves! Someone will have found it and sailed it away. The tornadoes will have wrecked it! This is lunatic. You're a fool, Tamo. For what? A pint of quinine? Was your father this mad?'

Maud flinched. There was that lie again, haunting her at every turn.

Tamo, with great deliberation, was folding his silk jacket inside out and rolling it in raffia to keep out the moth. 'My father,' he said, reverting before their eyes into a Malagasy native once more, 'my father was a ship's doctor. The health of this village rests on me,'

'Ah, I see! I see!' squealed Maud hysterically, leaping to her feet as rage and horror got the better of her. 'Now he means to cure the five thousand with five loaves and a pint of quinine! Look sharp, Nat! The Age of Miracles is upon us!' And she stormed outside, cutting herself yet again on the ironmongery of shrapnel strung across the path.

They sailed the following morning. During the voyage north, Quartermaster took Captain Sheller to one side and made him a proposition.

'Once you've taken possession of the iron ship, your honour, you'll be in need of a new master for the *Tenderness.*'

'I have a first mate can sail her,' said Sheller charily.

'And I'm sure he's a fine man. But I'm better. And I have a mind to leave the employ of *Mister* Samson,' said Quartermaster, down the sharp beak of his nose. 'I begin to feel the . . . error of my ways.'

'Ah. A penitent,' said Sheller sceptically.

'Nay. But I see the error of working for a swabbing tarpaulin like Samson.'

'I wonder you haven't cut his throat these five years since—a man of your . . . character.'

'What for? To take his place and have someone cut mine? Nay. I've been pistol-proof as quartermaster. But with a ship of my own—I mean a command of my own—I might turn a clean profit for that ship's owner . . . and leave him free to turn one of his own.'

'You? Captain of the *Tenderness*?'

'I wonder you don't work a whole fleet of supply ships by now, captain,' said Quartermaster obsequiously. 'And you a man with such a flair for your business. Yeah, I could quite put a life of crime behind me, to turn supplier in a ship of yours.'

Sheller snorted. But inwardly he had half a mind to agree. Quartermaster had more brains than ten Samsons, and there was no soft underbelly to the man: no sailor's superstition, addiction to drink or opium, no sentimentality, no conscience. Perhaps he *would* let Quartermaster have command of the *Tenderness*.

'Well, here's a test of your initiative, Mister . . . ' He waited for Quartermaster to supply his true name, to no effect. 'What do you suggest I do with Mr Tamo

White, Mr Hardcastle, and the girl after they have guided me to the iron ship?'

Quartermaster looked at the sky. 'Kill one and sell t'others,' he said unexcitedly.

Sheller nodded slowly. Yes, he would consider the man. He was particularly pleased to think of selling the navigator twice over, in two different ports.

'I'm hungry, Quartermaster. Business always leaves me hungry. Be so good as to break out some rations. I never eat ashore.'

'Very wise, sir.'

'Ah, what a wicked world we live in, Quartermaster,' said Sheller lugubriously. 'I sail half-way round the globe to bring men the necessities of life, and these same ungrateful sinners would poison me sooner than pay the market price for my commodities. Tell me it's not true.'

'The stew was poisoned in readiness for your coming, sir, yeah,' said Quartermaster with a strange glitter in his eye. 'Samson gave the command himself last night, when the drink was strong in him. I dare swear he remembers nothing at all about it today,'

Tornadoes had laid bare cliffs and uprooted trees as big as lighthouses. Mangrove roots had colonized whole acres of sea, so that green, leafy peninsulas jutted out from the shore where none had been seven years before. Even to Tamo, the task of finding the iron ship began to look impossible. 'Three granite outcrops,' Delilah had said, 'the third one beaked like a bird. And a groyne like a crocodile, with a plantain grove beyond.'

Here and there, freshwater streams discharged into the sea, colouring the rich lapis blue with a lighter turquoise. There were granite outcrops by the score, and it was possible to imagine any species of animal or bird in their craggy features if you looked hard enough. How could a groyne look like a crocodile? And if there was a plantation, did that mean local inhabitants? Inhabitants, in the course of seven years, could have found, sold, sailed or dismantled an iron ship from masthead to keel.

New sandbars had formed, making a nonsense of existing charts, and Hardcastle passed the voyage fastidiously annotating and emending them: he could not break himself of the habit. His anguish at being so close to Sheller and yet not able to take revenge made the muscles of his face stiffen, and he bit his lip continually, chewing the skin away from sore red patches. His hands shook as he wrote on the charts, and he yawned incessantly, as some do when they are afraid.

'I'm sorry,' said Tamo abjectly, to Hardcastle and Maud. 'I truly didn't reckon with Sheller making you come.'

'Of course he made us,' said Hardcastle disgustedly. 'As soon as he has the ship, he means to kill us all three.'

Tamo threw him a look which reproached him for saying such things in front of Maud. But Maud saw him do it. 'D'you suppose I didn't know that, Master White? It has all this while been clear as day to me that your plan has gone awry. I suppose you thought you would single-handedly capture this ship from Sheller and his crew of twenty and more, and cast him overboard like Jonah into the mouth of some sea monster, and take possession of his medicine cabinet and tools of chirurgery and become Saint Luke of the sea-lanes.'

'Sarcasm does not become you, madam,' said Tamo coldly. 'I see you would sooner I had stayed a—'

'Crocodile!' said Hardcastle. He was gazing ahead at a flat promontory of rock which interrupted the repetitive pattern of waves breaking against a shallow bay. The plantains on the clifftop were wild, not cultivated; there was no village nearby. The water in front of the rock was a pale milky blue, and at the point, a freakish current or fall of boulders had left a cave gaping out to sea. Just like the open mouth of a yawning crocodile.

'Three granite outcrops! Look! One with a bird's beak!'

'No, no. It should be the furthest one!' whispered Tamo, biting his knuckles in an anguish of uncertainty. 'No. No.'

'*Yes!* Your father—White would have been coming from the north!' exclaimed Maud. 'From Tamatave. Coming from that direction, the beak would have been at this end. It's the place, Tamo! You've found where he hid the ship!'

From the quarterdeck, Sheller was watching them, hawk-like, for some sign of recognition. The sight of it fired in his belly an excitement he had not felt for years. 'Is this the place?' he shouted.

'This is the place,' said Tamo.

Quartermaster and the first mate were studying the inlet through a telescope. 'The mouth's choked up with mangroves,' said Quartermaster.

'We can blast them out of the way,' said Sheller, punching at the distant coastline in his lust to have the ship hidden there.

'First my quinine,' said Tamo, mounting the quarterdeck.

'First my ship, dearheart,' snarled Sheller in his face, and pushed him off the ladder with one foot.

They no sooner heaved-to and lowered the jolly-boat than a host of horseflies swarmed off the mangroves and clamoured round them, hungry for blood. 'Hellish country,' muttered Sheller, clasping his collar close round his throat and swatting at them with his hat.

He and Quartermaster put out for shore alone—the two joined by cords of mutual mistrust which would not let them out of each other's sight. Every sailor aboard the *Tenderness* watched from the rail, intrigued to know whether the iron ship truly existed or not.

'Time to go,' said Tamo to his companions.

'What?'

'Time to quit the ship. Take our leave. Go over the side.'

Hardcastle threw back his head in a jerk of panic which had become reflex. His eyes swivelled to and fro between half-closed lids; he was a man undermined by months of fright and despair. 'Oh yes. Swim ashore, is it now? And walk home fifty miles through forests and swamps and hostile savages, and find Sheller waiting there, to finish what's left of us? Is that your grand plan, Master White?'

Shark, shark, shark, was all Maud could think.

'Well, when I said *leave,*' said Tamo, with a sudden demonic smile. 'I meant *give the impression* of leaving. Does that commend itself better to you, Mr Hardcastle?'

They took rope from a locker and slung it over the starboard rail, dangling it down into the water. All the while, Sheller's crew lined the port bow, pointing and making bets with one another as to the existence of the iron ship.

Then Tamo and Maud and Hardcastle went below and hid themselves in the bowels of the *Tenderness.* It was cool and dank down in the holds. The decking was treacherous, with manacles and fixed iron staples where Sheller secured his slaves for shipping.

The loot Samson's pirates had just traded for Sheller's goods was crammed in from deck to deckhead—a fortune in exchange for a few groceries and a little cheap hardware. Zaotralana's wealth had joined booty from other pirate settlements in the north where Sheller had already traded.

'The man must be as rich as Croesus,' said Tamo.

As they went forward, away from the hatchways, there was less and less light to see by. In the dark, Maud brushed against something big, yielding and prickly with hair, which swung away from her with a creaking of rope. She thought it was a hanged man. Around her, a score more ropes creaked from the bulkhead. A hold full of hanged men. Her lungs went too rigid to let her scream. Then she realized that they were the carcasses of freshly slaughtered cattle; fresh meat for the onward voyage.

Beyond was a hold stacked with rolls of something white, big as tree-trunks and, further on, where deck and deckhead were so close that they had to crawl, there was a sea of paper littering the floor. As they wormed their way into the forepeak, pressed side by side, Maud could feel that Hardcastle had crammed fistfuls of the paper inside his jacket and breeches, as if, like a scarecrow, his stuffing needed replenishing. Everyone had their own notion of civilization, she concluded. To her it was crochet needles. To Hardcastle it was paper. Perhaps he wrote messages to his wife and threw them into the sea in bottles.

Their hiding place—the forepeak—was the slender hollow of the ship's prow, where a single wall of planks let in the sound of the slopping sea.

They were no sooner settled than feet came running

in their direction—straight towards them, and they thought they must surely have been seen. But whoever it was out there, one bulkhead away from their pent-up breath and noisy heartbeats, stopped short of the forepeak and stayed to struggle with something bulky and awkward. Sheller must have left word for something to be brought up from below deck. The struggling, the grunts, the curses moved gradually away and the noisy silence of a ship at anchor settled over the *Tenderness* again.

BANG!

The aftershock of the explosion jarred her like a kick.

'What's that?' Maud gripped Tamo's arm.

'Sheller's blasting a passage through the mangrove roots. He wouldn't be doing that unless he had found the ship. It was there! It was really there!'

Maud let go her grip. She could not fathom his delight—as if it were he and not Sheller who was at this moment setting foot on board, taking command of the shining silvery ship. That was how she imagined it: like the Devil's magic ship in the old ballad:

Its sails were made of th' shining silk,
Its masts of beaten gold.

There was a splash of oars. Quartermaster's voice rang out from almost directly under the forepeak. 'Lower all the boats! Fetch ropes. Every man to the boats.'

Then Sheller's voice: 'We must tow her out. Every man to an oar! . . . Where's that brat White?'

That was when the three were missed.

The crew found the rope over the side, and threads of clothing snagged in the ship's rail. It was so exactly as at Tamatave: a rope over the side, no sign of life.

Sheller had them search the ship, but with no great zeal: it seemed all too plain what had happened.

'Devil rid them, the fools,' said Sheller. 'If they think to trip home through that jungle, they'll wish they'd stayed here with me.' He was angry: once again Tamo had lost him valuable merchandise. But his head was so full of the iron ship he had found, and of putting to sea in her, that he soon called off the time-wasting search. He needed every man jack in the rowing boats, towing the ship out of its hiding place on to open water.

Footfall by footfall, the *Tenderness* grew more and more silent. All its boats were lowered, all the sailors gone. In the darkness the carcasses swung, and the horseflies, finding their way by the smell of blood, were gorging themselves in the darkness.

16

Bottoming Out

Soon the rowers were all busy among the shattered mangroves, running towing ropes between the iron ship and the little rowing boats that must pull her out of her hiding place.

Only then did Tamo wriggle out of the forepeak, go above deck, and cut the anchor cable of the *Tenderness.* The tide was falling. She drifted imperceptibly off shore; they let the currents and tide carry them away from the gaping stone jaws of the crocodile, the impassive bird-beak of the granite outcrop.

'He'll come after us,' said Maud, climbing to the quarterdeck behind Tamo. 'Do you really mean to sail this all by yourself?'

He had pulled the Bible in its cork box from between the spokes of the ship's wheel, and it was spinning now, spinning mesmerically, first one way and then the other as cross-currents toyed with the rudder. 'I have you two to help me,' he suggested.

Hardcastle yawned uncontrollably, his mind determined on sleeping through whatever fate Tamo had brought them to.

'It was the ship you wanted, not the quinine at all,' Maud realized. 'But he'll come after us.'

'I don't want the ship,' said Tamo, snatching hold of the spinning ship's wheel at last, then sucking his stinging fingers. 'What does a doctor's son want with a ship?'

All Maud could think of was Nathan, left behind in

Zaotralana with King Samson and a rabble of pirates, of her hut and her animals, the rice which needed to be harvested, the melons which needed propagating. 'Are we going back? Are we? Sheller will come after us directly. He won't rest till he catches us this time.'

'Just wait till he tries!' said Tamo. 'Just wait!'

When, from the bow of the *Iron Maiden*, Sheller saw the *Tenderness* slip anchor, he raised such a roar that the horseflies rose in throbbing clouds off his back. His crew strained and panted at the oars of the tug boats, the mangroves clawed regretfully at the hull, not wanting, after seven years, to let it go, and the ship slowly moved forward. Sheller cursed and cajoled the men, threatened them, shouted offers of rewards if they would tow him on to the ocean fit to chase the stolen ship.

Then, when he reached deep water, he cursed his crew for not being aboard to raise the sails. Seven row-boats and thirty men he abandoned in the milky-blue bay on the edge of the mangrove swamp, for he could not bear to waste another second in picking them up. The *Iron Maiden*, as it escaped the inlet and came about, buffeted aside its own skiffs, and left the men in them wailing for Sheller—'Wait! Wait! Don't leave us!'

Sheller only shouted louder at the handful of men in the yards: 'Raise the sail and make chase, you swabbers!'

And then the sails unfurled. Tightly rolled and strapped against the yards for seven years, they were at last unfurled. And they fell in a powdery snow, eaten away to tatters by tropical ants and moths.

'There!' Tamo hissed triumphantly. *'Now sail your iron ship, Sheller!'*

Maud hugged him and whooped with joy. 'You knew! You knew all along!'

Hardcastle fumbled blearily with a telescope, hoping to focus on Sheller's hated face and see some mark of misery there to match his own. When he lowered the telescope, his eyes were flickering once more, to and fro behind half-closed lids. 'He thought of it, too. He's taken new canvas aboard. I can see it clear along the decks. There's men raising it already.'

So it came up behind them like a wounded whale. Its hull was not silver, as Maud had envisaged, but the dull, drab grey of lead, studded with rivets. Blood-red streaks marked the rusting of the iron nails. It took Sheller's tiny crew half a day to rig all the fresh sails, but even on a half dozen canvases, the *Iron Maiden* had been able to keep the *Tenderness* in sight. Now she was gaining all the while.

Quartermaster stood on the prow with a muzzle-loader, sniping at the three figures on the *Tenderness.* Any other ship's hull would have been so riddled by worm in seven years as to be barely sea-worthy. But of course, the *Iron Maiden* was lead-sheathed: she cut the water like a knife. Quartermaster's bullets began to embed themselves in the soft timber of the *Tenderness,* in the deck and mast. Hardcastle broke open Sheller's cabin and rifle rack and began to shoot back, but the muzzle shook visibly in his unsteady hands, and his bottom lip was bleeding where he had bitten it through.

At first, they mistook the rain for spray breaking off the waves, since the sea was rising. Then the clouds scrolled up over the land, and the gulls came overhead, beating westwards from a storm far out at sea.

The wind began to pluck up the wave-tops and twist them, like a woman spinning thread from a heap of blue-green wool—little twists of sea which broke off, travelled a short way, then fell back into the swell. The ship's wheel vibrated in Tamo's hands as he steered for deeper water; he did not want to be blown on to a sandbar.

The *Tenderness* turned for the open sea, so too did the *Iron Maiden*, though it wasted less wind in doing so, having an experienced captain at the wheel. The *Tenderness* creaked in its wooden joints—a noise as old as Noah's Ark. But the *Iron Maiden* roared—a weird, uncanny, hollow booming that carried over the water louder than the crack of Quartermaster's musket. The whole sea seemed to throb with the sound of the ship, the metal armour of a Goliath bearing down on the little wooden object of its wrath. Soon the noise was so loud that Tamo had to raise his voice above it.

'I'm sorry! I didn't mean this to happen!' he shouted. 'I never thought he'd take canvas aboard!'

His plan had been to maroon Sheller and his crew on a sail-less ship, while he made his getaway on the *Tenderness*. Maud almost admired him for it: it had so nearly worked. But now Quartermaster's bullets were striking the demi-cannon, the water barrels, the empty boat slings. The only comfort was that Sheller would not use cannon and risk sinking his own ship.

Aboard the *Iron Maiden*, men began to put their hands to their ears. The booming roar of the lead hull had developed an extra grating squeal, like a pig in the butchering. The mast thrummed, the vibrations travelled outwards along the yards, the new sailcloth, stretched tight and full of wind, trembled with the noise of drum skins.

'I wanted him to have it. It's no use to him anyway!' Tamo began to explain. 'The lead, you see . . . '

But the noise of the iron ship filled the whole space between sky and sea and obliterated his words. The swell continued to rise. The prows of both ships rose higher, dipped lower with every wave. The newly stowed cargo settled in the holds of the *Tenderness*. The carcasses of meat bounced on their ropes with each jarring drop of the hull. The wheel kicked in Tamo's fists; he knew that he was not rightly rigged for the wind and that he was putting the ship wrongly at the current, that because of him Sheller was gaining on them.

A bullet hit a fire bucket near him. Open at Tamo's feet, Sheller's Bible fluttered its pages until, one by one, they began to tear loose in the wind and fly upwards. A grey waterspout struck the ship—not ten feet tall, but it broke against the ship like chainshot.

The *Iron Maiden* gained another furlong; it would pass the *Tenderness* to windward and steal all the wind out of her sails—becalm her, take her. Take them.

'Get down! Hardcastle! Take cover!' But Charles was mesmerized by the great bulk of the ship invading more and more of his vision. Bullets gouged sunburst splinters out of the deck around his feet. The recoil from his own rifle kicked his head sideways. He was like the prize at the fairground that could not be dislodged: he incited Sheller's sharpshooters to greater and greater efforts.

The blossoming sails of the *Tenderness* began to shrivel and pucker. The iron ship was stealing her wind. Her bow-wave faltered. The gap was so small now, between the ships, that Sheller's bark of triumph was clearly audible: *'Now I have you!'*

Suddenly Maud broke from her hiding place behind the binnacle and began climbing the rungs of the mast.

She was staring back at Sheller's ship, pointing, her hair blowing straight up above her head in a pale stook. At the same moment, Tamo heard Hardcastle give a cry and thought he had been hit. Letting go of the wheel, he turned round, and was in time to see the *Iron Maiden* stripping herself naked.

She was sloughing her metal cladding, like a mussel being gouged from its shell, a great sheath of lead ripping itself away from the pallid white wood hull beneath. She stopped dead as the sea rushed confusedly in between sheath and hull, flaying metal from wood, skinning the carpentry carcass clean.

If all the rivets had sheared in that one instant, the sheath might just have dropped away intact, and left the wooden hull afloat, keeping out the sea. But some rivets near the rudder held. And so, as the sheathing tore loose, it twisted the whole framework of the hull, sprung all its wooden ribs, snapped the keel like a wishbone. The prow reared up vertically out of the sea like a harpooned whale, showing her underbelly—so clean and uncorrupted—to those gaping from the decks of the *Tenderness*. Then she went down. Stern first. Dragged to the sea-bed by a hundred tons of lead.

The sharpshooters and the other remnants of Sheller's crew leapt into the sea, but the sea itself was rushing to fill the hole left by the ship's downward plunge. A spiral suction drew everything back towards the epicentre of the sinking, where the mast gave one last stir of the ocean and snared men and flotsam in its rigging.

As the ship struck bottom, its empty holds belched out their trapped air, and a mountainous fountain of bubbles gushed to the surface, throwing up the scarlet and black and plaid of Sheller.

Even the sea had no stomach for him.

His tricorn was off, his wig, too; his boots were animated by the bubbling updraught; he danced on his own grave. Then the sea sewed up the small tear in its indestructible fabric, and nothing remained of the *Iron Maiden* but the ash of her decayed sails and some buckets and barrels from her decks.

The silence afterwards was shocking. Unsteered, the *Tenderness* came about, turning to face the wind, to ride out the weather free of Tamo's incompetence.

The stars abruptly came out, and since the wind was driving rags of cloud fast across the sky, the impression was of flints striking sparks.

'I knew,' said Tamo later. 'I found out. In England. At Graylake. It was all I could clearly remember of my—of Thomas White. His iron ship. Talk, talk. For weeks he talked about it. It sounded so . . . such a . . . so fanciful. An iron ship. I began to think it might have been a boast. A lie. But I went to the Navy at Greenwich anyway. I read. I asked questions. They knew about the experiments. And why they failed. Galvanic action, they called it. The lead eats through the iron nails. That's why there'll never be a metal ship. I knew it would happen. But not so soon. Not close by. Somewhere else. Sailing home to England, maybe.'

He had set out to kill Sheller, but there is something so infinitely dreadful about seeing a ship go down, that all Tamo's ruthlessness had sunk along with the *Iron Maiden*. Tamo White had sloughed his own iron cladding, and now he was raw and vulnerable, a boy out of his depth amid his own revenge. Hardcastle too looked hollow-eyed and sickly, as if the hatred he had borne Sheller had been his only source of energy.

They rode out both the squall and the night at sea, and in the calm morning turned for the shore. Tamo and Maud had no idea where they were. If, in being chased, they had overshot Zaotralana, they might have combed the coast for a month without finding it, and run aground in the search. But Hardcastle knew better. His painstaking charts spoke to him of headlands and coves, cross-currents and plantations. He found their way home.

At the sight of the familiar red cliff and the travellers' palms and the honeysuckles, the big outrigger canoes on the beach, Maud's heart filled with an affection she had not known she could feel for a mere view.

'Prepare to drop anchor,' said Tamo.

'What anchor?' said Maud. 'You cut the anchor cable.'

There was a spare plough-anchor in the hold. They struggled, they heaved, they attached ropes and hauled, but the anchor only wagged its iron tongue at them derisively: it was beyond their combined strength to lift it.

'We'll drift by! We'll drift by and never be able to stop!' shrieked Maud, unnerving the others with her noisy panic. Tamo was more of the opinion they would glide broadside into the *Ganesa*, moored in the bay, and sink both vessels, but he did not think it the right time to say so. Hardcastle made strange moaning noises in the back of his throat and said not a word, but went back to hauling single-handedly, futilely, on the plough-anchor till his hands were bleeding.

Tamo picked up a huge coil of rope—'something heavy, something heavy!'—and staggered under the weight of the hemp, unable to think of anything except that he should have taken down more sail. Too late now. Ought they to try and jump from the *Tenderness* to the *Ganesa*? The hulls were clearly going to clash. But the ship seemed to be moving with the speed of galloping horses, and when the two rails did touch, they exploded into splintering matchwood so that the children ran screaming in the opposite direction.

It was Maud who thought of the demi-cannon. She ran and began slapping on its iron breech with both hands. 'Tie it to this! Put the rope round this!'

Rather than tie knots, they looped the rope round and round the cannon, then rolled it forwards. 'Push! Push it over!' panted Maud, leaning her small weight against the wooden gun-carriage.

The cannon went overboard with barely a splash, and then, when the rope pulled tight, the ship dipped and heeled so ferociously that they all lost their footing and went sprawling into the scuppers. The *Tenderness* came to rest within twenty yards of a cluster of rocks, at the southern end of Zaotralana's bay. Almost all *The Revelation of Saint John* tore free of Sheller's Bible and blew along the deck and over the side.

Strange, they thought, that the sight of the *Tenderness* did not bring the whole pirate rabble running. Strange and unfortunate, because there was not a single jolly-boat or skiff left for going ashore. Then Nathan (whose whole world had been aboard Sheller's ship) burst from behind a tambourissa tree and came running down the beach, waving with both arms, his pinched face red with heat and excitement.

Tamo cupped his hands round his mouth. 'We have no boat to come ashore!' he called.

Nathan tried one outrigger after another, but they were sunk deep in the wet sand and would not shift.

At last he got a small dug-out afloat, and fetched them ashore in that.

When it was Hardcastle's turn to climb aboard, and Nathan called to him, he tossed back his head in that nervous flinch, and said not a word. It was as if the sound of his own voice would be too frightening.

Tamo went last down the knotted rope, bottles of quinine in one hand, the crook of his arm, and both pockets of his gaudy jacket. As he stepped into the dug-out, the look on Nathan's face was of breathless joy. 'You came back! You did it!' he said.

'I've done nothing,' said Tamo morosely. 'Nothing. I still have to be rid of Samson.'

'No. No! No, you don't!' cried Nathan, spitting on his palms and starting to paddle. 'Samson's dead.'

17
Amnesty

'He died last night,' whispered Nathan, as they lay on their stomachs and looked down on the village, unseen. 'A flux. It was vile. He came through the village with a pistol in each hand, looking for Delilah to kill her, and shouted for Quartermaster to help him. Howling and swearing.'

She did it, then. Twice over, said Maud to herself.

'The crew just barricaded themselves indoors and waited for the sickness to stop him. It was fearful. He shot a sifaka out of a tree—said it was the devil come for him. He tripped on the wires and fell into pits and cut himself on the snares, and all the while he kept roaring and swearing . . . '

'Poor sifaka,' said Maud.

'And now they're burying him. They want Quartermaster. They're waiting for Quartermaster to fire the shots. Where is he?'

'Gone to his own funeral,' said Tamo.

Between two traveller-palms whose leaves spread from the base like aghast hands, a grave had been dug for King Samson. His body lay on a piece of board—a door by all appearances—covered in a raffia sheet. A turban protruded from one end and his curl-toed oriental slippers from the other, while a spiral of flies circled over the round of his belly.

Gauche and uncertain, the pirates stood about, baring their heads then covering them when the sun burned their scalps. A Newfoundland slitter played something melancholy on a squeeze box and would not stop when the Dutchman wanted to say a prayer. Six of them lifted the door as far as the graveside, but no one wanted to touch the body. So, in the end, they rolled it into the hole with the soles of their boots.

'How old was he?' enquired one.

'Forty?'

'Thirty-three?'

'Twenty-one: don't let's waste bullets.' So a salute of shots was fired, which petered out at sixteen, an age Samson had probably never been. At the sharp crack of the muskets, birds burst from the tree canopies in a fountaining rainbow of colours—barbets and fodies, drongos and buttonquail, couas, woodpeckers and blue pigeons.

'Where's the queen? She ought to speak,' said the purser.

'She could say one of her learned pieces.'

They wanted Delilah. Sometimes the native wives shed tears over their pirate husbands. There was a story told how one had even stabbed herself for grief. It was a story of comfort to men like this. It encouraged them to hope that one day tears might be shed in their memory.

And all of a sudden, there she was: Queen Delilah. Tamo sat up, not caring whether he was seen or not. She should not have come out of hiding so soon! It was reckless. Besides, what did she owe Samson that she should honour his laying to rest by being there?

As stately and imposing as a Moorish galleon, Princess Andriamahilala walked out of the forest to the side of her husband's grave. She did not recite the Lord's Prayer or twenty-third Psalm, but she did deliver a funeral oration in her own peculiar language, while the men watched her round-eyed. They were so grateful to her for lending a little solemnity to the occasion—some sense of ceremony they could not somehow muster themselves.

'Oh, fat white pig,' [Delilah declaimed in Malagasy]. *'O lightless maggot. In heart you were smaller than the smallest. In spirit the sourest of the joyless. All the love you ever showed me fitted inside your fist. All the joy you ever brought me, you brought today. Carry this message for me to the Land of the Dead—to that other wretch who tormented me—to Thomas White. Say the two of you together do not make up one man. And may you fight and drink sour beer together for ever and ever. Amen.'*

'Amen,' said the crew, in awe of her oratory.

'Never rest with your ancestors,' Delilah went on, with bitter relish. *'Never insult our Dead with your company. Be alone. Apart. And never rise. Take these, and see what they will buy you now, King of Meanness, Lord of Nowhere, Least of the Dead.'* And she stripped her arms bare of bracelets and rings, pulled the necklaces from round her throat, the coins from her hair, pitching them all into the open grave.

The crewmen gasped with amazement. A savage throw away her baubles? They had rather assumed these women only married the likes of Samson for the presents that came of it. She must really have loved him! Thinking this was part of Malagasy ritual, the most superstitious even threw in small coins out of their pockets. But the thought of all that jewellery in the grave there, with Samson, that brought quite genuine groans of distress from them. The waste! The waste!

Twining her long hair into a plait, Andriamahilala piled it on top of her head and, holding it in place with one hand, walked slowly away, her big hips swaying with the voluptuous dignity of a princess.

After heaving two shovelfuls of earth on to the body, the first of the pirates weakened and set off to run. At once everyone was running. They collided with one another in the doorway of the longhut, cursed each other and their eyes as the darkness blinded them, then fell to grabbing up the loot of their dead king. He was under the ground now, and they were safe to help themselves. He had no rights left under any Ship's Articles.

Some settled for the prettiness of brass and copper, but others flung aside bowls and vases to dig up the earth floor of the hut, or tore apart Samson's clothes seam by seam, looking for precious gems. They grunted and panted and sweated with the exertion of the search, like a cage of apes excited by the banging of their bars.

Up at the top of the hill, Charles Hardcastle wrapped his arms across his face, drew his knees up to his chest and fell asleep against the hut wall, shutting out the spectacle and the whole nasty world.

'I have to be rid of these creatures, now,' said Tamo.

Maud examined his face and saw that Tamo had burdened himself with the welfare of the whole village. The son of the ship's doctor had taken it upon himself to free Zaotralana of pirates, and was afraid of being unequal to the task.

She wanted to say, 'It's not for you to do it. Not you alone.'

'I shall speak to the local men—make them see we have to fight. We have enough guns on the *Tenderness*. Pistols and muskets. I can arm them. If we wait till the crew are drunk . . .'

'No,' said Nathan.

'What, are you afraid?'

'No,' said Nathan. The illness had made his face

thin so that his eyes looked bigger and brighter. 'Yes, we could massacre them when they're drunk. Probably. A few dozen villagers might die. But we could. You could. Then we'd be no better than them—the pirates. I've been thinking. While you were gone.'

'Plainly,' said Tamo with a certain hauteur.

'We mustn't sink down to their level. We have to stay apart.'

'We can't just run away!' Maud protested, and Tamo, in his agitation, rounded on her:

'I thought you wanted to!'

'I've been thinking,' Nathan persisted doggedly. 'I won't be a party to killing anyone. I didn't like going at the seas. It scared the bowels out of me if you want the truth. I only did it because I was more scared of Samson and the quartermaster. But did those down there have any more choice than we did? Are you going to judge them? You don't know why they turned pirate. Who are you to say they ought to be shot for it?'

'They would kill you as soon as step round you,' said Tamo disgustedly.

'In that case, I'll be different. I'll keep myself from being like that. That's all I have to say.' And Nathan snapped shut his lips.

Maud sat between them on the ground. She looked at her brother, who was British and quite probably right, and only, for Heaven's sake, trying to be like his father. Then she looked at Tamo, the warrior, the strategist, the boy who, if he got his way, would become a hero of Malagasy folk-history. And she knew that there was not the thickness of a new moon to put between them. Neither wanted to see anyone else die; to see Zaotralana turned into a battlefield. Neither was old enough to bear it. She knew that both of them were children in comparison with her.

'There *is* a way to be rid of the pirates,' she said.

They both looked at her.

'There is a way, and we won't have to fight.' She waited until she was sure she had their undivided attention. 'The dead will do it for us.'

She pulled down from off a shelf her finest native *lamba*—a simple piece of woven raffia to wrap around her body for a dress. She laid it on the ground beside the sleeping Hardcastle. His jacket was open, and she began to pull out from it the crumpled papers he had stuffed himself with aboard the *Tenderness*. She looked as if she were plucking a chicken. On special occasions, the women of Zaotralana threaded tufts of paper or cloth or flowers into the weave of their *lambas*. She was making herself a dress to dance in.

'Your mother gave me the idea,' said Maud. 'She threw her jewellery into the grave because she knew none of the crew would dare go in after it. She was laughing at them.'

'So?' Tamo was bewildered.

'The people here, they don't want their ancestors to see what's happened to the village. But if they just could! If they just could! Trust me, Tamo. Do this one thing, and if I'm wrong, I'll take a pistol and fight the pirates with you.' She grabbed hold of his hand with hers and he looked down at it, startled, as if it were some windfall fruit that had dropped into his lap.

'Do *you* understand what your sister is talking about?' he asked Nathan.

But Nathan was tight-lipped and not prepared to answer. 'It's heathen,' was all he would say. 'I won't be party to it. I forbid it. Consider, will you, Maud Gull, what father would say?'

Maud jumped up and gave him a push in the chest with two fists. 'If I were in England I might dig him up and ask him! But I'm not, so I have to think for my—'

Then Nathan hit her. His open hand made a stark white shape on her face which, within a second, flushed red and livid. It did not make such a very loud noise, but Hardcastle woke at once, his eyes opening like signal lamps full of alarm.

'Look at you! Take a look at yourself!' Nathan was saying. 'Dressing up as a . . . wishing yourself a . . . Where's your maidenly modesty? Where's your Christian chastity and meekness? You are not the sister I cherished in England!'

'Is it quite civilized to strike a woman?' said Tamo, his hand on his swordhilt. He was utterly shocked.

'You hold yourself off, sir,' said Nathan. 'This does not concern you. It is between my sister and me.'

Maud breathed hard and fast through her nose. Her hand covered the mark on her cheek, her fingers smaller than Nathan's slap. Hardcastle got warily to his feet, eyes half shut against seeing yet more unpleasantness. He drew his jacket closed across his chest.

Maud wanted to cry, but all that came out of her was a giggle, a hysterical, uncontrollable hinny of laughter. There was her pompous little brother imitating a country parson—the voice, the stance, the hands on the lapels of his sailor-jacket. Was this what growing up was, then? Pretending to behave like an adult until the imitation became convincing? Hardcastle yawned, Nathan glared, and Maud giggled hysterically while abject tears ran down her face and Tamo stared at them. Maud's pet lemurs shrieked and gibbered, imitating human beings.

Then Hardcastle picked up one of the pieces of paper, and read it. On board the *Tenderness* there had been no light. Now, in the shade of the hut, he could just make out the print. Through a forest of elaborate curlicues the name of King George struggled to make itself legible and, below it, huge as a queen bee among a swarm of drones, the word PARDON.

His Majesty George, King of ye Union of England and Scotland, and of all colonies subject thereto, in this year of our Lord one thousand, seven hundred and eighteen, out of his great mercy, and that their misdeeds fall no longer to ye account of England, shaming her thereby, offers a gracious and free general PARDON to those bucaniers, corsairs and pyrates presently habitant east of ye Cape, being penitent of their sins and desirous to return to their native countrie.

Charles pressed it to his face, moulded the paper over his features. He picked up the sheets Maud had folded into fans, and poked them into the buttonholes of his jacket. He crammed his pockets, too. Then filling his fists with as many of the rest as he could carry, he stumbled down the hill towards the noisy rout going on inside the longhouse.

'Amnesty! There's an amnesty! A pardon! We can go home, boys! We can go home!'

Nathan and Maud crouched down, mesmerized, each holding one of the printed sheets, reading and re-reading it with the fingers of their hands, since their eyes were all on Hardcastle.

'Sheller deliberately kept them back. They gave him broadsheets to distribute and he kept the amnesty secret,' said Maud.

'Where's the profit for him, if his customers turn honest?' said Tamo.

'It's the hand of God,' said Nathan, overawed. 'He

reached out to save us. We shall all go home together—all sail into England free men. It's a miracle!'

'It's a year old,' said Tamo.

'What?'

'The pardon. It was issued last year. It may not hold. And besides . . . men differ.'

'What?'

'Men differ,' was all he would say. But he pointed down at the figure of Charles Hardcastle, running from slitter to Dutchman to second mate, grabbing at their jackets, thrusting the broadsheets into their faces.

Their hands were full of coins and trinkets. One had a copper vase on his head and looked like a *conquistador.* Another dropped Samson's etching of Windsor Castle as Hardcastle shouted into his face: *'Pardoned! We've been pardoned! We can go home! The King has pardoned us!'* For months the man had barely spoken. Now the children could hear his voice all the way from the hilltop.

But the crew heard nothing.

They ignored him. They pushed him out of their way. They took the pamphlet he waved at them and screwed it into a ball.

'Heard it before.'

'What's to say they'd honour it?'

'Lying tosspots they are, all of 'em.'

'What's that to us?'

Only one was interested—a little Yorkshireman who had never heard of King George and wondered if he truly existed. What had become of Queen Anne, he wanted to know?

Their minds were all on Samson's treasure. Hardcastle was in their way. Two men brawled casually over a pair of Samson's boots, kept one each, then pitched back into the search. It did not take long to pillage the longhouse of every one of their captain's personal possessions and to divide up such spoils as he had buried inside. The crew were in a mood to celebrate. On bad days—days scarred by terror or injury—they thought of home and wished they could be there. But today was not such a day, and Hardcastle was offering them nothing they wanted. So they pushed him, and threw punches at him, cursed him for a lunatic, and used the King's Pardon to stop up his babbling mouth.

For a few minutes, Nathan Gull had pictured himself home in England, a free man, washed clean in the King's forgiveness, climbing the steps of his father's vicarage, knocking at an open door . . . the Prodigal Son.

Now God's miracle had been turned down, declined with a spit and a curse. And Nathan was to remain a pirate still, till the sickness in his blood melted him, or a Turkish ball carried him overboard, or a fellow pirate's knife cut his throat for the sake of the buttons on his jacket. He wanted his sister to comfort him and tell him everything would turn out for the best. But just as he reached for Maud's hand, she abruptly stood up.

'They'll drink now, and have a feast tonight,' she said to Tamo. 'Tell your people to make *famadihana.*' She looked at Nathan coldly, her hand against her cheek. 'Tell them the ancestors need to dance tomorrow.'

Nathan said nothing. His hands hung down by his side. His eyes were hollow. This time it was Tamo who shook his head. Maud pursed her lips obdurately and stamped. 'Trust me. It will work. I know it!'

'If you say so,' said Tamo dubiously. 'But you tell them, Maud-*ala.*'

'Me?'

'I don't understand what you want—what you think will happen. Besides, they look at me, and they see a pirate now. I'm rotten with the same canker as those down there. No. It has to be you. They'll listen to you, Maud-*ala*, you'll see.' He reached out and touched the zebu amulet the *ombiasy* had given her and which hung from a thong round her neck. 'You'll see.'

Maud put on her *lamba* with its flounce of folded broadsheets, and fastened her sunbleached hair on top of her head. Her pet lemur, curious to see the leather toggle she pinned it with, climbed up to her hip, then her shoulder, then to and fro, fingering her hair, eating plantain from her fingers.

The crew were drinking Samson's fine wine, slopping it carelessly on the ground like blood from a wound. As Maud descended the hill, they caught sight of her, and whistled and shouted out, beckoning. As she skirted the central square, the branded man lurched up to her, breathing alcoholic fumes into her face. 'You be my Queen Mary. I'll be your King Will. Wassay?'

'I'm going to ask the villagers to make a feast—to mark the death of Captain Sheller.'

'Devil quit him, I'll drink to that!' said the pirate. The shiny, puckered skin of his burned forehead rucked as he grimaced his loathing for the supplier. The deaths of Samson, Quartermaster, and Sheller within the same day had left the crew like children unsupervised by grown-ups. Tomorrow they would be at a loss what to do, would cast lots or fight to decide on a new captain, frightened and helpless with no one to tell them what to do. But for now they would enjoy the freedom of a life without rules. Tomorrow they would go out to the *Tenderness* and strip it of Sheller's fabulous cargo. But today Samson's wine ensured that they could not negotiate the cliff path safely or even stand up without falling over.

Maud went past Noro's hut and the charcoal burners, up to the paddy fields where the women were picking new rice. The men were away fishing or hunting, in ones and twos, never allowed to muster in groups larger than three, by order of Quartermaster. But the women, who were no threat, had been allowed to continue their daily work much as before.

Maud stepped up on to the mud levy. The lemur sidled restlessly from shoulder to shoulder. One by one, the women straightened their bent backs and looked at her.

'I—'

Maud realized that the drunken pirate had scared out of her head any of the Malagasy words she had prepared to say. Her hand closed over the zebu amulet. She tried to think, as well as to speak, in Malagasy.

'I had a dream,' she began. 'A creature came to me and spoke. An aye-aye came and put his magic finger in my ear, and I heard. I heard the ancestors under the ground. I heard them asking for *famadihana*. I heard them asking to dance.'

The women turned side-on to her, sceptical, flapping at the flies around their heads with limp hands.

'You won't hold *famadihana* because the pirates are here. But I say, hold *famadihana*, and the pirates will not be here tomorrow.'

The faces which looked back at her had been used and abused in a hundred different ways since the coming of the pirates. They were blank, keeping their thoughts secret, giving nothing away. When Noro came up and stroked the lemur's fur, her mother followed and snatched her hand away.

'Inona no mba fantatrao momba ny fombancy?' she said bitterly. *What do you know about our customs?*

'I know you talk to the dead—tell them things,' said Maud. 'Ask them, then. Ask them if they want these *babakotos*, these apes, living in their village, marrying their granddaughters, eating their rice. Ask them. And if they don't, let them come up and see an end of it.'

Noro burst into tears. She was full of pity for Maud, and sank her face in her mother's breast. 'She's made a mistake, Mama. She thinks our dead can walk and talk and fight. She doesn't understand.'

'I haven't misunderstood,' said Maud. 'I've seen *famadihana*, remember? I know you love your dead. I know you're not afraid of the dead.'

The women looked about them at the lowering noisy forest full of spirits and ghosts. It was nonsense, of course. They were terrified of the restless, unpeaceful dead who howled at them out of the morning trees, who gibbered and loped through the evening shadows. Maud did not have the words to explain any better what she meant.

'I mean, you are not afraid of *famadihana,'* she said, struggling. 'Please! *Please!'*—then fell silent, defeated.

With a grunt, Queen Delilah, appearing from nowhere, pulled her great weight up on to the levy beside Maud. She laid a hand on Maud's shoulder, but Maud flinched and pulled away from her.

'The child means you are not scared to hold the bones in your arms,' Delilah said in her bullfrog roar. *'And she's right. Do as she says. She knows the ways of these dogs. She knows what will make them run.'*

The women began again to pick the new green rice. But when their hands were full, one by one, they extricated themselves from the paddy and, picking up their half-empty baskets, balanced them on their heads and swayed away towards the village. There was no way of knowing what they were thinking or why they had gone.

Once again, Delilah tried to put her arm round Maud, but the girl pulled away so sharply as to slip and fall off the levy. From down amid the rice, Delilah on the wall was a huge, dark shape blotting out the sun.

'What a matter, girl?'

'Did you poison him, too?' said Maud in English.

'What you say, girl?'

'Did you poison Samson, like you poisoned Thomas White?'

Delilah beamed at her, reaching out a hand to help her back on to the mud wall, starting to laugh in a way that shook all the meat on her bones. Maud did not take the hand.

'Lord, no, child! Man poison hissel'! Man poison my damn good cooking! Tryin' to kill that supplyin' devil. Then he get so drunk he forget! Eat it all hissel'!' And she started to laugh: at the stupidity of Samson, at the wonderfulness of fate.

Maud laughed too. She had nursed the suspicion for a whole day, without saying one word to the boys. Now the sheer relief started her laughing, too. She knew her brother would not approve, but she could not help it. The lemur on her shoulders took fright at the unfamiliar sound and bounded away across the heat-crazed mud. Maud had not laughed for months.

18

Wake the Dead!

A zebu was killed, and the meat portioned with great care into equal servings for everyone, including the crew. There was no whispering among the villagers, no conspiratorial plotting which the pirates might misconstrue as rebellion hatching. From first light, the air was simply full of the gentle plucked music of the *vahina* and single voices raised in song.

Though the sailors (who had gone to bed dead drunk) might have preferred silence, the music was hardly menacing. Drunk or asleep, they were vulnerable to assassins, and they knew it. Each new morning came as a relief: another night survived. Now they crept out into the sunlight, clutching their headaches in both hands, lids shut against the glare, and swore at the women pounding grain. But they were not unhappy, not uneasy.

In Tamo's plan of action, the deed would have been done by now, with knives, in the dead of night. Or else the young Malagasy men would be massing now in the woods, ready to storm their own village and slaughter the occupying forces, with heroic loss of life.

But this was Maud's plan. The only battle cries were the eery hoots of indris, the only sharp blades the solid rays of sun cutting diagonally through the leafy boughs. Everywhere, people were smiling and singing, dressed in white (which dazzled but did not alarm the pirates) and there was a smell of meat cooking.

Today the crew would off-load Sheller's supply ship, precariously moored by rocks in the bay, and argue about who had what. Maybe they would elect a new captain, find out the truth of what had happened to Quartermaster and to the iron ship. Women smiled at them and brought them a breakfast of tripe congealed in fat—which is enough to make a man retch, but not inclined to make him nervous. Though they swore at the old women and taunted the girls, the crew were not unhappy. Such was Maud's plan.

When a procession casually formed and villagers strolled over towards the Village of the Dead, Maud and Tamo went with them.

'What's happening?' the crew asked.

'A celebration. A feast day,' Maud replied.

Nathan would not go, of course. He stayed in his hut, as obdurate as a snail closed up in its shell, reading King Samson's Bible—it was the only thing the crew had left unclaimed after pillaging the longhut. 'You are no longer kin to me, Maud Gull,' he had said with all the sombre gloom of a priest declaring excommunication on a heretic. 'This is a sacrilege. I forbade it, but you choose to defy me. From today on, never speak to me. No sister of mine would do this wicked thing.'

He had thought that would bring her round. But she went ahead despite him. And now, sitting in the dark hut, listening to the music build, it was Nathan who felt excommunicated, alone, cut off. His comfort must be in righteousness, in being right, and he set about finding the Biblical proof that he was. It was not so easy as he had thought. His father could have called the texts to mind as easily as the Lord's Prayer. So could Mr Thrussell at Graylake. Nathan wished he had listened more closely, studied more assiduously. But he would find the verses. Thus he crouched over the Bible: a fourteen-year-old theologian, teenage Defender of the Faith in a heathen land. The Reverend Gull in miniature.

'. . . *Regard not them that have familiar spirits, neither seek after wizards, to be defiled by them . . .*'

Games of cards and dice had started up among the pirates in the sunlit centre of the village when the procession came back from the Village of the Dead. Thirty or more stretchers were borne along on a current of song, like the notes on a stave of music, black resting on white. Dark tattered bundles of cloth were carried to the doors of individual houses and set down amid drifts of new white silk or pale raffia cloth. There was a smell, a strange, sweet smell, confused by the smell of cooking. And there was a hubbub of happy voices.

And the villagers really were happy now. What had begun nervously was taking on a life of its own. It was so long since they had kept *famadihana,* so long since they had acted independently of the men who had taken over their village, taken over their lives. There was a liberation in doing something uniquely Malagasy, a ritual the foreigners knew nothing about.

The crew watched with only half a bleary eye, incurious as to why people usually so cowed, timid and gloomy, were singing now and laughing. The English girl was among them, she also in a white *lamba,* singing some hymn:

'O salutaris hostia,
quae caeli pandis ostium,
bella premunt hostilia,
da robur, fer auxilium.'

'Saviour, whose selfless death threw wide
The gates of Heaven to Man below;
Our foes close in on every side;
Thy help supply, thy strength bestow.'

The dead 'king's' fat wife, noisy as a bullfrog, swayed her hips in a never-ending dance, her arms outstretched to either side, her hands full of flowers. When the stretchers were set down, they were at once surrounded by laughing family groups wielding unmanageable sheets of blowy cloth.

The pirates who had slept late came to the doors of the huts, to investigate the noise . . .

'. . . *Thus saith the Lord, Learn not the way of the heathen . . .'* read Nathan, up in his dark hermitage. *'The dead praise not the Lord, neither any that go down into silence . . .'*

'What is it? *Christ! Take it away! What are you doing? What is this?'* The Dutchman, fuddled with sleep and yesterday's wine, gawped at the body of a young child, part decayed, part preserved, as it was thrust at him by a proud mother.

'Izy no Fanja. Fanjanay!' This is our Fanja. Our Fanja.

Newly woken, the purser stepped outside to breathe the air. At once a short, neat parcel, newly wrapped, was laid in his arms like a present. He pulled the wrappers off with a brutish, greedy curiosity—and a pile of human bones clattered to the ground around his feet. The purser made a noise like a stabbed pig, and forced his way past men, women, and child, running for the square.

As he ran, he collided with other pirates, all horror-stricken, half-convinced they were hallucinating. But the most alcoholic delusion was nothing in comparison with the arcade of horrors in store for them. As they ran, they tripped over dead men, and skeletons swaddled like newborn children, tripped over bowls of water where tiny, frail old women were washing the massive thigh bones of their ancestral warriors. In the passageways between every hut the crews were greeted by a dead body hoisted up high, peering with eyeless sockets out of a gap in its shroud at the strange new fortifications and booby traps. A Newfoundlander ran home again, only to find the grandmother of the house showing his bedroll and belongings to another awful item of putrefaction. '. . . And this is where he sleeps, and this is what he stole, and this is where . . .'

They drew their pistols, but what enemy was there to shoot? The dead are proof against powder and shot.

There is a superstition common among sailors that if a dying man speaks your name, you too will soon be dead. And here were their names being whispered into the rotted ears of three dozen carcasses—an entire graveyard being politely invited to look them over . . . *'These are the men who live in your house now. They butchered your sacred animals last month; they use your outrigger; they are holding us hostage . . .'*

In the middle of the village square, the pirate with P branded on his forehead came face-to-face with Maud Gull. She was dancing with Noro and her family—a swaying, shuffling dance so casual as to conceal any nervousness. But at the pirate's approach, Noro froze and began to back away. Her mother drew the child behind her. For a moment, P tasted once more the comforting power of the bully. Then Maud took from

Noro's father the white bundle he was carrying: the bones of Noro's grandmother. 'This,' she said to the parcel, in English, without a note of resentment in her voice, 'this is the man who eats your rice and sleeps under your roof.'

P pulled twin pistols from his belt. The pallor of his face made the burn on his forehead even more livid red. 'You get that filth out of here! You get it away! Keep away from me!' Maud did not move.

Tamo saw what was going to happen and drew his sword. But he was not carrying a gun, and he was too far away, much too far away to prevent it . . .

Pointing both pistols at Maud, P fired point-blank.

Nathan was reduced to thumbing idly through the Bible, his eyes on the pages, but his mind struggling to make sense of the noises outside. Would the pirates really be so terrified by the dancing dead as to quit Zaotralana, leave their fortified treasure houses and run for the open sea? In their time as pirates they must have seen such horrors . . . Was *famadihana* any worse? Then he found himself wondering, if Maud's plan did not work, what reprisals the pirates would take on Zaotralana for the scare they had been given. His twitching fingers came to rest idly on Matthew's Gospel. The verse beneath them said, '*We have piped unto you, and ye have not danced; we have mourned unto you, and ye have not lamented.*'

At that moment, the sound of flintlock pistols firing brought him to his feet and set him running. Outside, the dangling metal grazed his head. The thorns embedded in the path slit the soles of his shoes. Scarlet fody flew out of the bamboo, like drops of blood.

* * *

The branded pirate gaped at Maud. All the singing had stopped. She lay on her back, under the white parcel of bones, the zebu amulet thrown up into her hair by the impact of landing. Noro came out from behind her mother. The villagers, their ancestors still balanced high on their shoulders like toddlers at a fair, came crowding in towards P. Up on the hilltop, a boy started to yell and run down the slope.

After ten seconds, or twenty (who could have said?) Maud stirred and opened her eyes. There was a pain in her chest and cloth covering her face and a great weight pressing down on her, as though she were already buried. All the breath had gone from her lungs. She tried to breathe, but could not. Was this what it was like, then, to be dead? The soul aware, the body no longer able to move? She could even hear the voices of the living, Delilah wailing and keening as though she had lost a member of her family. But no one came—only the ticking sound of flies landing on the raffia over her face.

Then a little brown hand—a wizened claw, as of a child long dead, grabbed hold of her hair and began tugging at it, tugging so that her skull banged up and down on the ground. Did the dead rob each other, then? 'Ow!' she said, and the air rushed back into her winded chest.

The cloth was pulled from over her eyes, and she saw the no-noseholes in the centre of the wizened face. It was a lemur trying to steal her zebu amulet. With one enormous effort, Maud pushed the parcel of bones off her chest: P could not possibly know with what revulsion she found herself pinned to the ground by Grandma Noro.

He only saw that she was getting up, and knew that the pistols in his hand were empty and that he was alive in a charnel house. Dead generations of Malagasies were mustering to destroy him. In one clumsy movement which twisted his ankle and filled his open mouth with blowflies, he turned and set off to run. He ran like a man in a nightmare, whose legs are deep in quicksand. To right and left, out of the corner of his eyes, he could see his fellow pirates running—all heading for the bay, all making for the boats.

Their fists still clutching cards or dice, cooked beef or the butts of empty pistols, they ran for their ship. Jawless skulls grinned at them, jogged after them, as the villagers tried to offer them home-brewed beer. Having no idea what the cups contained, they imagined horrific ingredients, knocked the beer away and kept running. The villagers sang louder now, and drums were beating—loud, incessant drums which started the coua birds shrilly crying.

All along the beach, offerings of food had been laid out, at first light, to feed the dead of the sea—drowned fishermen whose bodies could not be turned and who had to dance alone on the sea-bed. The food-offerings had attracted shark into the surf and crocodiles on to the strand—massive crocodiles the size of canoes. Terror engulfed the pirates who, leaderless and taken unaware, screamed with the strain of pushing rowboats down yards of dry sand, across wet clogging sand and into the awkward surf. They fought each other for places at the oars.

Sheer habit might have taken them aboard the *Ganesa*. But Sheller's ship lay so much closer and (if their wits had not deserted them entirely) they knew it to be crammed with valuables. The dark shapes of sharks escorted them all the way out to it. A dorsal fin scraped against the wood. The crocodiles, startled by the commotion, closed their panting mouths, flexed their massive bodies, and scuttled into the surf.

All along the clifftops, the dead were dancing—fat white bundles or long white mummies, dancing in the sunlight, peering out of their no-eyes at the glittering sea, singing with their no-mouths, speaking potent curses, for all the fleeing pirates knew. They belonged underground; all this decay and disintegration. It was too grotesque for words. Animal cries from the excitable jungle became, in their overheated imaginations, the hoots of spirits and ghouls.

The Odyssey rowing past the singing Sirens never laid on canvas so fast as the *Tenderness* with its crew of terrified sea-bandits. Not a drop of blood had been spilled. But then that was Maud's plan.

Noro's father reverently rewrapped the freshly washed bones of his mother. One of P's bullets had gone wide, but a scorch marked where the other had entered the wrapping before splintering the tibia and ribs of the skeleton and lodging in the dense pelvic bone.

'Tell your grandmother thank you,' said Maud to her friend.

'You tell her,' said Noro. 'You speak our language.'

'Yes. Still.' Maud hesitated. 'I'm not Malagasy,' she said.

The bones were not all from a woman. Within Noro's family grave, the oldest skeletons had long since become jumbled together. As Noro explained, the person who danced was not Grandma but a representative of Grandma—an amalgamation of ancestors. What mattered was that the past be allowed to dance in present-day sunshine, hear the news, stir up memories and lend its energies to the living. As Noro put it, 'It wasn't Grandma who protected you. It was lots of her.'

As the realization of their freedom dawned on the people of Zaotralana, an even greater mood of celebration broke out. They did not understand what had so terrified the pirates; they could simply perceive that their ancestors had somehow freed them: their ancestors and Maud. They wanted to fête her, to fill her hair with flowers.

But Maud did not feel triumphant. The despond which follows a bad fright made her heart ache behind the bruises on her chest. Nathan had sworn never to speak to her again, and Tamo had lost the *Tenderness*. The crews might even come back tomorrow for their abandoned treasure.

'Will they?' she asked Tamo. 'Will they come back?'

He put his arm round her shoulders. 'No. If they had taken the *Ganesa* they'd have come back for the *Tenderness*. This way they've got so much, they'll forget what's left behind.'

The dead began their cheerful procession back to the cemetery. Not until they were all gone from sight—every parcel, every mummy, every stretcher and shroud—did Nathan emerge from behind a garden wall. He was holding a pistol in one hand and a sword in the other, and looked as wrecked as the iron ship. He darted out like one of Maud's lemurs, and almost leapt into her arms, hugging her so hard that it winded her again. 'I would have killed him if he'd killed you,' he said not once but over and over again. 'I would have killed him if he'd killed you!'

'Tut tut,' said Maud reprovingly. 'Remember your Bible: *Vengence is mine, saith the Lord.*'

19

Fate

'There were once four men living on the Earth. The first was a hunter with a spear, the second a trapper with a snare; the third lived by picking fruit and berries, the fourth by planting rice. Naturally, as soon as hardship struck, each man thought he would be happier if only he could change places with his brother man. One bad day, when all four were equally discontented, they went to God to ask for a change of occupation. But when they got there, squabbling and trying to shout each other down, God was busy pounding rice. "I'm too busy to discuss it today," he said. "Come back tomorrow. In the meantime, look after this for me." And into each man's palm he poured a handful of rice.

'On the way back, the hunter saw a fossa and, dropping the rice, went after it with his spear. The trapper saw a bird overhead and stopped to set a snare: needing both hands, he laid the rice down while he rigged it. When he turned back, the ants had carried every grain away. The fruit-picker saw a delicious mango overhanging a river. As he clambered out along the branch, the rice fell from his pocket into the water and the fish ate it.

'The fourth could think of nowhere better to put the rice for safe-keeping than to bury it in the ground, and there it took root and sprouted.

'Next day, God came by. "Where's that rice I left with you?" Three hung their heads, while the fourth pointed to the new green shoots. "Aha!" said God. "This shows that a man must follow his fate. Do as you were born to do, and as your fathers did before you." After that, every man was content . . . or if he was not, then it was his fate to be miserable.'

When Tamo sat down from telling this story, the villagers nodded and murmured their assent. They had heard it a hundred times before, but, for them, newness was not the issue . . . Stories, too, needed to see the sunlight every so often, to be turned over, to be communally remembered.

Maud had never heard the story before, but she nodded too, as Tamo sat down and received little tokens of appreciation from his audience for his *kabary*. She might have known the Malagasies would have such a story. A man must follow his fate. Do as you were born to do and as your fathers did before you.

Another man began the story of a child's pet grasshopper which died . . .

The day's heat recoiled and red kingfishers were darting up and down the river, catching flies. Stripe-tailed lemurs promenaded in the striped shadows of the trees, picking up nuts and fruit. Chickens pecked in the centre of the circle of people, as if gleaning words dropped by the storytellers.

Nathan was not there, of course. He did not understand the language sufficiently well, he said, and besides, he was making ready for the voyage. What that entailed, Maud did not know; all the treasure the pirates had left behind was already stowed on board the *Ganesa*, and she was already provisioned. Nathan's other belongings hardly merited packing.

Maud watched Delilah—Princess Andriamahilala, rather—stroke her son's hair, blissful in their reconciliation. Maud had not *wanted* to tell Tamo how his mother had poisoned Thomas White. Murder was such a very big trespass, and so terribly un-British. Still, she had known what joy the news would give him, Tamo being neither Christian nor British. Now he thought his mother was the miracle of the age. He had proof of her love for him: she had been ready to commit murder for his sake.

Some sort of retribution ought to light on Delilah, thought Maud. But it would not. Maud found she did not want it to, either. Now she thought of it, her own father's littler crimes of unpaid bills, undisclosed bankruptcy, had probably been committed for the very same motives—out of love for his children.

At the end of the next story, Maud got up and went to the hut. She found Nathan sitting helpless in the garden, unable even to get inside and retrieve his Bible. 'That *thing* is in there again. That creature Tamo thinks is his father's spirit.'

Maud ducked indoors and let her eyes adjust to the dark. The chameleon squatted among the flowers, in the shrine corner of the hut. Its colour was dark and shadowy, its profile prehistoric. She *knew* it was not Thomas White: not his reincarnation nor his prowling spirit. But Thomas White was buried in a melon patch in Tamatave, and she would never be going there again. So Maud said to the chameleon, in a whisper, 'It was me. I told Tamo that you weren't his father. I wanted him to have a different Fate. I'm sorry. I realize you cared about him too. That's why you sent him to England. You wanted him to have a better life than you. And he will have! He will! But after the fortune-telling . . . afterwards, he thought he had to be the same as you. And you didn't want that, did you? . . . So I lied. I started up the lie. I'm sorry.'

The chameleon swivelled its bulbous eye, looking impartially into all four corners of the hut, into the past, the present, and the future. With a couple of kicks Maud managed to open the eastern door—the door the dead go out by, the door where Death comes in—and the chameleon walked slowly out on its knuckles, on its awkward, bandy legs. As the light touched its scaly body, the skin fluoresced into the yellow-green of the evening grass, and the mouth unfurled its prodigious curled orange tongue, like a dragon loosing fire. But it spoke not a word in reply—simply coiled its tongue away again into the deep hollow of its jaw.

When she looked round, Nathan had come inside. He was so happy. 'We'll be home by Christmas, think of it!' he said, wrapping Samson's Bible in a remnant of orange silk. 'Hardcastle will see his baby, and I shall pay off father's debts—every one of them. We'll be rich, Maudie! Well, not rich, perhaps, but comfortable. Yes, rich!—If we can keep hold of it all. Hardcastle says he can take us into the sea-lanes and hold us there till we meet with a navy ship or some such. We'll say how it was—that we were held hostage by King Samson, and only got free when . . . '

Maud did not argue. She could see that her brother had already adjusted the truth, and that 'going at the seas' was now as unreal as it had ever been when he daydreamed of pirates during his lessons at Graylake.

' . . . You shall have fine dresses and a carriage to carry you to church on Sundays, and put all the ladies to shame who slighted you . . . '

'I'm not going,' said Maud.

'To church?'

'To England. I'm staying here.'

Nathan's mouth dropped open. 'You want us to stay?'

'Not us. You go. You and Hardcastle must go. It's where you belong. But not me.'

His face rucked like a scuffed carpet, his nose wrinkling, his eyes narrow, his teeth slightly bared. 'You want to stay with Tamo.'

'I want to stay here.'

She had not known she was going to say it, but all of a sudden, for the first time since the *famadihana*, her ribcage was unlocked, her heart free to expand again. 'Think, Nathan. What does England hold for me?'

'Christian duty!' He said it like a cat pouncing on a rat.

'Why? Is God an Englishman?' she snapped back.

Then she put out a hand, to be reconciled. She did not want to argue; not if they were going to part. 'Listen. In England . . . in England I'd be just a girl. And that's to say . . . I'd have to be . . . I'd have my fate decided: what I might and mightn't do, what I could and couldn't be. It's comical—don't you think it's comical? Here, Tamo thinks he has to bide by his fate, but I can be whatever—'

Nathan did not take her hand, but turned on his heel and walked out. Where he slept, Maud had no idea.

Next morning, Nathan woke in the arms of a tree. Above his head, a swarm of emerald green wasps had formed themselves into a gigantic pendant ball, the surface continuously moving, like the ocean currents on the face of a green planet. It was a mass of buzzing life, a single shimmering entity made up of individual shining bodies. And it was grotesque. In shape and colour it was like his first sight of 'Madagasikara' on

Sheller's maps: Madagascar, which swarmed with life-forms he did not recognize and could not stomach. Madagascar, whose intricate language and customs he would never understand. Madagascar, which suspended over him an everyday threat of sudden death. He pulled off a piece of bark, and threw it at the wasp-ball, which exploded into a green storm—a deluge—a monsoon of wasps.

Falling out of the tree, Nathan ran for the sea, and did not stop running till he got there.

The rising sun was still afloat on the horizon, a golden bee-sac of honey. Even so, everyone was there, on the beach before him. Hardcastle was already carrying fresh fruit aboard an outrigger. (The crew had taken all the jolly-boats.) Tamo made him a present of the ivory gimballed compass; Maud had crocheted a cap out of white flax, for his baby. It was strange how tall the navigator seemed to have grown now, in comparison with them. He reassured Maud repeatedly that he would 'take good care of her brother'. She wished him good weather and a fair voyage.

No one mentioned the impossibility of man and boy sailing a large ship across oceans to a fixed destination. They were banking on meeting another vessel. And nobody asked what would happen if the vessel which found them was crewed by pirates.

'Be sure and have some quinine by you always,' Maud said, turning to Nathan as if he had been there all along. She had brought him Samson's Bible, wrapped in its orange silk.

'You keep it,' he said and, after a moment's hesitation, she folded her arms around it again, and hugged it to her chest.

'Thank you. I'd like to have it.' She was wearing a pale *lamba* which no longer slid down around her waist for lack of curves to hold it up. Her skin was bronzed, the hair piled on top of her head was sun-bleached gold, and her feet were bare. Nathan found it faintly shocking that his sister had changed so much without him noticing. Now, when he pictured her, it would not be 'poor mousy little Maudie', dusty and frail. It would be Maud-*ala*, among tambourissa trees and tamarisks, frowning against the strong light off the sea, a lemur in the crook of her arm or on her hip, or pounding rice, throwing the pestle high up into the face of the sun.

Nathan leaned forward and whispered shyly in her ear. 'Will you marry Tamo? One day?' But she only laughed, and tossed her head back and looked at him sideways out of narrowed eyes. He felt excluded once again, this time from something bigger than Madagascar and the Malagasy way of life.

She was not laughing when she kissed him goodbye. 'Thank you for bringing me here,' she said. 'Remember me in your prayers.'

And as the outrigger moved briskly away, sail flapping between the V-shaped mast, and Maud stood in the surf with her dress floating round her knees, Nathan nodded to himself. Yes, he was to be congratulated on that. All over the world, he knew, British botanists were shipping rare plants from continent to continent in an effort to make them grow other than where God planted them. Nathan had transplanted his sister, and for a frail little specimen, she had flourished remarkably well. He observed as much to Hardcastle, but the navigator was busy thinking of things further afield.

Tamo stood on the cliff path, by the defunct cannon. He was wearing his flame-coloured jacket, and plainly visible. Soon he was joined by a paler figure, and both waved for a long time to the *Ganesa* as she drifted, sparsely rigged, out to sea. But before Nathan had lost sight of discernible detail, the two were back down by the shoreline, gathering shellfish in company with other villagers, looking up now and then to see him on his way.

20

Benefactor

Not far over the horizon, they were threatened with cannon by a British East Indiaman and, surrendering instantly, were boarded by the captain and second mate. Sufficient crew were put aboard to enable the *Ganesa* to follow the Indiaman as far as Mauritius. Nathan and Hardcastle told how they had escaped from a pirate stronghold on St Mary's Island. The one was so well-spoken, the other so young that no one doubted their word.

In Mauritius, the rescuers claimed salvage, sold the ship and kept the proceeds. But neither Nathan nor Charles nor their bundles of luggage were searched.

They reached home in mid January, amidst snow flurries which made the land look no more stationary than the sea. After a three-month voyage, it felt none too firm under their feet, either.

None of Sheller's threats had been carried through. No warrant existed for Hardcastle's arrest as a pirate. They were never even called on to test the validity of King George's amnesty. England, preoccupied with worries of its own, digested them without a hiccup, and they were wise enough not to attract the curiosity of their neighbours.

Nathaniel Gull lodged with the Hardcastle family on his return to England. He had nowhere else to go, and the navigator's little house in Tilbury was comfortable enough for the time being. Soon, both supposed, they would find somewhere more in keeping with their wealth.

But though they talked often about the move, they could not agree on where this larger house should be. Nathan wanted to live within sight of the sea, whereas Hardcastle most emphatically did not. In fact he foreswore his profession sooner than go to sea again, bought a printing press, and advertised for an engraver to partner him in printing maps. Maps of Wales, maps of the lanes of Cornwall, maps of Hereford and the Western Isles.

To the engraver's confusion, Hardcastle would always insert, near the edge of any map, one extra road—some minor highway or bridle path which did not exist. When asked what it was, Hardcastle's only reply was to say, 'The way out.'

His baby son was a big, florid boy with knees like melted candlewax and large, solemn eyes. He accepted the father he had never seen as amenably as any new piece of furniture entering the house. He saw no strangeness in the way the man sometimes snatched back his head as if from a blow, or dropped his eyelids at any loud noise, or curled up and went to sleep in the corner of a room and in the middle of the day. The baby did not wonder, and the man's wife did not comment. Nathan glimpsed the amnesty leaflets which Hardcastle carried in every pocket of every coat and waistcoat, and folded into a thick wad over his heart, but he made no mention of them—of anything—to his landlady. There was an unspoken agreement in the house that Madagascar, and what had happened there, was never to be spoken of.

On one matter Heskia Hardcastle did speak. She pronounced one night at dinner that she would take no profit from pirate plunder. She did not care, she said, how Nathan squared his conscience, but she would not have booty under her roof, nor buy food with it, for the food would taste of blood. Hardcastle laid down his spoon; it was a comment calculated to cast a gloom over any meal. Glumly Nathan sat with his head on one hand, pushing the pease porridge about his bowl. Maud would never have let him be rich either, he thought dismally. And yet something had to be done with the . . . *spoils of war,* as Nathan chose to call them.

'What would you say, ma'am, to a bequest? An educational foundation, say, for fatherless boys.'

Mrs Hardcastle beamed. She thought it an excellent idea. At the back of his mind, Nathan laid aside a sum of cash for the education of baby Toby. He had learned, if nothing else, that the most rigid principles gave way when it came to children. Mrs Hardcastle would undoubtedly let Toby be educated with pirate gold.

It was then that Nathan's plan began to take shape, though he put off the necessary journey till Easter, when the roads would be better for travelling.

Besides, he was ill in March. Malarial fever sat on his chest like a fossa, scratching at his eyeballs, subjecting him alternately to the gibbering cold of winter and to sweaty tropical heat. He dreamed he was in Madagascar, waiting for Maud and Tamo to come, jamming shut the eastern door of the hut with his feet. He woke with his heels pressed against the foot of the bed, reached for the bitter taste of the quinine, and drank his regular morning toast: 'To you and me, Maud-*ala*. What shall we two do today?'

He liked to imagine that no more lay between them than the thickness of a wall, and that next door, in a somewhat sunnier room, Maud was also waking, dressing, feeding her animals, cooking the rice . . .

imagining her brother to be in the next-door room. In a way it was true. All it took was a different way of looking at the world.

Easter.

The woods were white with fountaining may. The ground under the trees was a haze of bluebells; gardens, as Nathan passed them by in the coach, were hatching out a dozen yolk-yellow varieties of flower.

The other passengers on the post coach shifted uneasily, and at Kettering asked the driver if 'that youth' could not be asked to ride on the roof. The driver declined to ask. He did not want Nathan sitting up next to him, either.

Nathan took a sip from the flask at his hip and pretended to be asleep, to put them more at ease. He wore a moss velvet jacket bald at the elbows, a broad garish cummerbund (with pistol), a tricorn hat, and borrowed boots. From under the hat, six or eight matches—hemp cords dipped in saltpetre and limewater—dangled down to either side of his face.

The iron gates of Greylake College held out against the chaos of spring, but for a few drifts of daffodils below the ha-ha, and the unmanly pink blossoms of the orchards. The trees to either side of the long drive showed an elegant English reserve: no lemurs, no scarlet fodies, no wasps in emerald shimmering balls. An ordered woodland for an orderly species.

For one sickening moment, it occurred to Nathan that Thrussell might have died or retired, and that the journey had been for nothing. But the headmaster was unchanged. In fact, to walk into his office was like walking through the portals of sleep into a remembered time.

'I have returned recently to this country from abroad,' he said, pitching his voice as low as it would go, 'and may be forced to quit it again at short notice.'

Thrussell said nothing; he was making estimate of the shabby barbarian who had entered his office. He showed no glimmer of recognition for the boy he had expelled.

'A man in my manner of work shouldn't leave his assets dangling. Leastways, that's the opinion of my banker. My godson, for instance, needs educating.'

'Quite! Quite!' Thrussell modified his first impressions. There was money here, if no breeding. 'Quait! Quait!' he repeated, growing more refined in reaction to the sunburned youth wiping his nose on his sleeve. 'Where exactly does your business detain you, Mr . . . ah . . . Ra—' He quailed from attempting his visitor's foreign name.

'Ratovoantany. Madagascar, sir. I'm a roving kind of man, you know. On Madagascar. A privateering manner of a man.'

For a moment, Thrussell stood open-mouthed at finding himself face-to-face with a pirate. A pile of books slid spontaneously off his desk, by which Nathan judged he must have wedged his leg against the desk to master his alarm. 'Well, and what a remarkable turn of events, Mr . . . ah—'

'Captain.'

'Captain. You are not the first . . . ah . . . businessman from that little island who has entrusted his ward to us for a Christian education. I seem to recall one—'

'No coincidence,' Nathan interrupted him. 'Thomas White's son, yes. Blackguard Tamo, as we call him. He commended you to me.'

Thrussell's face broke into a grimace of dubious

relief, and he mopped it with a handkerchief. 'A charming lad. I remember! So . . . self-assured . . . '

'As to a Christian education, I couldn't say. We have customs on Madagasikara. Customs and practices.'

'Practices? I'm sure we could accommodate . . . '

'He might, for instance, bring with him the bones of his grandfather.'

'The—'

'In a sea-chest. For turning, you know.'

Thrussell made a noise in his throat like a sob.

The sharp ache of hysteria bit at the back of Nathan's gullet. The man's stupidity, the man's entire ignorance, was baiting Nathan on to an extravagant tomfoolery he had never intended. He went and stood looking out of the window at the orderly school grounds, and breathed deeply, recovering himself.

'Anyway. The matter which brings me here, Doctor Thrussell, is that I have it in mind to bestow some money surplus to my needs on an educational establishment.'

Thrussell grew dizzy at the sudden passage of so many different emotions through his antique heart, and had to sit down. 'A noble sentiment indeed!'

'To provide schooling for the sons of impoverished parents—like mine were.'

'Pirates? Did you say pirates?'

'Parents, sir. The sons of impoverished *parents.*'

'How very!' was all Thrussell could say. He jammed his fingertips together, and his stomach gurgled with pleasure.

' . . . to be named in memory of a great man.'

'Yes, indeed!' Thrussell hastened to agree. 'The Ratovo—Scholarship.'

Inwardly, he was spending the capital already, building here, renovating there. His quill began to scribble involuntarily, wording his letter to the Board of Governors, telling them of this his *grand coup* on behalf of their school.

'No. Not in *my* name. In the memory of a better man than me. I met his son. On Madagascar, you understand. He too was going at the sea.'

'At the—?'

'A pirate, like myself,' the youth by the window translated, his back still turned on Thrussell, his voice a little strained. 'My scheme is to honour his father—a much loved man of God, by all accounts.'

(Whose God Thrussell had ceased to care. All that money coming to Greylake!) 'Admirable! Most commendable! Yes!'

The pirate shook out his lace cuffs with great deliberation. 'Consequently, Doctor Thrussell, I came here to offer your excellent teacher of Classics, Mr Pleasance, the post of Headmaster at The Reverend Edmund Gull Charitable School, Gravesend, which I intend to open next Michaelmas. He has done me the honour of accepting. Don't expect him to be at his desk on Monday.'

With a dull crack Thrussell's quill broke, and when Nathan looked round, the headmaster's face was lightly spattered with ink. 'That—'

Nathan took off his hat, and the matches fell to the floor among Thrussell's fallen books. They looked one another in the eyes and Nathan, to his lasting astonishment, found he felt no fear at all. What was this small, spiteful hypocrite after Sheller and Quartermaster, the sea and sickness and sin? Nathan held up a finger to his lips, to pre-empt any ill-advised outburst by Thrussell, and said in a low, good-humoured whisper, '*De mortuis nil nisi bonum, magister*. Never speak ill of the dead. Their sons will come back to haunt you.'

* * *

Afterwards, Nathan changed into his own clothes, packed up the absurd costume (but for the boots which were too heavy to carry) and travelled on to his home town. His father's grave was not marked, of course: just one among countless paupers' graves. So Nathan simply walked up and down the general area, saying aloud what he had done, how he had redeemed his father's name, how the debts were paid. The graveyard was full of birdsong—the gentle, sweet, unobtrusive twitter of drab English birds, and the grass was puddled with primroses. A church spire, stolid and monumental, overshadowed his every movement. For the first time since his return, Nathan felt the ground steady under his feet, ballasted with generations of English Christian dead.

Hardcastle and Toby met him off the coach, and they walked home through Tilbury. A playbill pasted to a wall advertised a revival of Charles Johnson's *The Successful Pirate* at the Drury Lane Theatre. But Nathan had no wish to go and see it. The fictional exploits of buccaneering men had lost their magic for him. Besides, there were other pirates on view in Tilbury that spring.

One, unredeemed by any amnesty, hung from the gibbet at Tilbury Point, tugged at by a brisk breeze off the river. His body had been bound in chains, daubed with tar and encased in a cage, denied Christian burial as a warning to the living of the hideousness of death.

It did not have quite that effect on Nathan. 'It's Easter,' he said to Hardcastle.

'A week since,' said Hardcastle.

'When they went to the tomb to rewrap Christ's body . . . '

Hardcastle threw Toby in the air and caught him repeatedly, making the child laugh and laugh.

' . . . except that it had gone . . . ' said Nathan.

'Raised to glory,' agreed Hardcastle, rubbing noses with the baby.

' . . . out into the garden.'

Suddenly it seemed to him that the tarry skull of the pirate on the gibbet might not be shouting a warning after all—that his decaying corpse might no longer be suffering the torments of the gibbet as his executioners liked to suggest with cage and chain and padlock. There were amnesties other than the King's.

The man might simply be singing: singing and dancing in the bright, brittle Easter sunshine, held up in mid-air not by chains but by invisible hands or on invisible shoulders.

Geraldine McCaughrean is one of the most highly-acclaimed living children's writers. She has won the Carnegie Medal, the Whitbread Children's Book Award (three times), the Guardian Children's Fiction Award, and the Blue Peter Book of the Year Award, and is known and admired for the variety and originality of her books, as well as her stunning storytelling skills.

Among her other books for OUP are *The Kite Rider, The White Darkness, Stop the Train,* and *Not the End of the World.* In 2005 she was chosen by the Trustees of Great Ormond Street Hospital for Children to write the official sequel to *Peter Pan.* The result was *Peter Pan in Scarlet* which was published worldwide to huge critical acclaim in 2006 and became an instant classic.

Geraldine McCaughrean
Winner of the Whitbread Children's Book Award
The White Darkness
'Astonishing' Guardian

ISBN 978-0-19-272618-6

Captain Oates, hero of the Antarctic, has been dead for nearly a century. But not in Sym's head. In there, he is her constant companion, her soul mate, her adviser. It is as if he walked out of the Polar blizzard and into her mind. In fact, if it were not for him, life might be as bleak as the Antarctic Wilderness.

When a short family expedition spirals out of control, Sym is forced to ask herself a question that becomes a matter of life or death: is it madness to stake one's happiness on someone who isn't there?

'A breathtakingly fine novel'
Bookseller

'McCaughrean's imagination is fierce, tireless, unpredictable'
Observer

'Astonishing'
Guardian

ISBN 978-0-19-275432-5

Everyone knows the story of the Ark. The flood rising, the animals entering two by two. Noah. But what about the women and children? Did they all accept Noah's orders to ignore their friends and neighbours struggling in the water?

When Timna does the unthinkable—when she defies her father and saves a life—she knows her fearful secret may bring death and disaster on board. If it does, one thing is certain. There will be nowhere to run.

'A tour de force by a brilliant writer'
Guardian

'Finely written, hugely challenging and rewarding'
Jan Mark, *TES*

ISBN 978-0-19-271881-5

For Cissy and her family, a new life is beginning on the prairies of Oklahoma. It's 1893 and for them and their fellow settlers, a bright future seems set to arrive along the Red Rock Railroad track. But when they refuse to sell their homes to the greedy railroad company, its boss swears his trains will never stop there again. How can the little town of Florence hope to survive without the railway? Its inhabitants might as well pack up and go back where they came from.

But Cissy and her neighbours vow to *make* the train stop—to do whatever it takes, to risk whatever they must, no matter what consequences come hurtling around the bend . . .

'for a really good read, look no further than this excellent, unpredictable and engrossing novel from a genuine master of the imagination.'
Independent

'This funny, sad and insightful novel . . . has all the hallmarks of a modern classic.'
Guardian

'. . . a tense, fast-moving adventure story, sustained to the very last page'
Financial Times

ISBN 978-0-19-275528-5

Haoyou knows that his father's spirit is living high above him in the sky over Ancient China. He also knows that now it is his turn to follow his father—so, strapped to a kite, Haoyou is sent to fly among the clouds and the spirits of the dead.

This amazing story is unlike anything else you have ever read. Packed with action, adventure and a real taste of life in Ancient China, *The Kite Rider* was the winner of the Blue Peter 'Best Book to Keep Forever' Award and the Smarties Prize Bronze Award, and was shortlisted for the Carnegie Medal.

'a marvellous soaring story that gives you a glimpse into another world'
Guardian

'A masterpiece of storytelling'
The Times

'an author incapable of writing a dull sentence'
Nicholas Tucker, *Independent*

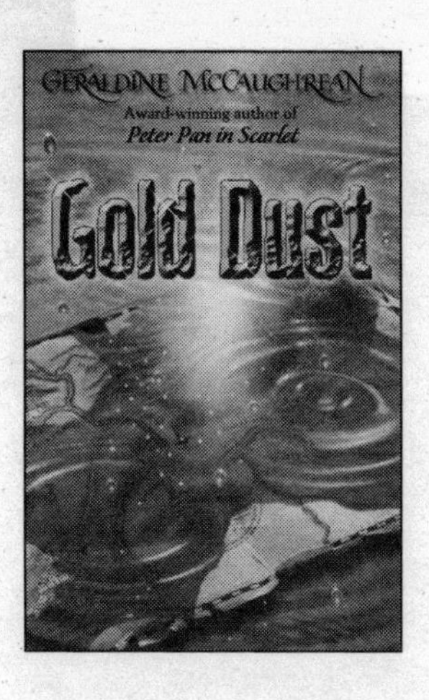

ISBN 978-0-19-275529-2

Inez and Maro can't believe their eyes when a hole appears outside their father's shop. Before long, there are holes all over town, undermining the buildings, undermining everyday life. There are strangers, too—desperados and entertainers, gunslingers and money-men. Rumours are rife: of monsters, murder and dreams come true.

It's started . . . the secret's out. People are coming from all over the country with a glint in their eye and hope in their hearts. And the word on everyone's lips is GOLD.

The action is non-stop in this thrilling adventure which won the Whitbread Children's Book Award.

'This novel is pure gold dust'
TES

'a rich tale of the lust for money that undermines an entire Brazilian town'
Guardian

'This novel is a feat of imagination and genuinely awe-inspiring'
Books For Your Children

3 8002 01546 0258